Copper Script

KJ CHARLES

This is a work of fiction. Names, characters, places, and incidents are either the product of the author's imagination or are used fictitiously. Any resemblance to actual persons living or dead, business establishments, events, or locales is entirely coincidental.

Published by KJC Books

Edited by May Peterson

Cover by James T. Egan of Bookfly Design

Print layout by Black Jazz Design

ISBN: 978-1-912688-27-2

For Metylda, with huge thanks for the title!

Chapter One

London, Autumn 1924

Detective Sergeant Aaron Fowler massaged the base of his skull. It didn't relieve the pain in his neck, because that was sitting opposite him in an expensive suit.

"Paul," he said. "I'm sorry to hear your fiancée has broken your engagement. It's not a police matter."

"You aren't *listening*," said his cousin, Mr. Paul Napier-Fox. "She didn't break it off of her own accord. She was manipulated, and I want the fraud who did it held to account. Isn't there a Witchcraft Act?"

"Witchcraft," Aaron repeated.

"Oh, you know. Spiritualism. Fortune telling. Money by false pretences."

Aaron's work with the Criminal Investigation Division covered such things as murder, rape, burglary, gang activity, sedition, extortion, and terrorism. Spiritualists weren't his problem, he wasn't fond of Paul, and he'd had a long day. He couldn't remember when he'd last had a day that wasn't long. "It's not a CID matter. Go to the police station if you have a complaint."

"I can't make a fuss about witchcraft to a pack of bobbies," Paul objected. "I'd sound like a madman. But this fellow told a lot of damned lies about me. He took Babs's money and span a great lot of lies and she swallowed every word. She broke off the engagement because of my character! What character, I said, and she said *Mr. Wildsmith told me all about you*. I've never met the fellow in my life!"

"What has that to do with the Witchcraft Act?"

Paul made an exasperated noise. "He claimed to know my character through magic! Surely that's not allowed. And I tell you what, Ronnie, Mater's on the warpath about it. She said you should do something and she'll have a word if you don't."

Several thoughts jostled for pre-eminence, among them how very much Aaron detested being called Ronnie; that Mrs. Ursula Napier-Fox could usefully be employed in Special Branch to put the fear of God into the most hardened subversives; and, regrettably, that Paul might have a point.

"If this fellow claims to have magical powers," he began, and then checked, "What exactly does he claim?"

"He said he could tell my character and intentions from my handwriting. It was a few lines about my costume for our masquerade engagement party!"

"Graphology."

"No, I was going as Henry the Eighth."

Aaron massaged his neck again. "Graphology is the practice of analysing handwriting. I dare say it's a lot of rubbish, but it's legal."

"Slander's not legal," Paul said stubbornly. "Babs broke off the engagement because of this damned fellow, with Mater already planning the flowers. I worship the ground she walks on and she didn't even let me explain! And it's not the first time, either."

"That you couldn't explain yourself?"

Paul glared. "That this fraud has put the cat among the

pigeons. I heard he was behind Letty Villiers giving poor old George Pursthwaite the push. All the best girls are going to this fellow and having their heads filled with poisonous nonsense."

Aaron had no interest in the love lives of the smart set, but this story was starting to prick at him. "What benefit is this man—Wildsmith?—getting from this?"

"Money, of course. He charges a fortune for a consultation."

"Is it mostly female clients?"

"Well, the fair sex are gullible, Lord love 'em."

Aaron was more concerned by *vulnerable.* Spiritualists and the like, a group in which he was quite prepared to include graphologists, tended to be very good at coaxing secrets out of the people who came to see them, especially since the world after the war was populated by people who were desperate to believe in something, or anything. Those drawn to visit a mystic could easily be persuaded by atmosphere and cajoling to reveal far more than they had intended, and he'd heard some nasty stories of exploitation and extortion, from which women were generally more at risk. It was hard to prove, hard to prosecute, and not his professional line, but he couldn't feel happy to ignore it.

"A colleague of mine, Sergeant Hollis, has a bit of a line in Spiritualists," he said. "The best thing is if you trot up to see him. King's Cross station."

"King's *Cross*?" Paul demanded, rather as if Aaron had suggested Zanzibar. "I'm not going to King's Cross! And anyway, Mater wants you to do it. Family and all that. Discretion. Don't want my business spread all over town any more than it is already, what with Babs can't keep her mouth shut. I suppose it runs in the family but why women have to gabble on and on endlessly, never a pause for breath, talk talk talk and gossip gossip gossip. A man can't hear himself think. And I'll tell you what else—"

Aaron had already stopped listening. He had no interest in helping Paul, who had grown from a thoroughly horrible boy to a vain and self-centred man, and he was well aware of his professional obligations as laid out in the Police Handbook: *An officer must not make enquiries unconnected with official duties, nor in his official capacity meddle with the private affairs of individuals.* His aunt Ursula would be enraged if he refused to help, but Aaron wasn't greatly concerned by that either; he could always unplug his telephone for a week.

He really had no reason to involve himself at all, except that this story was making his nerves prickle.

"All right, I heard you," he said, across Paul's ongoing monologue. "I shan't speak to this fellow in an official capacity— Don't argue with me, Paul, I haven't finished. I won't do anything officially, but I will talk to this Wildsmith purely as a private individual. I'll go for a chat and see how the land lies, and if I think there's anything dubious, I'll take it to Hollis myself. That will have to do, because it's all I'm going to do. Understood?"

Paul sniffed. "I suppose it's something."

Mr. Joel Wildsmith, Scientific Graphologist, lived in Great Percy Street, Pentonville. It was highly convenient for King's Cross nick, or indeed a spell in prison.

Aaron had made an appointment by letter, which he'd

typed, and signed with a false name. He knew how mediums and the like operated, often going to extraordinary lengths to find out information about clients, and saw no reason to make things easier.

He regarded graphology in the same light as astrology, phrenology, Spiritualism, and religion, which was to say, he accepted that their believers were sincere in their faith, and considered it none of his affair unless they attempted to foist those faiths on himself. Aaron had not grown up in a habit of placing reliance on higher powers, universal meanings, or natural justice.

He did believe in service. He'd served his nation at war, and now served its people as a police officer. He carried out his duty as best he could, to uphold the law and help redress a balance that felt permanently tilted against too many people, and that gave his life meaning.

Or, at least, it should, even if some days, the pursuit of justice felt as far-fetched as any astrological fantasy.

He shook the thought off as he approached the rather shabby boarding house at 22 Great Percy Street. A char in a smutted apron let him in without ceremony.

The narrow hallway smelled of cabbage. It wasn't the sort of place one might think a Scientific Graphologist would live: Aaron had rather imagined either a pristine laboratory or somewhere book-lined with leather chairs.

He went up to the first floor and knocked at the indicated door. A red-headed man of medium height answered, holding a mug of tea. "Mr. Thurloe? Please come in. I'm Joel Wildsmith."

He indicated the hatstand with the mug, rather than taking Aaron's coat or hat. Aaron took half a second to disapprove of the poor manners before he realised Wildsmith only had one hand. The other sleeve, his left, was empty at the end.

It wasn't unusual: London was full of men who lacked hands and arms and legs and eyes, and that was the damage you could see. It wasn't even the most notable thing about him. That would be the moustache, which was horrible.

It was an obtrusive, bristling moustache, so absurdly over-large for his face that it made Aaron's own face itch just to look at it, and aggressively ginger. If one could look past it, his hair gleamed copper under the gaslight; he had eyes of so light a brown they were somewhat unsettling, thick eyebrows the same shade as the moustache, and a roundish face that probably made him appear slightly younger than he was. Aaron guessed late twenties. He might have looked like a curate or a clerk if it wasn't for the moustache; given that self-inflicted disfigurement, he looked like nothing so much as a dishonest bookie.

Aaron took his time to hang up his coat and hat, digesting his impressions as he looked around the room. It was a small bedsit, with a kitchenette consisting of a single gas ring and a sink, a bed in the corner behind a screen, a little gimcrack wardrobe, two threadbare armchairs, a small table with a single kitchen chair. The table bore a scrawled-upon notepad, a pen, and some sort of metal device with leather straps and a hook that couldn't possibly be what it looked like. There were no pictures on the walls, no photographs, nothing personal. It was bleak.

"Have a seat. Tea?" Wildsmith asked.

Lower half of the middle class, Aaron thought. "Thank

you," he said, on the grounds that a sensible officer never refused tea.

Wildsmith managed the making of it with great efficiency, using his elbow to turn on the tap via the lever attached. He lit a match for the gas by holding the matchbox to his side with the same elbow, and striking the match with his right hand. It all looked very practiced. Aaron glanced again at the thing on the table.

"Prosthetic," Wildsmith said from the gas ring.

Aaron hadn't realised he'd been observed. "I beg your pardon?"

"That contraption. It's a prosthetic. If I strap it to my arm, I can crank the hook affair tight to hold a pen or what-have-you. I can't say it makes writing particularly easy, but here we are."

"You've still got your right hand."

"Everyone says that," Wildsmith said. "It was the first thing the doctor told me in hospital, actually: 'Good job it wasn't the right, eh?' I'm left-handed."

Aaron had known a few cack-handers at school and in the Navy, but they rarely announced it quite so assertively; Wildsmith sounded almost belligerent. It seemed particularly forceful for a man who visibly wasn't left-handed any more. "Ah. Rotten luck."

Wildsmith made a noncommittal noise of response. It was a very familiar noncommittal noise to a police officer, or to anyone after the war. *Yes, it is, isn't it? Dreadful, actually. Close to unbearable. Still, mustn't grumble!*

The graphologist made the tea, added milk and no sugar on request, and brought over the mug, then reclaimed his own mug and took the other armchair. "So, Mr. Thurloe. What can I do for you?"

"That's the question," Aaron said. "I understand you're a...what was it?"

"Graphologist. I read handwriting—not in the way everyone else does, I could hardly charge for that." That was very clearly a practiced line, probably to head off the weak joke that would otherwise be inevitable. "I analyse handwriting and tell you what it reveals about the character of the writer."

"How?"

"It's a scientific study. I look at emphasis, angles, length of lines and shape of letters, how they connect—"

"And what does that tell you? If I put a long tail on my *g*s, you infer I have a short temper?"

"It's an aggregate of impressions," Wildsmith said. "Your writing betrays your past, your character, the mood you were in at the time. I need a page at minimum to get a sufficient feel."

"And what do you do this for?" Aaron enquired.

"Money. It's ten shillings per half hour."

"I meant, what's the purpose of your service?"

Wildsmith leaned back in his chair. "That depends on the client. Sometimes people want to know more about prospective employees, or spouses. Maybe you can't get along with a colleague and you don't understand why. I can give you an insight into their feelings that might help you."

"Based on what? You say it's a scientific study, but what's your qualification?"

"Are you here under duress, Mr. Thurloe?" Wildsmith asked.

"I beg your pardon? No, I'm not."

"You chose to approach me. I didn't solicit you, and nobody is forcing you to believe in my work or use my services. You're welcome to ask questions, but a bit less aggression, if you please."

Aaron took a steadying breath. "Excuse me. You came highly recommended, but I can't help feeling sceptical."

Wildsmith tilted his head, acknowledging the words rather than accepting an apology they both knew Aaron hadn't made. "To answer your question, there is no degree course in graphology, though there are plenty of very well-researched works on the subject. I'm self taught. My clients serve as my references, and if you think I'm entirely off target, you can always refuse to pay."

"You allow that?"

"I can't easily stop you," Wildsmith pointed out. "Why don't you tell me what you're after? If you tell me your concerns—if you're considering people for a job, or a lodger, or what-have-you—I'm more easily able to look for what you want."

Or what I want to hear, Aaron thought. "I'd rather not give details about the individuals. I've three letters I want to you to have a look at."

"If you prefer," Wildsmith said indifferently, and reached out his hand. Aaron made to pull the letters out, then paused. "Wait. What about the ethics of this?"

"What ethics?"

That said it all. "You're reading private communications for one thing. And you're passing judgement on people you haven't met, who haven't consented to have you look at their hands."

"If you think the materials ought to stay private, don't show them to me. You chose what to bring. I do guarantee discretion, and if it's any help, I don't much look at the words: it's the shape of the letters, the feel of the hand that interests me. And as for passing judgement—you've come here for me to do this. If you have qualms, the door is behind you."

"You don't have qualms?"

"I have rent."

Blunt, not to say a touch aggressive. He had what Aaron's father would have called *front*, a way of meeting the world jaw-first. Aaron had no objection to that; he found bluntness more appealing than charm. Not to mention that Wildsmith's presentation of himself as a practical man doing a job came across as more convincing than any amount of highfaluting scientific claims.

Wildsmith probably knew that very well.

Aaron gave it a second, allowing himself to look torn, then he handed over the first paper.

Wildsmith took his time, those light brown eyes—ochre, Aaron thought might be the word—roaming over the text for several minutes. His mouth moved slightly, so far as Aaron could tell under the horrible moustache. The silence stretched. Aaron was good at silence, and very capable of sitting in a room with a suspect till their nerve broke, but he had to admit that Wildsmith was doing an excellent job of ignoring him completely.

He looked around the room again. It really was bare. His own digs weren't precisely cosy, but he had a photograph of his sister's wedding, and a reproduction Constable on the wall. Admittedly that had been a gift from his sister as a joke when he joined the police force, and he only hung it out of habit, but it was there.

Wildsmith looked up at last, and scrunched his face up, as if blinking something away. Aaron thought it looked affected.

"This is a very decent man," he said. "I assume man, the hand looks extremely—"

"Man, yes."

"He's—what's the word—stolid. I think he's the sort of fellow you could tell about a problem in confidence, though I don't know if he'd come up with any particular ideas himself to fix it because he's not imaginative at all. Really not. Almost whatever the opposite of imaginative might be, actually." He squinted at the paper. "I bet he's terrifically practical in whatever he does. Probably he's good with his hands. In personal terms, I expect he'd be a solid friend. Maybe you wouldn't go to him for advice on your love affair, but I expect he'd buy you a pint while you talked about it. Not a romantic husband, I wouldn't think, but a useful one. How can I put this: I bet he's never bought his wife flowers in his life, but he'd happily dig her a rose bed if she wanted one."

Aaron felt himself jolt, and cursed internally as those bright, light eyes caught the motion. Wildsmith gave it a second without comment, as if waiting for him to speak, then moved on. "At work, this is probably one of Nature's NCOs. He won't come up with brilliant new ideas that change everything, but he will make sure it runs to the best of his ability. I wouldn't expect him to handle disagreements with any particular flair, but I doubt you'll find him in a fight either. Insults tend to bounce off men this self-sufficient. In a word, he's reliable."

Aaron stared at him. Wildsmith gave a tiny shrug. "That's my opinion."

"Based on his handwriting. What, precisely, about the angle of his letters or the way he joins them tells you he dug his wife a rose bed?"

Wildsmith exhaled. "I'm trying to say, this is the hand of someone who does sensible, practical things, for good or ill. I'd imagine he'd propose with a 'What about it, old girl?' rather than sweeping her off her feet, but he would also be there in sickness and in health, like you're supposed to. This is the hand of a reliable man."

Aaron made himself nod slowly. "I see. How can you be sure?"

"I can't be *sure*. I'm not offering guarantees, I'm telling you my impressions."

"Extraordinarily detailed impressions."

Wildsmith shrugged again. Aaron took the letter back, mind racing.

There were tricks of the trade: flattering statements that sounded plausible to anyone, leading questions to help the faker draw truths from an unsuspecting client, and of course private investigation to get information another way. He found that last very hard to believe, given he'd supplied a false name and only made the appointment yesterday, and his brother-in-law Roger, whose letter this was, lived in Sheffield.

Not investigation, then. But it was, surely, possible that there was enough in handwriting for Wildsmith to judge that a writer was steady but unimaginative—not to mention forming a judgement on the content, a detailed and lengthy list of furniture to be sold from Aaron's father' cottage—and that he had elaborated the rest of it out of the air from those two points.

As it happened, Roger had proposed with the words, 'What do you say, old thing?', and had only ever bought Sarah flowers on her direct orders, but had indeed recently dug their cottage a rose bed. But that was sheer coincidence. Or, perhaps, an indication that Roger was a 'type'. People were often predictable and behaved with remarkable similarity: much of policework came down to knowing patterns. Graphology—which was to say, quackery—was doubtless the same and it didn't do to start reading anything more into what were, admittedly, some extremely well-targeted guesses.

"Interesting," he said. "What about this?"

He handed over the second paper, which he'd written himself. He'd copied out the opening of *Bleak House*, inspired by last night's weather. Good luck to Wildsmith wrenching anything personal from that.

The graphologist once again went into a brown study, eyes intent. Aaron sat back, considering him.

Wildsmith was dressed adequately but not well: clean, but without any great effort at smartness. He wouldn't consider himself poor, but he clearly counted the pennies. That was hardly surprising. It was difficult enough for able-bodied men to find work these days, and maimed ones were common enough that nobody would give him special treatment. If he couldn't do manual labour and he couldn't write, he would be in something of a bind. No wonder he'd turned to graphology.

Still, he was personable enough and there were jobs as salesmen. He didn't have to descend to this rather shabby pretence, and particularly not since it did real harm.

Wildsmith's assessment of Roger's letter had been superficially very convincing indeed. A more credulous person would have taken that a string of inferences and lucky guesses as evidence of mystic knowledge or astonishing powers or what-have-you. If Wildsmith had been equally lucky or cunning when he was pronouncing a verdict on Paul's letter, his fiancée—doubtless an idiot, given she'd agreed to marry him in the first place—might well have taken every word as gospel truth.

In fairness to Wildsmith, an engagement that could be broken on the unsupported word of a third party had probably not been destined to succeed. But that didn't entitle this man to throw out praise or condemnations based on how people crossed their ts.

His thoughts were broken by Wildsmith's long exhalation as he looked up.

"Well?" Aaron said, and was annoyed to realise he felt a touch of anticipation.

Wildsmith paused. Then he said, "I would like to know the context. Are you asking about a job, a friend, a man marrying your sister?"

"Just give me your impressions."

Wildsmith gave a small hmph of annoyance. "Fine. Well, this man—this hand—good Lord, it's like he's wearing a corset."

"Excuse me?"

"Metaphorically. Tight-laced. He is so held in, so tense—I'm surprised he can breathe." He clenched a fist illustratively at his chest. Aaron felt his own lungs tighten. "It's like he's got his teeth gritted, all the time."

"Repressed. Is that what you mean?"

"That's one of those psychoanalysis words, isn't it? All sorts of things bubbling away and you want to marry your mother?"

"Something of the sort."

"I couldn't say about that. He's certainly struggling with something, and there's a whole lot of tension because of it. So much tension. He's keeping hold of himself till the muscles seize up. It makes my neck hurt."

Aaron stared at him. Wildsmith made a face. "There's a lot more here too, don't get me wrong. It's an intelligent hand, and there's a lot of force of character. And it reeks of honesty. Not quite as plain and straightforward as your other chap necessarily, but I think you could rely on him in a hard spot, and trust him to do the right thing, even if it was difficult. This is not someone who fiddles his taxes. An upright man with a lot to him, but I don't think the world is working terribly well for him."

"Does it for anyone?"

"Ha. But, you know, some people live with that, and some people struggle with it, and this is a struggler. I think...I feel like he's unhappy? Yes. I think he's really quite unhappy."

Aaron's chest was squeezed tight. He manoeuvred his hands towards his pockets as he sat in a casual sort of way, to avoid massaging his neck.

"Well," he said. "That's certainly interesting. Do you have any idea why?"

"I couldn't begin to speculate. I'm just saying what I see here, not how he got there."

"How he writes a capital F doesn't give it all away?"

That came out a little less lightly than it should have. Wildsmith said, "I told you, I take an impression of a personality at the time of writing. It's not a life history. And my impression is, this is a man with an awful lot to him, but if your sister wants to marry him, she should consider what she's getting into."

"That's a damning thing to say of a stranger."

"I don't mean it badly! I'm just trying to say that this chap's got a lot going on inside that's a challenge for him, therefore it's liable to be a challenge for someone who loves him. I'm not saying he's not worth it, not that at all. I think...I think, if you could..." He looked back at the paper. "Actually, I think it would be absolutely worth it. There's so much pent up, so much feeling. God. If someone could just cut those laces for him, I bet he'd—"

He clamped his mouth shut on that, the copper eyebrows shooting up. Aaron said, "He'd what?"

"Nothing."

It wasn't nothing: he looked decidedly self-conscious. "You were saying something."

"Rambling," Wildsmith said, not entirely convincingly. "Thinking aloud. My point *is*, this is a man with a lot to him but a lot to sort out too, and that might be hard to live with. Or it might not, if he keeps it all in, but that's not much of a life if you ask me."

Aaron's hand, concealed in his pocket, was clenched into a fist so tight his knuckles strained against the cloth, the skin. "Rather less favourable than your first assessment, then," he said as easily as he could.

"Depends what you want him for. Honestly, you might

well be able to work with him and not notice a thing: people can be remarkable at hiding themselves. More tea?"

Aaron did not want more tea. "Yes, please."

He tried to breathe out, watching Wildsmith as he moved around the kitchenette. *Relax. Relax.*

There was no way on earth that Aaron's handwriting proclaimed his interior life to anybody with the eyes to read it. Fortune-tellers made sweeping statements that everyone could nod along with; probably lots of people spent their lives trying to reconcile contradictions and needs, attempting to keep their unruly thoughts and wants in check. Well, Aaron knew they did, because his job dealt with the ones who didn't bother.

Wildsmith did not know him, or anything about him, and if it felt like he'd slit Aaron's chest, peeled open his ribs, and taken a clinical look at the insides, that was part of the well-oiled deception. Persuasive statements that half the population might apply to themselves. A lucky guess.

He took the second mug of tea with a murmur of thanks, and, as Wildsmith sat, said, "What about you?"

"Had plenty, thanks."

"Not tea. What about your handwriting?"

"You mean, what does it say about me? I've no idea. I couldn't tell before I lost my hand—it was like trying to listen to your own voice—and now I don't suppose it says anything much except *This man hates his prosthetic*. Are you all right, Mr. Thurloe? You looked a bit shocked."

"Surprised," Aaron said. "You cast an interesting light on some things I hadn't considered. It's given me a lot to think about."

Wildsmith gave a quick smile, barely visible under the

moustache. "Glad to be of use. You mentioned judgement before. I really don't try to sit in judgement, or claim the right to do so. But I do think, if I can help people understand one another a bit more, that's got to be a good thing."

"What if you feel compelled to judge? If a young man brings in his sweetheart's letter, and you conclude she's a bad lot?"

"I don't know I'd use that expression," Wildsmith said. "I might read deception, or anger, or greed, or selfishness, but I'd try not to extrapolate that to *This is a bad person*."

"But there are bad people. You can't deny that. The prisons are full of them."

"And the rest," Wildsmith said, with unexpected feeling. "The average gaol will offer you bad people, people who made lots of bad decisions, people who made one bad decision, and people who were just very unlucky on one particular day."

"True," Aaron admitted. "But they all committed offences, all the same. They made the choices that put them in gaol, when other people made different choices in similar circumstances."

"Similar circumstances? Like when the hungry child wickedly steals a penny bun from the baker's, whereas the well-fed banker standing next to him nobly chooses to pay?"

"'The law, in its majestic equality, forbids the rich as well as the poor to sleep under bridges, to beg in the streets, and to steal bread.'"

"Exactly!" Wildsmith said. "Did you just think of that? It's jolly good."

"Anatole France." Aaron had been required to learn that line by heart. "I quite grant you that some people have fewer and harder choices than others, and that we could reduce crime if we reduced poverty. So let's leave aside your hungry child, and look at your well-fed banker who's planning to flee for South America having robbed his investors for years. Is he not a bad lot? Or do you decline to judge him too?"

"He stinks," Wildsmith said. "But even so, it's worth looking at the why and the wherefore, isn't it? Otherwise you're saying *They're a bad lot because they make bad choices, and they make those choices because they're a bad lot.* Whereas I think it's more useful for me to say, oh, *This person is writing with contempt*, or *They don't seem to believe they're doing anything wrong*, or *This feels like they're telling lies.* That way, perhaps my client can understand more about what's going on, based on their own knowledge of the person and situation. Perhaps you might even work out how to change things—how to appeal to the better parts of their nature, or to understand what motivates them and offer something else."

"You think so?"

"Well, it's possible. I had a client who was having awful trouble with his employer, a very highly regarded professional man. He was a brute and a bully on my client's word, but his hand reeked of fear. He felt deep down he wasn't good enough, and he took it out on his staff. So I told my client to praise him. He said, *Don't be absurd, I'm a junior, my praise would mean nothing to such an important man*, but all I could see was someone desperate to hear he was doing well. I said, just try it. He did, and the chap's now eating out of his hand."

Aaron frowned. "That sounds very like pandering to a man who ought to behave better."

"Yes, he ought to, but he wasn't," Wildsmith said. "And *you* might prefer to be screamed at daily rather than lower yourself to grease the wheels, but my client just wanted to go to work. What he needed from me was a way to do that, not a condemnation of his employer's character. Do you see?"

Aaron saw quite a few things, one of which was that Wildsmith was very good at what he did, which was nothing to do with handwriting. He clearly understood people, and particularly the two most potent human desires of them all: to be found interesting, and to gossip about others.

"What about this chap?" he asked, and held out the third paper. Wildsmith took it, and started to read.

The difference was dramatic. Within a few moments his shoulders rose and hunched like a cat's, and his jaw and neck tensed visibly as he read. His mouth worked silently, and then he said, "No."

"Excuse me?"

"No. Absolutely not. Don't hire him, don't let him marry your sister, none of it."

"Why not?"

"Christ, can you not read?" Wildsmith demanded, and then, immediately, "Sorry. Sorry. It's—look, forget what I said just now, I'm making a judgement. This man is bad to the bone."

Aaron sat very still. "Why?"

Wildsmith gave the letter a little shake, as if trying to dislodge dirt. "He's wrong inside, horribly wrong. There's a disconnection. This is someone who doesn't care and who likes to do—to hurt— It's pulling the wings off flies, but that's all he does or wants to do. It's cruel and it's clinical—and he's *entertained*— Oh my God. What the fuck. What is this?" He shoved the paper back at Aaron. "What the hell have you brought me?"

Aaron took it automatically, and rose to his feet as Wildsmith sprang to his. "Calm down. And look here—"

"No, *you* look. If you know this man, then do something about him. You need the police, not a bloody graphologist! And do it *now*, because I will bet you the contents of my bank account that he has hurt people, and he will hurt people again."

"Are you serious?"

"Yes," Wildsmith said through his teeth. "I suppose he's what you really came about? Well, I've told you your suspicions are right, congratulations, now bloody do something. Take it away. *Go* away. Pay me first," he added.

Aaron fished out two ten-shilling notes, in the hope that paying up would lead to calming down. "Wait. Could you tell me more about this?"

"I do not want to—" Wildsmith stopped himself, inhaled very deeply, and went on with a thin veneer of control. "Please, just go to the police. Ask them to spare five minutes from their busy schedule of harassing the Irish and entrapping men in public conveniences, and look at this fellow. I'm sure you can make someone listen to you, you seem like the sort. If they investigate him they will find something."

"What something?"

"Something horrible," Wildsmith said flatly. "This man's wrong all the way through. He's done terrible things and he doesn't care. If they hang him for it, he still won't care. He needs to be stopped and he won't stop till he's made to, so go to the police and *make—them—look*." He jabbed a dictatorial finger on each of those words. "And if you need a starting point—oh hell, I don't know. Helplessness. Children. Animals or children. You need to go. I've a headache."

He shoved Aaron's coat at him, then his hat, and Aaron found himself outside in short order. He stood in the night air, steadying himself for a moment and then set off home with a lot to think about.

There could be no doubt of Joel Wildsmith's skills. This last display was proof positive: he was unquestionably a fraud, and a shameless one at that. *A little bit too clever, Mr. Graphologist*, Aaron thought savagely.

He'd known who Aaron was. That was the key to the whole thing, and all his explanations made sense in the light of that. Probably the spiritualist-confidence fraternity exchanged notes on police? Or maybe this whole thing was an asinine practical joke on Paul's part, and if it was, Aaron was going to give his cousin the sort of dressing-down that led strong men to emigrate. There was an explanation along those lines, even if Aaron didn't yet know exactly what it was, because Wildsmith had quite clearly known the author of the third letter.

Children. What a damned filthy thing to use as a deception.

They'd found four small bodies wrapped in sacking under Wilfred Molesworth's kitchen floor, and he had shown no remorse, no guilt, nothing at all. He had been a mild-mannered little man, blinking behind his spectacles as they levered up the floorboards, and he had blinked mildly just the same way while the hangman put the rope round his neck.

The papers had had a field day, of course. Probably one

of the rags had reproduced a letter or some such: that might have been how Wildsmith had recognised the hand. From a newspaper photograph several years ago.

That was clutching at straws. Nonetheless it was, must be a trick, and he would find out how Joel Wildsmith had done it—how he'd known, and, as important, what he knew. And he'd do it carefully, because the man was a sufficiently brilliant confidence trickster to be positively dangerous.

He'd damn near persuaded Aaron with his first demonstrations, and he'd damn near got his liking as they'd talked. Aaron had wanted to argue more, had had all sorts of points to make and things to say. He'd felt like it would be enjoyable to thrash things out. He had in fact found the man remarkably easy to talk to: it was why he'd stopped.

Yes, Wildsmith was very good indeed. Why, when he'd read Molesworth's letter, he'd gone quite grey, the blood visibly draining from his face. Even the greatest actors couldn't do that on command.

Trick, Aaron thought again, and strode furiously down the road.

Chapter Two

Three days later, Aaron had reached no brilliant conclusions. He had looked further into Mr. Joel Wildsmith, or rather, asked Sergeant Hollis to have an informal look for him, since he didn't want to put Paul's complaint through official channels quite yet. Hollis was in the uniformed branch, a solid rugby-playing sort with an unexpected speciality in mediums, palmists, and fortune-tellers.

"Graphology is a new one on me," he admitted over a pint of Aaron's buying. "Is there anything to it?"

"I couldn't say." According to Aaron's hasty reading, such luminaries as Disraeli, Sir Walter Scott, and Robert Browning had believed in the power of graphology, but they were a pack of writers and not to be relied on for common sense. "I dare say one can draw some impressions from people's handwriting, but not to the extent this fellow claims."

"Mumbo-jumbo crystal ball stuff? Or is he the scientific type, and it's all jargon?"

"Neither. Presents himself as a very plain, straightforward, normal sort of chap."

"It's a good trick if you can pull it off," Hollis said. "Be a particularly good trick for this one: he's a queer."

Aaron took that in with a tiny judder of shock he hoped didn't show. "Is that so? I wouldn't have thought it."

"Well, the magistrates certainly thought it. He was picked

up for soliciting in a public convenience a couple of years ago. Did two months."

That explained a certain amount of the attitude. "Hmph. Anything else?"

"Nothing I could find. Unremarkable war. Ambulance division in Flanders, invalided out in '17. No other complaints against him. If he's as good a fake as you say, he's rather come out of nowhere."

"Is that unusual?"

"The good ones tend to be splashy. You know, make a hit, get a clientele among the smart set, face in the papers, prices up."

"He's reached the smart set already," Aaron said.

"Maybe you've caught him early, and we can pluck him before he ripens. What's your interest? It's not CID's usual hunting ground."

There was perhaps a bit of an edge to that, since the relationship between the uniformed division and CID tended to be prickly. "It's not official interest at all. The fellow ruined my cousin's engagement." Aaron outlined Paul's predicament. "I went to see what was what, and found him a bit too clever for my liking. But that was in a private capacity, of course, and as you say it's not my area, so I thought I'd better bring him to your attention." And that would teach Mr. Wildsmith to playact his *Tell the police!* scene.

"Fair enough," Hollis said. "I'll keep an eye out. How's life in CID anyway?"

It was about as positive a result as Aaron could have hoped for, except for the news of Wildsmith's proclivities. If the man knew who Aaron was—and he must, it was the only thing that made sense—and he was queer himself, and he'd come up with that business about self-control…

That didn't add up to anything that made Aaron happy. His neck twinged.

He went back to see Paul that evening. "I've been following up your fellow. The graphologist."

"I should hope so. I hope you plan to throw the book at him."

"I need some information first. What exactly did he tell your fiancée ?"

"Oh, a lot of stuff he had no business saying. She lapped it up, of course. Really, Ronnie, women are—"

"What did he tell her?" Aaron repeated.

"Well, I'm not going to tell you," Paul said, ruffled. "The point is, he wrapped her round his little finger, and that sort—"

"Was it true?"

Paul's eyes widened. "That's a damned offensive remark. Just because you're a bobby, you don't have to forget your manners."

"I don't know what he told her, but it seems to have hit a nerve with you, and it certainly did with your fiancée. So I am asking you, was it true?"

Paul's mouth tightened mulishly. Aaron tried not to roll his eyes. "I'm not asking for fun. If this man is making up lies, he's a charlatan, but if he's digging out secrets and using them, then we're looking at obtaining money by deception, and we might even have a blackmailer on our hands. So I'm going to ask you again. Was what he said factually accurate?"

"If you must," Paul muttered.

"And what was it? I don't care," Aaron added. "I don't give a damn: I just want an idea what this fellow is up to."

"Oh, all right. You'll keep it to yourself? He told Babs I had another girl."

"That's all? Nothing more specific?"

"Since you ask, he told her I'd been with a girl just before I wrote the letter."

"Been with?" Aaron repeated blankly.

"You know what I mean. Or maybe you don't," he added snidely. "Gone to bed with. Like normal men do with girls. Do I have to draw you a picture?"

"He told her that you bedded a woman, and, what, wrote a letter to your fiancée as soon as you'd finished? And you're saying that's true?"

"You needn't be so prissy," Paul said. "It's the nineteen twenties, you know. We don't all have to behave like Victorians any more."

"Rolling out of one woman's bed to make plans for your engagement to another woman sounds more Georgian to me," Aaron said. "If not Tudors—wait. Your engagement party was a costume ball? And you were going as Henry the Eighth?"

"Oh, don't you start. Babs made a rotten fuss about that when she gave the ring back. Threw it at me, actually."

Aaron didn't blame her. "Are you positive Wildsmith made that specific accusation? You're sure he didn't say something like *You were thinking of other women when you wrote*, and you filled in the gaps? A guilty conscience can do that." Not that Aaron saw much sign of a guilty conscience in Paul, but one never knew.

"Oh, no, Babs had it exactly," Paul assured him. "She said

she gave my letter to this fellow and he told her the writer had just been to bed with someone. Well, that's why I admitted it. One thing if she'd said *Is there someone else*, a man can handle that sort of conversation easily enough, but being told precisely what had happened threw me for a loop and I said something stupid like *How did you know?* Denied it after, of course, but it was too late by then. She didn't take it well at all. Said it was bad enough that I couldn't be trusted or what-have-you without some ghastly little oik telling her I'd written my letter with sticky hands."

"He said that?"

"No, I think that part was Babs."

Aaron attempted to claw his way back to the conversation he wanted to have. "Are you in the habit of writing letters to one girl after bedding another?"

"Good Lord, Ronnie, you make it sound like a compulsion. We—Babs and I—needed to agree on the costumes rather urgently, that was all."

"So the only people who could have known you wrote the letter in those circumstances were you, your lady friend—anyone else? Servants? A spare lady in the room?"

"There's no need to be sarcastic."

"And did you brag about your conquest? Tell a friend, make a story of it?"

"Good heavens, man, what sort of fellow do you think I am?"

Aaron restrained himself. "Who was the other woman?"

"I'm not telling you that," Paul said. "Have some decency."

Wildsmith had been right about Aaron's self-control to the extent that he didn't spring on his cousin and throttle him. "For heaven's sake, man, use your head. If you didn't tell anyone about this letter, and nobody but this woman saw you write it—"

"Well, but she didn't either," Paul said with an air of mild triumph. "She'd already left. Having her hair done, you know, rushed off. And before you ask, I certainly didn't tell her I was going to write to Babs. It was hardly her affair."

Further questioning revealed that he'd put the letter in his pocket when he went to the post box rather than carrying it along the street in his hand, and that the lady friend was married to an elderly and very rich man from whom she had no intention of being parted till death did them.

Aaron left his cousin with one very strong conviction, which was that Paul could go to the devil. Other than that, he was bewildered.

If Paul was a reliable witness, and that 'if' contained multitudes, Aaron could think of no plausible way Wildsmith could have known about the circumstances in which he'd written his letter. *He just got out of bed with another woman* wasn't the sort of thing psychics tossed out as guesses: it was far too specific. But to know it as fact would require the sort of surveillance Special Branch might provide for a Soviet spy.

This didn't make any sense. None of the explanations he could think of made sense.

Sherlock Holmes said, *When you have excluded the impossible, whatever remains, however improbable, must be the truth.* It was impossible that Wildsmith could actually tell a child murderer or a recently unfaithful fiancé from their handwriting, therefore he must have dug up the information that would allow him to fake it. But surveillance of that quality took men and time and expertise, which was to say money. You might do it to impress a suitably influential client—Aaron had a vague idea that Paul's ex-fiancée was a Bright Young Person—but the problem was, Wildsmith couldn't have predicted he'd find anything to make such an outlay worth while. And if he had money to spend and wanted to make an impression on the smart set, why would he live in a miserable room in Pentonville rather than renting something decent, somewhere fashionable?

GK Chesterton had taken issue with the Holmes quotation. He'd said that if you told him the Prime Minister was haunted by a ghost, that was impossible, whereas if you told him that the Prime Minister had slapped Queen Victoria on the back and offered her a cigar, that was merely improbable, but he knew very well which of the two was more likely to be true.

Which was all very well, but Aaron didn't believe in ghosts. He reminded himself of that several times as he walked home.

The next few days were rather too busy for Aaron to worry about the graphologist's impossible fraud. He had to appear in court for the prosecution of George 'Dapper' Melkin for unlawful killing.

Dapper, a violent brute with a penchant for flashy waistcoats, was of the Brummagem Boys, a Birmingham outfit that had an ongoing dispute with the local Sabini gang. A Sabini man, one James 'Nippy' Nicholls, had died following a recent fracas; Aaron had two eye witnesses and a bloodstained gentleman's walking stick, hollowed out and the end filled with lead, to put Dapper on the spot.

He was pleased about that. It had been a good collar, and more, he had a deep dislike of the gangs. The racecourse terrorists, as the newspapers called them, had originally confined themselves to extorting bookmakers, cheating racegoers, and fighting one another over who got to do those things in which area, but their size and reach had grown markedly since the war. The Sabini gang alone could call on some three hundred men in Clerkenwell, Finsbury and King's Cross. Since the same area only had a policing strength of around six hundred, that was too damned many gangsters jockeying for power, offering 'protection' to shopkeepers and bookmakers, sticking their fingers into nightclubs and gambling dens and other such pies. Aaron had read of the problems in Chicago and New York, with their areas where the law's writ didn't run, and he did not want to see it happen in London.

He did not, therefore, mourn Nippy Nicholls' death, but he did relish the opportunity to send Dapper down as he deserved.

It mostly went well, except that Dapper's barrister made a spirited and deeply insulting attempt to suggest that the King's Cross police in Aaron's person favoured their local gang over the interlopers from Birmingham. Aaron kept his temper despite the provocation, the judge slapped it down hard, and Dapper got twenty years.

It was a good result. Less good were the newspaper stories the next day. Not much else was on, and Aaron found his picture in several of the papers, along with a lot more of his life story than he wanted.

"*Firebrand Fowler's Son Abandons Unions, Takes On Gangs,*" Detective Constable Challice read aloud in the mess. "That's a bit tortured. *Sabini Gang 'Protected In High Places'* with quotation marks so it's not libel. That's not very nice, but the article isn't too bad overall. Oh my goodness, listen to this. 'The latest heartthrob isn't a film star: he's a policeman. Darkly handsome DS Fowler's Italian good looks—'"

"You have to be joking," Aaron said.

"No, honestly, it's in the *Pictorial.* They've done a sketch. You look like Valentino. Well, *you* don't," she added with a critical glance, "but the sketch does."

DC Helen Challice was the second woman to join the Met's Criminal Investigation Department, the only one based at King's Cross. It was generally felt that women should not work on crimes of violence and murder, so she was usually set to cases more suitable for the gentler sex. Aaron could imagine Challice had an advantage when it came to interviewing a three-year-old whose father had given her gonorrhea, or a thirteen-year-old who'd been raped by four men in a row and was now pregnant, but he had no idea in what way those cases were supposed to be easier on the investigating officer. She couldn't be more than twenty-three or so, but after six months in the job, she already looked older.

He'd come across her sobbing in an office one night, and been sufficiently reminded of his own sister that he'd first attempted comforting words, and then just brought her tea that was basically hot sugar syrup until she stopped crying. Once a few days had passed and she'd realised both that he hadn't made her wobble into station gossip, and that he didn't intend to make advances off the back of that unexpected intimacy, they'd settled into as close to a friendship as Aaron had at work.

She was a self-possessed young woman, with the brisk confidence of a Head Girl or a hockey captain, and she was looking at Aaron with an air of concern. "Are you not pleased? I'd have thought being compared to Valentino would be quite the boost."

"I'd rather not be in the papers at all. They will drag things up that don't matter, and I'd rather just do my job."

"Valentino, though? I wouldn't mind it if the papers said I looked like Clara Bow."

"I bet you would if they said it when they should be talking about a good collar," Aaron pointed out. "And it's rather insinuating, isn't it? The lawyer accuses me of being in the Sabinis' pocket and then the papers say I look Italian..."

"Do you think that's it?" Challice gave the *Pictorial* a quick scrutiny. "There's nothing in here about the Sabinis at all, though, it's just their New Faces section."

"Oh. Well, that's not so bad." Aaron was perhaps a little over-sensitive on the subject of his family; skin tended to be thin where it had been previously rubbed raw.

"Really, I think it's fine," Challice assured him. "It does say you're related to man-about-town Paul Napier-Fox, whose recent engagement—"

"I don't want to know," Aaron said from the bottom of his heart. "Please stop."

"Oh, all right. It seems a bit of a waste, though. Half of CID is desperate to get their pictures in the paper and here you are with stories coming out of your ears and you don't want them. Really, we should make the most of it. Put you on posters. DS Fowler, the Face of the Department."

There was a snort from the door. It was Detective Inspector Davis, wearing his usual expression of aggressive disgust. "You and your lady friend admiring your press cuttings, Fowler?"

"Oh, that was just me, Inspector," Challice said with the bright, friendly smile she usually adopted with Davis. "Was there something, sir?"

He didn't trouble to reply to her. "DDI wants a word, Fowler. Now will do."

Divisional Detective Inspector Colthorne was a tall, imposing man in his forties, distinguished if not handsome, with a shrewd air that suggested a stockbroker before he got complacent. He'd been promoted from Detective Inspector in C Division (Soho) a few years ago, and was now the senior officer of G Division (Finsbury, Islington, King's Cross, and Clerkenwell). He had an authoritative rule but an easy manner with it, and was generally considered a good chief, a laugh when he wanted to be, though possessed of a wicked temper if you were fool enough to cross him.

Aaron didn't quite share the general admiration. He'd been a constable under Mr. Colthorne in Soho before they both moved to King's Cross, and never managed to get on with the man. That, he had to admit, was down to envy. He wasn't easy or genial himself, didn't have the knack of charm or banter, and probably could never have been popular anyway since he came with far too much baggage attached.

Gossip about his father and his extended family always went before him, and he was wearily accustomed to the simultaneous necessity and impossibility of proving himself. *Yes, my father was Terry Fowler, the union man. Yes, my mother's family is upper-class as it comes. But I'm still a copper.*

"Well, Fowler," Colthorne said. "Congratulations. Excellent result yesterday. Good to get Melkin off the streets."

"Thank you, sir."

"A disgrace about that brief's insinuations, though. This tactic of abusing an honest policeman and impugning his character ought to be severely punished by the Bench."

The DDI had been the object of a similar accusation during the war years, Aaron vaguely recalled; clearly the experience had left scars. Aaron was grateful for the sympathy now. "Thank you, sir," he repeated. "It was rather unpleasant. Of course the defence has to do what he can for his client, but to be accused of corruption or collusion with criminals—it strikes at the heart of why we do the job."

"And, I'm sorry to say, that sort of slander follows a man around for a long time. Mud sticks."

"I hope not, sir. What they said of me was entirely baseless." The DDI's brows drew together, and Aaron had a sudden, horrible feeling that he might have sounded as though he was implying something about other accused officers. "It's often the way, if they've nothing else to fall back on," he added hastily. "Grasp at straws to discredit the prosecution."

"I don't know if I'd call it grasping at straws," Davis said. "You're Italian: naturally the brief would see the Sabini connection."

"I'm British, sir," Aaron said evenly. "And my only connection to the Sabini gang is having arrested some of them."

"Of course it is," Colthorne said jovially. "There's no point fretting about this sort of thing, Fowler; it's just part of the game, and we all have to take our knocks, you as much as anyone else. And aside from that, you did well enough out of the papers. Flattering stuff in the *Pictorial*. One for the scrapbook, eh?"

"Sir," Aaron said, exquisitely uncomfortable.

"And worth following up, perhaps," Colthorne went on thoughtfully. "The Press like a face, a personality. If they've latched on to you as the Valentino of King's Cross nick, we could use that. Why should C Division get all the column inches? A monthly article, perhaps—"

"No," Aaron said, the word coming without thought. "That is, I should prefer not to have anything to do with the Press, sir."

Colthorne cocked a brow. "Come now. You must have given half a dozen interviews yesterday."

"I gave the usual briefing after the verdict, sir," Aaron said stiffly. "Nothing else." He was doing this wrong, he knew. Colthorne's tone was jovial; he was probably only joshing, and Aaron should be taking it as banter, but he couldn't. "I really wouldn't want to be in the papers," he repeated doggedly.

Colthorne leaned back in his chair, assessing him with a look. "I'd have thought you were used to it. Firebrand Fowler and Bright Young People—"

"That's nothing to do with me, sir."

"Your family is nothing to do with you?"

Aaron was damned if he was going into that. "Not at work. I can't help what the papers say; I'm just trying to do my job."

"Glad to hear it," Colthorne said, evidently deciding the conversation wasn't worth pursuing. "A good collar, and a good result. Davis tells me you've a few days' leave booked? Well deserved. Enjoy yourself."

Aaron always took his days off because they were his right and you used your rights at work, but he didn't have much to do with them. He generally went to stay with his sister in Sheffield, or had her little family descend on his flat in Lisson Grove, but he'd heard just the day before that his niece had come down with scarlet fever. He therefore occupied the first morning by purchasing a variety of books, toys, chocolates, and whisky in Debenhams for the benefit of the whole family and getting it all shipped up. Then he went to the dentist, then to the cinema, and with all his avenues of entertainment now exhausted, he turned his thoughts to Joel Wildsmith.

He'd been too busy to consider the graphologist for a while, but now he was at leisure, the problem nagged at his mind. He simply couldn't see how Wildsmith could have found out as much as he had.

He bought a book on graphology. It assured him he could come to a full understanding of a person's character simply by considering the differences in writing styles:

Some of pressure (strong, weak, irregular, decreasing in the downward direction, sudden dot-like pressure), differences in the degree of legibility, regularity, connection, size, width, fullness, extension upwards and downwards, differences of the writing angle (slant to the right, upward angle, slant to the left), of the speed between the movements, differences between good and bad spacing, between angles and curves, between a rising and sinking tendency of the letter basis...

"Makes perfect sense," he muttered to himself, and flipped randomly to a later page, which informed him that writing the date rarely expressed the writer's libido as thoroughly as other numerals could.

Sod this. He put the book on the table, although he felt like throwing it across the room, and headed off to Pentonville. He didn't make an appointment. If he had to hang around for a while, he would: it was worth it to retain the element of surprise.

In the event, the char said Mr. Wildsmith was home, and let him in. He knocked at the door. A handsome man answered.

Aaron stared. Wildsmith, sans ghastly moustache, stared back at him.

It made all the difference. Without the foliage he had a lovely mouth, with a perfectly curved upper lip and a full lower one. He had a good nose, come to that, and his strikingly light eyes under the thick reddish brows were an intriguing, even dominating feature when the moustache wasn't demanding all the attention.

"You shaved," Aaron said, like a fool.

"Of course I shaved. Would you wear that thing longer than you had to?"

"Had to?"

"I lost a bet," Wildsmith said, sounding as though he had

explained himself as often as he was going to. "Hello again, Mr. Thurloe, and by that of course I mean Detective Sergeant Fowler. I saw you in the papers. Aren't you glam."

"May I come in?"

"Have you a warrant?"

"This isn't an official visit. I'm calling as a private citizen."

"You did that last time. I'm not a great admirer of policemen who pretend to be private citizens. It tends to end badly for the people they lie to."

Wildsmith leaned against the doorway as he said that, and crossed his arms in a belligerent manner. A split hook protruded from his left sleeve. He had a pencil clamped between the two halves of the hook.

"Are you busy?" Aaron said. "Shall I make an appointment?"

"No, you should go away."

"This is a private call. A pound an hour, wasn't it?"

"Are you going to leave or do I have to call a constable? Not that a mere constable would dare enforce the actual law against a detective sergeant," Wildsmith added sourly. "But he'll have to find some fumbling excuse not to carry out his duty by removing an importunate nuisance, and at least that will be funny."

"I don't think I'm being importunate, although you're certainly being obdurate," Aaron said. "For the third time, I'm not calling in an official capacity. I'd like to consult you on a graphological matter, and I'm happy to pay for your time."

Wildsmith looked at him. The fingers of his right hand drummed rapidly on his other sleeve. "Tell you what. You can come in if you tell me something."

"What?"

"The pieces of writing you gave me. Whose hands were they?"

"None of your affair," Aaron said, instinctively defensive.

"Fine," Wildsmith said, stepped back, and closed the door.

Or tried to. Aaron had been a police officer too long to have doors shut on him, and his foot was firmly in the way. "Hold on there."

"No. If you're acting as a police officer, I'll see your warrant. If you aren't, you come into my home on my conditions, which are, I want to know who wrote those papers."

Aaron weighed it up rapidly. He wanted answers, and he had nothing else to do, and Wildsmith had shaved.

"All right," he said. "But let me come in first."

Chapter Three

"Tea?" Joel said grudgingly.

He didn't want to give Detective Sergeant Fowler tea. He wanted to have told him to sod off and shut the door. But he'd let the man in now, and that meant some things had to be done. He hadn't served in a war for people to go around not offering other people tea.

Joel could use a cup himself, having spent a miserable couple of hours doing his accounts, trying to persuade his left arm to work with the prosthesis, as though a pencil clamped in a hook was a substitute for the press and shift of fingers. He'd been assured it would become second nature soon enough: why, he'd be able to use a fountain pen one day! You saw pictures of men welding with prosthetics, so a pencil should be nothing. His notepad, covered in scrawls and skids, gave the lie to that.

His arm was uncomfortable, too. The muscles were twinging, which hopefully just meant they were getting stronger, but the end of the stump was a tiny bit sore, and that was never good news. He wanted to take off the prosthetic for relief, but he wasn't doing *that* in front of a sodding copper. Instead, he loosened the hook enough to pull the pencil out, and set about getting the kettle on. He had a feeling that behind him Fowler was looking around. Probably at his inept efforts at writing, maybe at his bleak room. There was very little chance he was looking at Joel's arse.

Which was for the best. He didn't like or trust police, he really hadn't liked that hellish hand Thurloe-Fowler had sprung on him last time, and he had a strong feeling he wasn't going to like whatever Fowler wanted now.

He *had* rather liked the look of the man, at least before he'd learned he was a copper. Fowler was a tall man, decent shoulders, in good trim. He had black hair cropped regrettably short, perhaps to hide curls; the sort of skin that would brown easily instead of going painfully pink in April sun as Joel's did; liquid dark brown eyes. Not a Valentino, despite the Pictorial's claims, but extremely easy to look at, all the same.

Even easier if he smiled more. He'd initially held his mouth tight and hard in a decidedly unappealing way, but when he'd been startled it had softened and rounded and... oof. Joel could be a fool for a man like that.

If that man wasn't a rozzer. Which this one was. So fuck him, and not in the good way.

He brought over the tea—milk, no sugar—and took his own chair. "Well. You want something."

"Yes. It's to do with a client of yours."

"I'm not discussing my clients' business. That's confidential."

"I understand, but as it happens, I already know what you told her. Or rather, I have been informed what you told her. I want to know if that information is accurate and, if it is, how you knew it."

Joel narrowed his eyes. "That still sounds like me discussing a client's business, and also like none of yours. You said this wasn't a professional call."

"It's not. Her fiancé is my cousin. Rather, her ex-fiancé. She broke it off after what you said of him."

"I can't help that, and—do *please* try to listen—I'm not discussing my clients' business. Shall I write that down for you?"

Fowler's mouth tightened another notch. "My cousin says you made certain assertions about his conduct. I want to know if what he said is true."

"Liar, is he?" Joel said in a friendly manner.

Fowler did not react with the expected how-dare-you. He sounded quite unconcerned as he said, "One can't expect Smith's account of what Jones told him that Brown said to be reliable. And people are particularly prone to exaggerate in these circumstances."

"What circumstances?"

"Fortune telling," Fowler said, with a touch of bite. "You say 'I see a woman wearing blue' and it quickly turns into 'He saw Aunt Elsie in the blue hat she always wore.'"

He wasn't wrong, but it was still rude. "I don't tell fortunes, or see visions. I analyse handwriting."

"According to my cousin the conclusions you reached were extremely specific and highly unlikely. I'd like to know if and how you reached them."

"Oh, well, that's easy to answer," Joel said, with bright helpfulness. "I used graphology."

Fowler's jaw clamped. "You looked at his handwriting and saw intimate details of someone's personal conduct shortly before the letter was written."

This was unquestionably the Barbara Wilson job. Joel probably didn't need to worry about client confidentiality—she seemed to have told half of London about her affairs, judging by the nine new clients, all of them raving about how he'd caught out that dreadful Paul Napier-Fox—but he wasn't going to help the police, or at least this policeman, as a matter of principle. "I did a graphological analysis and gave the results."

"And was my cousin's conduct expressed in the writing angle? The curve on the vowels? A sinking tendency of the letter basis?"

Someone had been doing his homework. "Yes, all that," Joel agreed sarcastically. "I read handwriting, Detective Sergeant. I don't spy on people to get my answers, if that's what you're getting at, or have a team of shills to dig out information like one of those Spiritualist operations: there isn't the money in graphology. I just have a knack for hands." He glanced at his left sleeve. "Ironic, really."

Fowler's dreamy-dark eyes could look rather menacing, he discovered. "So you look at a scrawled note and it gives you a profound insight into someone's character and recent actions. I don't believe you, Mr. Wildsmith."

Joel eyeballed him right back. "I don't care, Detective Sergeant Fowler."

Fowler took just a fraction of a second on that. Joel couldn't fault his self-control. "And I specifically don't believe that graphology can tell anyone what you supposedly said of my cousin. How would that work? Did his handwriting look different to normal?"

"Since that's the only time I've seen his handwriting, I really couldn't—oh, was that meant to be a trap? Jolly good. But pointless, because I'm not lying. I've told you what I do, and if you don't believe me, that's your problem. You can watch me all day and night and you won't find me sending out spies, or picking pockets for information or whatever else you suspect. I'm just good with handwriting."

"*How?*" Fowler demanded.

Joel leaned back. "Before we continue this, Detective Sergeant, we had an agreement. You were going to tell me who wrote those papers."

"No—" Fowler said. It sounded involuntary, almost like he'd tried to cut it off.

"Yes. I agreed to talk to you on that basis, so you can make a down payment now. If you're going to change the deal, the door's behind you."

He saw the twitch of feeling on Fowler's face, annoyance quickly leashed. "Very well. The first paper was written by my brother-in-law."

Joel nodded approvingly. "Good choice. Decent chap. I'd let him marry my sister."

"My sister didn't give me a say in the matter," Fowler observed. "He has, by the way, just dug her a rose bed."

"That's nice?"

"You specifically said a rose bed. You said he wouldn't bring her flowers, but—"

"Good Lord, man, you can't imagine I could tell that from his hand," Joel said. There was no bottom to most people's credulity but he'd expected different from Fowler, somehow.

"Of course I don't. That's why I'm here. I want to know how you knew that."

"I *didn't* know that. It's an example I use a lot because people grasp it. I say, this is someone who does practical things to show love, he's not one for gestures. So he won't buy you flowers, but he will dig you a rose bed. People understand examples better than abstract words."

"Why roses specifically?"

"Because I don't know anything about flowers, that's why. I couldn't spot a dahlia in a police identity parade, but my family home had a rose bed."

Fowler exhaled. "And roses are about the most popular flower in the country, so you've a good chance of the example striking a chord. I dare say that's very persuasive to clients."

"Are you suggesting I should use metaphors that are completely alien to people's experience?" Joel enquired. "Anyway: brother-in-law, how nice. More importantly, what about the third one? Have you reported— No, wait, you're a rozzer. Have you arrested him?"

"As it happens."

"What for?"

Fowler hesitated for a few seconds, and finally spoke with clear reluctance. "The third paper was written by Wilfred Molesworth."

Joel took a second to place the name then sat bolt upright. "Molesworth? Kids under the floorboards Molesworth? And you made me *touch* that? Jesus! What the hell did you do that for?"

Fowler's brows had gone steeply up. "It was just a letter. There was nothing telling in it."

"It was his *hand*. I read characters from hands and I do not want to read the characters of child murderers, certainly not without warning. Don't ever do that to me again."

Fowler had a sceptical look, as if he thought Joel was play-acting. He could go screw himself. Molesworth's writing had been like plunging into a mass of cold grey cobwebs—sticky, clinging, crawling. "He hanged, didn't he?"

"Yes."

"Good. Maybe try catching the next one before he racks up four children."

That came out with a touch more venom than, perhaps, it should have, because Fowler gave just the tiniest flinch. His voice was deliberately level when he said, "I suspect it was more than four. He wouldn't say, though, and now he's dead."

Joel paused on that, considered his face. "I don't remember the case well. It was in the papers when I was in hospital getting the remains of my hand taken off, so I wasn't paying much attention."

Fowler gave a tiny shrug—not indifference, more like helplessness. "We found four bodies under the floorboards, and they had not had easy deaths. That's all we ever managed to discover. We only caught him through sheer luck in the first place. None of the missing children had even been reported, poor little wretches."

"So how did it come out?"

"Oh, Molesworth's next door neighbour marched into my police station and said she thought he was a murderer. That might be written off as spite or feuding or eccentricity, but there was something about her; she was truly unsettled. I went round on a pretext, had a nice chat and a cup of tea, and when we were done I popped into the kitchen to rinse the cups. There was a smell, and it didn't require a lot of police work from there." Fowler grimaced. "It was counted as a success, but as you say, there must have been an opportunity to catch him earlier. Something that could have been done."

"You can't solve a crime before it's been discovered, I

suppose," Joel said, and then wondered how the blazes he had found himself offering comfort to a rozzer. "Except when you entrap people into them, or frame them up, of course."

"Naturally that would make it easier," Fowler said, with some sarcasm. "Did you recognise his hand?"

"Who, Molesworth? From where?"

"You tell me."

"Oh, for God's sake. How many times must I say—"

"Until I believe you," Fowler said over him. "If it was possible to glance at a man's writing and say *This is a child murderer*, we'd have squads of you people looking over samples from everyone in the land."

"Then thank God it isn't," Joel said. "And I didn't say he was a child murderer. I said there was something horrible about him and he liked to hurt people, and I guessed children because—" Because he'd felt something vile and squirming. "Because that sort of personality targets the weak, the helpless: that's part of the fun. His hand stank of it and if you can't see that, it's not my fault."

"I *can't* see it, because it's just handwriting. And in my view, the best way to judge a man's character from his writing is if you already know who he is."

Joel clenched his fist, and felt the twitch in his left arm that suggested he'd tried to clench both. "What's your idea? That I've memorised samples of every lunatic murderer's handwriting in case a police officer under a false name asks me to look at a random piece of paper?"

"Of course not."

"Then what are you suggesting?"

"I don't know!" Fowler said, with sudden, explosive

frustration. "I want to know how you come up with this stuff, how you work it, because you have presented me with an absurd claim. You didn't simply say that Molesworth had this or that characteristic: you recoiled as though I'd presented you with a dead rat. Therefore, you *knew*."

"I knew what he was, not who he was!"

"That isn't possible."

"Well, it is sodding possible, because I do it. I just look at handwriting," Joel said savagely. "I think, *What kind of person would I be if I wrote like that?* I *imagine* being the person who wrote like that, and then I tell you what I feel like. That's the big secret you're after: I put myself behind their pen, rather than in their shoes. I don't know why it works—Christ, I don't even know that it works at all, except that everyone tells me I'm right. And I certainly can't teach you how to do it, any more than you could teach a colourblind man to see in colour."

Fowler stared at him. Joel glared back. "Don't look at me like that. It's not my fault."

"If you're unqualified—"

"Who's supposed to qualify me? Was I wrong about any of your letters?"

"But you're asking for money to do something akin to palm reading. Drawing conclusions and making things up."

"Fine. That's what I'm doing. It's still not against the law." He'd checked that carefully, and was quite sure that if he didn't claim supernatural powers, he was in the clear. "And if I'm just making it up, the laws of probability suggest I must be getting a majority of it wrong so I'm not sure why you care about a few lucky guesses landing compared to all the mistakes you're about to tell me I made."

If Fowler's mouth got any tighter, he was going to need to see a dentist. He put a hand up to massage his neck, taking a couple of deep inhalations as he did it. "So you looked at Molesworth's handwriting and thought, this is a warped and evil man. You looked at my brother-in-law's and thought, this is a decent, reliable one. Any particulars you cited were chance. Very well. So how did you make a highly specific accusation about my cousin? Or did his fiancée invent it?"

Joel was tiring of this. He had other appointments, accounts to do, and an aversion to interrogation. "Shall we stop messing about? I'm not talking about my client, but your cousin is Paul Napier-Fox, yes?"

"Yes."

"Fine. I was presented with a letter rambling about a costume ball. I said the man who wrote it was selfish and deceptive. I said he wrote it with immense self-satisfaction, as if he'd got one over on her. Specifically, I said it felt like he'd just rolled out of bed with someone else and was feeling jolly smug about it." He glowered at his opponent. "Are you telling me he had?"

There was a silence, then Fowler said, "As it happens, yes."

"Oh, for Christ's sake."

Fowler made a noise that suggested something had ripped. Possibly his brain, possibly his trousers, who could say. "That specific detail—you cannot claim that's the same as a rose bed. People don't *do* that."

"Apparently your cousin does. I didn't think much of him," Joel added. "I'd choose my cousins more carefully if I were you."

"You didn't answer my question."

"I don't know what you want me to say. The letter didn't have a glob of spunk on it or whatever you may be imagining. The writer felt smug and sneery and, I don't know, careless, the way you do after a good screw, and...it was how it felt. That's all."

"A lucky guess."

"Yes!" Joel said, a bit too loudly. "A lucky guess. A dramatic illustration of what a rotten fiancé would do, which you tell me is what your rotten cousin actually did. How is that my fault?"

"Do you gamble?" Fowler asked.

"With all the spare money I have lying around? No."

"Perhaps you should. On your telling, you're an extremely lucky man."

"Yes, I often think that," Joel said, absolutely deadpan, and saw the flick of Fowler's eyes to his left arm.

A little silence. Then Fowler said, "What would you do in my place?"

"As a proud member of the Metropolitan Police? Beat someone up for a confession, I expect."

"Does your mouth ever get you into trouble?" Fowler enquired, and it was the most unguarded he'd sounded yet. It made his own mouth look really rather good. "It's not a marvellous idea to talk like that."

"Is that a threat?"

"No, it is not. This is a free country, and you can talk as you wish. I just hope you aren't quite so provoking in your daily life."

"My daily life doesn't include coppers," Joel said. "As for what I'd do in your place... I hope I would realise that the graphologist whose time I'm taking up couldn't possibly have intimate knowledge of my cousin's post-coital correspondence or my brother-in-law's horticultural pursuits. That I'm fretting about a couple of freak coincidences, and everything else can be explained by the fact that said graphologist is as talented as he is good-looking."

Fowler began a response but managed to stop it on the first plosive, though it was *very* plosive. Joel probably shouldn't be winding him up to this extent. He was too rigid, and that sort of self-control was liable to explode.

Which reminded him.

"Anyway, I've held up my end of the deal," he said. "I've told you how I do it, and what I said. Now you tell me, who wrote the second paper?"

"Why do you want to know that?"

What he'd have liked to say was *That hand was hot as hell and I want its owner's name and address. Any ideas?* It was the kind of stupid risk he might have taken a few years ago, reckless and angry, a wild punt with a magnificent fuck on one side of the scale and God knows what dangers on the other.

He was probably too old to be that stupid. But not *that* much too old, so... "I was intrigued," he said. "Well, it's an intriguing hand. Corseted, I think I said, and someone ought to cut the laces. Does that sound right to you?"

Not a twitch, not a flicker. Fowler's face was unnaturally still.

"And you promised to tell me," Joel added. "Are you going to break your word, Detective Sergeant?"

"It's...a friend's. A friend of mine."

Ooh, the rotten liar. In both senses, because a child could spot the fib there. "That's interesting. A lady friend?"

"Excuse me?"

"I was wondering if she's single?"

That had come out of his mouth too fast for his brain to stop it, and he thought, *Oh shit*, as the dark red bloomed on Fowler's cheeks.

And then the bastard said, "Are you interested?"

"I'm a single man myself, Detective Sergeant," Joel flipped back. "Footloose and fancy-free. And I appreciate a well-filled corset, so I thought you might introduce me."

"What if I told you my friend was an octogenarian gentleman with six cats?"

"I'd say you were lying through your teeth. If one is allowed to accuse the police of such a thing, even when it's clearly true."

"I'm here in a private capacity," Fowler reminded him. "I can't put you in touch with my friend, I fear."

"At least pass on my advice. Get someone to cut those laces for you before you pop." He gave it just a second, and finished, "...is what you should tell her. If you're that sort of friend."

He was pushing this, he knew, but he could no more resist the temptation than fly. "Don't you think?" he added. "Better out than in, don't they say?"

"That reminds me," Fowler said. "When we discussed my friend's handwriting you said *I bet* and then stopped. What did you bet?"

It was ridiculous he should have remembered that, or expected Joel to remember. It was even more infuriating that Joel did.

"Oh, I don't think I should say," he temporised. "I spoke without thinking. I wouldn't want to be disrespectful to a lady."

"I won't repeat it," Fowler said. "I'd just be interested to know."

"Still. It was trench talk, if you know what I mean."

"I was in the Navy, but I expect it's much of a muchness. Say what you meant. I shan't take offence on my friend's behalf."

"Well, if you insist," Joel said. "When I read your friend's letter, I thought that was someone who, in the right circumstances—the right hands—would bang like a barn door in the wind. Oh, will you look at the time: I've a client arriving any moment. It's been an absolute pleasure, Detective Sergeant. Drop by whenever you're passing."

He ushered the slack-jawed policeman out. Then he put his back to the door, slid down to the floor, and laughed himself sick.

Chapter Four

Two days later, the memory of the look on Fowler's face was still giving Joel pleasure. It had been immature and stupidly risky, but what was life without a bit of fun?

If he wanted a serious answer to that question he should probably ask Fowler. Lord above, that man needed relief. He clearly wasn't joyless—if he hadn't been playing along by the end, Joel would eat his hat—but talk about self-control, a thing Joel respected more in the breach than the observance.

He should be glad of it in this case. He'd already done two months for soliciting a policeman, albeit by accident; a repeat offence was the absolute last thing he needed.

Anyway, he had better things to think about. The trickle of Bright Young Clients continued, thanks to Miss Barbara Wilson's enthusiasm, or Mr. Paul Napier-Fox's overactive prick, depending how you looked at it. Joel had added three quid to his savings this week alone, and his balance was looking positively healthy.

He did feel the occasional twinge of conscience. Fowler was quite right that he had no qualifications and no proof that he could do what he claimed. Joel's only defence was the fact that he could do it.

He didn't know where it had come from. He'd been an outlier all his life: red-haired, obdurately left-handed, a flamboyant show-off at least by the dour standards of his family, but he'd never considered himself psychic or any such damn fool thing. Heaven knew how badly his brother and father would have taken that, since they had been quite sufficiently embarrassed and enraged by him as it was. They'd demanded conformity and obedience; his mother and sister had supported those demands in order to keep the peace. Unfortunately, Joel was not one of Nature's peace-keepers. It had become necessary to leave home at sixteen; he had found a job in a newspaper office, sorting through letters from members of the public; and that was where it began.

So many letters, in so many hands. Rambling and ranting, fury about trauma and trivia, endless pedantry, cries for help, long screeds into the void. All of them ended up on Joel's desk, and after a while he'd realised that he was sinking into them, ignoring the text in favour of the personality behind it.

He'd actively tried to do it at first. It added interest to the day, and felt like a challenge, trying to pick out the whispers of character that underlay the droning or jabbering on the page. He even read a couple of graphology books but found them meaningless. It wasn't the angle at which you crossed a t, it was the motivating spirit in the way it was dashed or forced or drawn.

He'd pursued it as a diversion, nothing more. Looking at hands, dreaming himself into other people. Only, as he practiced, the whispers of character when he read rose to a murmur, and then to a call, a cry, a shout, a shriek.

He'd left after three years: he simply couldn't stand the barrage any more. He was looking for work in an office where everyone used typewriters when the war broke out.

And now here he was. He couldn't work with handwritten text because to have needs and hurts and worries screamed in his face all day was intolerable. He also couldn't write legibly, type at acceptable speed, or do anything requiring dexterity, because the doctors who'd promised his right hand would soon acquire the facility of his missing left had lied through their teeth. *You should have been using your right hand all along*, he'd been told several times, with an implication of *Serves you right, you persistently left-handed wretch*. As for manual labour, the clue was in the name and he'd never liked heavy lifting anyway. He thought he might be a good salesman, but that thought had occurred to a lot of men with physically incapacitating war wounds, and many of them were better spoken and better educated than him.

With a suitable prosthetic he might do a factory job, but he didn't have any prospect of getting one. There were too many able-bodied men looking for work, and too many mutilated ones who already had the experience if they could find a workaround, and thousands upon thousands who lacked both usable skills and usable bodies and desperately needed support. And there was nothing like enough money to provide for them all: Joel had spent a year or more fighting to get the hook. The Ministry for Pensions had made things entirely clear in their literature at the end of the war. "You are going back to ordinary civil life," the leaflet had said, "and it is up to you to make yourself as fit for that work as possible." Which was not exactly in the spirit of the election promises about making Britain a fit country for heroes, but here they were.

Joel intended to make himself fit for civil life and work. He had a plan. But for that he needed money, and so he'd turned his talent to account. He could read character in handwriting: if you called it graphology, it sounded like something you could charge for. As such, he'd built up a bit of a reputation and a growing clientele, enough to afford this poxy little room all to himself and start to accumulate savings. He was a respectable member of society if you didn't look too closely and Fowler's disapproval was neither here nor there.

He had just one client this morning, a regular. She ran a secretarial agency and was sufficiently concerned about the morals of 'her girls' that she wanted all potential new recruits assessed for decency. Joel wasn't surprised she couldn't keep staff. He picked out three submissions he thought had enough force of character to stand up for themselves, and sent her on her way.

He was frying sausages for lunch when there was a knock at the door. For a moment he considered not answering. It was lunchtime, damn it, and he wasn't expecting anyone.

On the other hand, his last unexpected visitor had been Fowler. Joel turned off the gas ring, went to the door, and came face to face with a policeman in uniform.

His stomach plunged instantly. For all the bravado he'd put on with Fowler, the sight of a uniform still made him feel sick and fearful.

"Mr. Joel Wildsmith?"

"Yes?"

"My name's Sergeant Hollis. May I come in?"

"Why?" Joel asked.

"Just a chat, sir."

Joel did not want him to come in at all. He also didn't want his landlady to take the hump about policemen cluttering up the halls, so he stepped back and Hollis let himself in.

"I was just making lunch," Joel said, with an absurd sense of shame at being caught preparing food. "What's this about?"

Hollis glanced at the kitchenette, but if he thought he was getting asked to sit, let alone offered a cup of tea, he could fuck off. Joel had his limits. "Bit of a question, sir. I understand you interpret people's writing. Fortune telling, sort of thing."

"I use the principles of graphology to analyse handwriting. It's nothing to do with fortune telling: it's a scientific study. There's books on the subject."

"There's books on palm reading too."

"There's books on all sorts of subjects," Joel said sharply, and bit back the urge to give 'miscarriages of justice' or 'police corruption' as examples. "I don't do magic or tell fortunes, and I don't claim to, either."

"Mmm. We have received a complaint that you made a series of slanderous allegations against a gentleman on the basis of his handwriting."

Shit. "I haven't made any allegations against anyone," Joel said. "I give assessments of character based on handwriting. I don't ask who the handwriting belongs to."

"I expect people tell you, though. No? This is my fiancé, this is my superior...?"

"That's up to them," Joel said. "For all I know they're not telling the truth. And I don't think it's slanderous to say *This hand suggests weak character*. I think that's free speech."

"Oh, undoubtedly, sir. But making a specific allegation of immoral conduct against a gentleman which cause his fiancée to break the engagement—that sounds like slander to me, and I suspect there's a very material claim for damages there."

Joel was rapidly approaching panic. He couldn't be sued for slander: even if he won, the lawyers' fees would eat every penny of his painstakingly accumulated fund.

This had to be the Paul Napier-Fox business. But Fowler had said he'd been right about Napier-Fox's post-love letter, and it wasn't slander if it was true.

Of course, it wouldn't matter if a thing was true if a Detective Sergeant and his posh cousin stood up in court and denied it. Joel knew exactly what value truth had to a policeman in the witness box. If Fowler said Napier-Fox had never admitted any such caddish thing, and Barbara Wilson gave only Joel's stupid bloody insight as the reason she'd ended her engagement, he was screwed. Could you be gaoled for slander? He couldn't remember. He felt cold all over, dizzy with fear, and with Fowler's betrayal.

Not that he knew the man to call it a betrayal. Maybe he'd panicked him with that stupid fucking flirting: Christ, he was a fool. But still, for Fowler to side with his shitty cousin to the point of telling lies in court—

Joel shut his eyes and took a deep, steadying breath.

He'd had an extremely good look at DS Fowler's handwriting, and if that man was going to err, it would be on the side of insufferable rectitude. He surely wasn't going to perjure himself to help a shitty cousin sue; that simply didn't mesh with anything Joel had seen. Which suggested there was more to this.

"I don't know about that, Sergeant," he said, as calmly as he could. "I'm no lawyer. I'll have to look into the matter.

Only, do correct me if I'm wrong, but isn't slander a civil matter?"

He said that with a look of intelligent curiosity, and held it on his face till Hollis said, "Yes, sir, it is."

"Not the Met's area, then."

"No, sir."

Joel didn't say anything to that at all. One of the journalists at the paper had advised him, in a moment of slightly inebriated expansiveness, that silence was the greatest weapon. If you were silent in a negotiation or an interview, the other party felt compelled to fill the gap. So he simply stood without a word, keeping his eyes clamped on the policeman's face despite the head-to-toe social discomfort, setting his back teeth to make himself not speak.

Hollis broke first. "Very well, sir. Just giving you a word to the wise. When people claim they can do the impossible, especially if they make allegations about their betters, that's a good way to get in a lot of trouble. We keep our eye on that sort of thing."

"Glad to hear it," Joel said. "Very responsible. Is there anything else I can do for you? In that case, good afternoon."

He shut the door behind Hollis, heart thudding. Then he went back to his half-cooked sausages, stared at them for a while, and threw them in the bin. It was a horrible waste of meat, but he'd lost his appetite.

By mid-afternoon, the waves of panic had subsided a little, which allowed the jagged rocks of his personality to re-emerge. He was deeply, intensely pissed off that a copper had threatened him in his own home, over a civil matter, when he'd told nothing but the truth. He was not going to be pushed around by a uniformed bully boy, and he intended to do something about this.

The question was what.

A formal complaint was not a possibility. He wasn't going to poke the hornets' nest, not with his record. But he *was* going to complain to the only policeman he knew, and ask him what his cousin was up to and if he seriously intended to support it. After all, Detective Sergeant Fowler had come round to Joel's home and accused him of dishonesty. He should have a chance to see how that felt.

He dug out Mr. Thurloe's typed letter asking for an appointment. It bore an address of a mansion block in Lisson Grove, which wasn't too far. He'd go and pay a visit.

Joel turned up at about seven. He didn't know what sort of hours detective sergeants worked, but they must go home eventually.

He'd realised on the way there that there might be a Mrs. Fowler. That would be a good thing: he needed to keep on the straight and narrow. Provoking Fowler had been fun—a *lot* of fun—but he'd probably have cold feet by now, he certainly would when Joel turned up at his home, and when some men got cold feet, they used them to kick with. Joel needed to keep it professional, demand what the hell was going on, and hope he'd read Fowler's hand accurately.

Tollemache Mansions, Lisson Grove proved to be a newish three-story block of flats in yellow brick overlooking a little garden square, a short walk from Marylebone Station. It was quite a lot nicer than Great Percy Street.

Plush for a policeman, Joel thought, and wondered for a second if Fowler was on the take before remembering his hand.

There was a line of doorbells, with Fowler at number three. Joel didn't ring. He waited for someone to come out, smiled his way through the building's front door, made his way up to the first floor and flat three, and rang the doorbell.

Fowler answered it, and the look of startled horror on his face was some compensation for the day Joel had had.

"Hello, Detective Sergeant. Could I have a word?"

"What are you doing here?"

"There's policemen popping up at my place at all hours. Turnabout is fair play, isn't it?"

Fowler narrowed his eyes but stepped back. "Come in."

It was a distinctly swisher place than Joel's. The kitchen was an actual separate room, as was the bedroom. Nice for some. There was a single picture on the walls, a print of some country scene, and a couple of photographs around the place; otherwise it had a rather plain look. There was no sign of female occupation. Or of another man either, or of anyone who particularly cared about their surroundings. Joel lived in a bleak empty room too, but at least he did it to save money.

"What can I do for you Mr. Wildsmith?"

"It's what you may be doing to me," Joel said. "I had a visit from a Sergeant Hollis today. He let me know that Paul Napier-Fox is liable to sue me for slander. I wondered what you knew about that."

Fowler took that in for a few unblinking seconds. Then he said, "Sit down."

Joel took the sofa, since there was only one armchair,

which looked to be the room's most-used seat. Fowler hesitated, then said, compelled, "Tea?"

"Had too much today, thanks."

"Whisky, then?"

That was slightly unexpected. "Are you allowed to drink on duty?"

"I'm not on duty. And our conversations have never been official."

Fair enough. "Thanks."

Fowler poured two whiskies—generous amount, good heavy glasses, splash of water—and passed one to Joel, then took his own seat. "Explain. This business with Paul first."

"Well, I don't know for a fact it's him," Joel temporised. "Sergeant Hollis informed me that the Met have received a complaint about me causing a lady to break her engagement to a gentleman with a specific allegation of immoral conduct. He said there's a claim for slander and material damages that the gentleman will be pressing."

"Have you provoked any other ladies to break their engagements recently?"

"One," Joel admitted. "But only your cousin's affair matches the circumstances Hollis described, so I'm assuming it's him."

Fowler frowned. "He can hardly claim slander, given he did exactly what you said he did."

"Well, that's my problem," Joel said. "There's no proof he wrote that letter post-coitally except his own admission."

"Which he made to both me and his fiancée. You could call us both as witnesses."

"I could. But he's your cousin, and the lady might not choose to wash her dirty linen in public."

"I believe she's been hanging it, and Paul, out to dry all over London," Fowler remarked. "But in any case you don't need her. My testimony will be enough."

Joel blinked at him. "You mean that? You'd speak on my behalf?"

"Not as a character witness," Fowler said, perhaps a touch bitchily. "But Paul told me in so many words that he bedded another lady before writing to his fiancée. I'm not going to deny that on the stand— You thought I would." His face changed as he said that. "You came here because you thought I'd, what, refuse to tell the truth? Claim that he never said it? Perjure myself in court?"

"I wondered," Joel said, a little defensively. "He's your cousin. The police lie."

Fowler started to say something. Joel distinctly heard the fricative of an *Ffff* before he stopped himself, jaw muscles tightening visibly. "I do not lie on oath. If I'm called I will tell the truth."

That rather cut the legs from under Joel's grievance. "Right. Yes. Well, thank you. I, er, didn't mean to insult you."

"You didn't think insulting my professional integrity would insult me?"

The budding efforts at peacemaking instantly withered. "As it happens, I have personal experience of the Metropolitan Police in the witness box, and maybe you're an honest copper but I can assure you, the one who testified against me wasn't. I suppose everyone who is accused of anything insists that the policeman lied, but this one *did*. And if that leaves me with a prejudice against the police, I'm sorry to hurt your feelings, but that does tend to happen when you screw people over."

"It doesn't help you to assume bad intent of an entire group based on an experience with one man."

"That's true if you say it about Jews, or Greeks, or redheads," Joel said. "I don't think it applies to people who choose to do a particular job. Come off it, Detective Sergeant. You don't believe there's any corrupt police?"

"I know very well there are," Fowler said, clipped. "A small minority. People love to say that one bad apple spoils the whole barrel, but I would say that most of my colleagues do a difficult job with dedication and good intent. If you encountered someone else—" He paused there for a second, then went on deliberately. "I am aware you were convicted. And of what."

Of course he was. Of course he'd looked. Joel's heart was thudding with a peculiarly unpleasant combination of fear and anticipation. "Are you."

"You're saying the charge was trumped up?"

"Yes."

"How?"

"Do you actually want me to answer that? Because I will be obliged to go into details which you might not want to hear."

"Go on."

Joel shrugged. "Public lavatory. Minding my own business. A gentleman indicated I might want to suck his cock. It seemed like a good idea at the time and there was nobody else there, so I obliged him. He seemed to enjoy himself; he certainly made sure he finished before he arrested me."

He'd been watching Fowler's face as he spoke. It was unreadable, rigid.

"I objected on the obvious grounds, and he and his mate gave me a slapping about for it. Then when it came to trial, he stood up and assured the court he was innocently minding his own business when I accosted him. No possibility that he solicited me, and of course no mention of the part where he came in my mouth. My defence counsel advised me that my story would be an admission of gross indecency if they believed it, and slander of an upright servant of the public if they didn't, so either way I'd be looking at a longer sentence than what I'd get for importuning, so I just had to sit there and take it. The judge gave me my two months as per, and the bastard smirked at me when I got taken down."

Fowler contemplated his face for a long moment. "What's his name?"

"Are you joking? Plenty of them do it. You know they do. Hanging around to entrap people—"

"I can't stop that practice. But you've told me of a gross abuse of power, and if he's done it once, he'll do it again. Abuses are like mice: they don't come in the singular." He tipped his head, looking at Joel with a distinct challenge. "If you're telling the truth you'll know his name."

"Constable James Sefton," Joel said. "Big chap, brown hair. Marylebone Station. If he finds out I've been talking, he'll probably come after me."

"I can raise questions without naming you. Leave it with me."

He actually sounded like he meant it. "Thanks," Joel said, stifled. "That would—if you could do something about that —" Fuck. He wasn't going to cry. Only, it had been so frightening and humiliating and shitty, and nobody had listened or cared at all.

The policeman was looking at Joel's face closely. Too closely. He was going red, he could feel it, but he was *not* going to cry.

"I will look into it," Fowler repeated very calmly. People probably found his deep voice soothing. "And I will also bear witness to Paul's admission if that's required, but first I will let him know that I'm ready to do so. If he goes ahead with a slander suit in the circumstances, he's even stupider than I realised, and more to the point, he'll need an equally stupid lawyer. Unless he has anything else to complain of?"

"Not that I know of."

"Then I don't think you need worry. Now, what was this about Hollis? Slander isn't generally a police matter."

"That's what I said. He turned up and made a lot of threatening noises on the theme of it being unwise to make unsupported allegations about my betters. He didn't have anything else. There *isn't* anything else."

Fowler humphed. "I'll talk to him."

"You know him?"

"I do, yes. It's, ah, possible he thought he was doing me a service by warning you off."

He looked slightly embarrassed, as well he might. Joel glowered, then reminded himself Fowler was—not on his side, as such, but being decent. "Yes, well. If you could disabuse him of that?"

"I will talk to him," Fowler repeated. "If you've done nothing more than make some very lucky guesses, you've the right to go about your business unimpeded. That said, your line of work seems very likely to bring you trouble of this sort. You might consider that."

"Thanks for the advice, but I don't have a great deal of choice," Joel said. "And, you know. Thank you for..." *Being honest* would probably offend. "I realise you don't believe in what I do, and you didn't have to listen to me at all, so—thanks, that's all."

He made to rise as he spoke. Fowler said, "No, wait."

"What?"

"Well—finish your drink. That's decent Scotch."

"Shame to waste it," Joel agreed automatically. It tasted like most Scotch to him, which was to say burning leaf mulch, but he settled back and sipped at it.

Settled back into the sofa of a policeman's home. What the blazes. He'd have expected Fowler to welcome his departure, not delay it. He wondered whether he was obliged to make light conversation while he finished his drink. "Family well?" he tried. "Roses coming along?"

"It's November," Fowler pointed out, with what felt to Joel like a similar awkwardness to his own, then relapsed into silence. Maybe this was a new interrogation technique. You put someone in an embarrassing social position and they confessed everything just to get out of it.

"So is there a Mrs. Fowler?" he asked, mostly out of desperation.

"No. No, I'm not married."

"Didn't think so. The place lacks a woman's touch."

"I've seen where you live," Fowler riposted. "You could put up a picture or two."

"Yes, hammering in a nail is very much a one-handed job."

Fowler winced. "Of course. I'm— No, hold on. You've surely friends who would do that if you asked."

"What do you know about my friends?"

"Someone bet you to grow that moustache. Only a friend would be so malicious."

Joel couldn't repress a grin. "Fair enough. Yes, I know people who would wield hammers for me. To be honest, a picture feels like more commitment than I want to make to that hovel."

"That seems entirely reasonable," Fowler said. "At ten shillings the half hour, I'd have thought you could do better."

"It's a fine rate if you have enough people paying it. Once I'm turning clients away, I'll move somewhere more salubrious."

"Just you? There's no Mrs. Wildsmith?"

It was a perfectly reasonable question of the light conversation type, and yet there was something about it, or the asking, or the way he was watching Joel's face, and in that instant, something sprang to delicate, tingling life. Joel found his lips curving.

Not that he was going to do anything stupid. He'd only just got out of one lot of trouble, and he had too much sense to screw a policeman again, especially not knowingly, and it wouldn't do to alienate Fowler, who was going to help him.

Unless Fowler was expecting a quid pro quo. He had, after all, asked Joel to stay. He didn't seem the sort of man to demand it, but if he thought Joel was interested...well, he might not even be far wrong. Those dark liquid eyes, the mouth that needed to slacken and gasp—Joel had a lot of ideas about that mouth.

None of which he would be putting into practice, because he'd learned his lesson about obliging coppers.

"Afraid not. Probably for the best." He knocked the last gasp of whisky back on that, and rose before he did anything stupid such as suggesting another drink. "I'd better go. Thanks again. I won't say you've restored my faith in the police..."

"Yes, well, I lack faith in graphologists," Fowler said, with a smile that didn't look quite right. Disappointed? "Goodbye, then, Mr. Wildsmith."

"The difference between police and graphologists is, you've never caught me in a professional lie. I'll show myself out," Joel said, and got out of there, leaving the tall, dark figure lonely behind him.

Chapter Five

Aaron had one last day off to fill. He might have gone to an art gallery, or a museum, but in fact he found himself heading over to Marylebone nick, in order to ask about the policeman who had supposedly taken advantage of Wildsmith.

'Supposedly' was an awkward word there. Aaron was well aware some of his colleagues profited from their positions. Accepting petty gifts, free food and drink, was a matter of routine; Aaron wouldn't take more than a cup of tea himself, but didn't comment when his colleagues accepted a packet of sausages or a bunch of flowers for the wife, for fear of being seen as a prig. He wasn't aware of corruption on a larger scale in G Division, but he knew bribery was rampant in Soho, where the criminals had more money. He'd also heard of colleagues taking payment in kind from ladies of the night in return for looking the other way, which was a very euphemistic way to say extorting sexual services and not doing their job.

On Wildsmith's telling, this Constable Sefton hadn't even refrained from doing his job once he'd had his way. No wonder Wildsmith was so angry: he'd not just been trapped and abused, but also cheated.

If the graphologist's account was accurate, of course. Aaron had a deep reluctance to believe it: being in the force with such men would feel like a stain on himself. But it didn't do to flinch from painful truths, and if you decided that anyone who accused the police was lying, you had stepped onto a path that led to some very dark places.

So Aaron would check up on this Constable Sefton with an open mind, and see if the fellow had any question marks hanging over him. Perhaps that would help him decide whether he could trust a word the graphologist said.

He couldn't decide that currently, and as a result thoughts of Wildsmith wouldn't leave him. The way he switched between cockiness, outright aggression, and a sudden vulnerability that the prickliness was clearly protecting. The quickness to laugh, or to anger. The unfeasible claims. The wide, joyous smile.

Not the smile. That was definitely not Aaron's affair.

He needed to reach a conclusion on Wildsmith for his own peace of mind, and whatever that conclusion might be, he also needed to stay away from him. That conversation in his dingy room had been too much: Aaron had been left speechless, deeply alarmed and, unfortunately, extremely aroused.

Bang like a barn door in the wind. The cocky little swine.

It had been a provocation only. He was sure of that, because an invitation would have been beyond reckless. But the provocation was enough to make any sensible man conclude he should keep away, and Aaron had meant to do exactly that until Wildsmith had turned up at his door.

He'd probably had to let the fellow in, but he didn't know why he'd asked him to stay; he'd regretted it immediately. It wasn't as though Wildsmith had wanted to be there. He'd left as quickly as was possible, and with that parting shot.

You've never caught me in a professional lie. Maybe Aaron should try to do just that. If he could work out what

Wildsmith was and how he was doing it, maybe that would get the blasted man out of his head.

He found an acquaintance at Marylebone police station, one Inspector Cassell, and asked for a quiet word.

"Constable Sefton?" Cassell said. "That turd."

"Oh."

"Rotten to the core. Suspended from duty last month. Won't be back if the DDI here has anything to say about it, but you know what a pain in the arse it is to deal with this sort of thing under the Chocolate Soldier."

That was Sir William Horwood, Commissioner of the Metropolitan Police. He'd gained the unaffectionate nickname as a military man who had survived a famously bizarre assassination attempt involving poisoned chocolates; among his many unlikeable characteristics was a flat refusal to believe accusations of police corruption or wrongdoing. It infuriated those who wanted the Met to be better, and also those who wanted it to look better. "What did Sefton do?" Aaron asked.

"Had his hand out. Now we're having to look at all the men he was usually on duty with, the filthy bastard. Do you have something on him? I want to make the sort of example of him everyone else won't forget in a hurry, and every little helps."

Aaron gave him Wildsmith's account, without a name. Cassell heard him out but shrugged his shoulders. "Sounds about right. We had a couple of similar complaints from street-walkers. No use to me, though."

"It's indecency on his part, and on my witness's story, it's clear incitement."

"They always claim incitement. I'm not getting bogged

down in a he-said-she-said with queers, or dragging in a hard-to-prove misconduct charge that he can use to muddy the waters."

"What Sefton did was tantamount to assault."

"It's hardly assault if your chap signed up for it."

Aaron felt his gut clench. "Under false pretences. And he paid dearly for it."

"Shouldn't have broken the law, then. I dare say he feels hard done by, but he got two months for soliciting when it might have been two years for gross indecency. The important thing is that we get Sefton dismissed from the Force, and we will, no matter what the Commissioner thinks. Why did this come to you?"

"In the course of another case. I said I'd look into it."

"Well, he can bring a complaint if he wants to admit to an offence, but he did less time than he might have, and the man responsible is losing his position anyway. I'd say your fellow is best off keeping his mouth shut. In more ways than one."

He laughed at his own witticism. Aaron's neck muscles spasmed so hard they hurt, but he made himself smile too.

That meeting didn't put him in a better mood. He told himself that Cassell was an honest man, a good copper, doing the right thing overall. Perhaps one in a hundred of their colleagues would find anything wrong in his casual dismissal of Wildsmith's experience, and Aaron just had to live with that because it wasn't going to change. The knowledge didn't make their conversation easier to swallow.

It did, however, add one more tally mark on Wildsmith's side of the ledger, even if having told the truth about his conviction didn't make his graphological claims any more plausible. Notwithstanding, Aaron made the time to drop round to his cousin's flat that evening and let him know that any attempt to bring suit for slander was doomed to fail.

"You must be joking, Ronnie," Paul said. "You can't be serious. You know this fellow lied about me."

"He said your letter read like you'd just rolled out of bed with another woman. You admitted to me that you did exactly that."

"But *he* didn't know that!" Paul protested. "You said yourself it wasn't possible for him to know. So he was making it up, and making things up about people is slander."

"Not if you hit on the truth, it isn't. Your complaint is that he accurately described something you did, and I really can't help you with that."

"Then what use is it having a policeman in the family?"

"I couldn't say."

"Anyway, you're missing the point," Paul said. "This Blacksmith fellow—"

"Wildsmith."

"He owes me damages for my reputation, and for spoiling my marriage. Babs's people are well oiled, you know, and awfully well connected. It would have been a jolly good thing for me and instead I've been made a laughing stock through no fault of my own—"

"Oh, come off it," Aaron said. "No fault?"

"She wouldn't have known if it wasn't for that little swine!

And he can't be allowed to go around making wild what-do-you-call-ems."

"Statements of fact?"

"Accusations. Oh, come on, Ronnie, you'll stand by me, won't you?"

"In what way?" Aaron enquired.

"He made this absurd allegation with no way to back it up. If I bring suit and you help me out, we can teach the little devil a lesson about slandering his betters."

Aaron had been offended when Wildsmith suggested he would lie on oath for his cousin. He wasn't offended now, since he hadn't expected or hoped for anything better, but he was annoyed. "I'm going to pretend I didn't hear that. Don't embarrass either of us by repeating it."

Paul reddened. "Oh, that's very fine, when your side's been nothing but an embarrassment to the family for thirty years. I did think you might be able to look into a clear bit of sharp practice, or simply stand by your own blood when I'm being traduced by some wretched guttersnipe. I suppose breeding will out."

That led to a frank exchange of views, during which Aaron reminded Paul about the laws governing perjury and his intent to see them applied given the chance. He left in a thoroughly bad temper, and all the more frustrated with his failure to understand how Wildsmith had done it. He had no objection to falling out with his family on principle, but he didn't want to do it for the sake of a cheat.

He arranged to buy Hollis a drink the next day, to let him know what was what. It was a slightly embarrassing meeting at first, since Hollis had intended to do Aaron a favour, and Aaron didn't want to seem unappreciative.

"The problem is, Wildsmith was right," he explained. "My cousin simply hasn't a leg to stand on in terms of a complaint, however the man got or guessed his information. And, between us, I wouldn't help Paul stand on it anyway. He's behaved like a swine and been found out, and if he doesn't like it, that's his hard luck."

"Fair enough," Hollis said amicably. "Well, I'm happy to leave it if you think best, though we can't have these people perpetrating frauds left and right."

"I don't know that Wildsmith is a fraud," Aaron said. "At least, not in the sense of rifling people's pockets for letters or bribing the servants for information. To be honest, I'm beginning to wonder if there's something in it."

Hollis squinted at him. "Really?"

It didn't seem entirely unreasonable, now Aaron was used to the idea, that handwriting might betray personality on a large scale—vanity, or cruelty, or some such—and he was sufficiently familiar with the way mediums worked to see how Wildsmith could magnify a few generalities into something that felt impressive. But then there was Paul's indiscretion, or what he'd said of Molesworth—or even what he'd said of Aaron's own hand...

He wasn't going to think about what Wildsmith had said of his hand right now.

"He was unquestionably correct several times. Maybe he's just damned acute, I don't know. I tell you what, it would be blasted useful if it *was* true. One could present a graphologist with letters from all the suspects in a case and ask him to pick the culprit."

"Ha! A judge might have something to say about that," Hollis said. "Then again, I expect people said as much about fingerprints thirty years ago. Do you really think there's something there?"

"Not to convict on. But if he could offer reliable insights, as part of the whole picture—"

"If. You know, Fowler, these people have the devil of a way of seeming plausible. You say he was right a lot, but I've seen mediums at work, and it's amazing how the memory turns a few banalities, a lucky guess, and a bit of observation into miracle-working."

"That's undeniable. What we really need is a blind test," Aaron said. "Make sure there are no clues for him to seize on at all and see what he comes up with."

"How would you do that?"

Aaron had thought about this, possibly rather too much. "Give him writing from a lot of suspects in a case, and some from unrelated people too," he said promptly. "Get him to say who he thought was guilty. But the thing is, we'd make it an *unsolved* case, one that was ongoing, with the man who gave them to him not involved in any way."

"So he couldn't read your face for the answer, or even suspicions," Hollis said thoughtfully.

"Exactly. And mark the papers with numbers and somebody else has the key. So even if he found out what case it was, he still wouldn't know who had written which paper. Get him to write his opinions down, so there's no misremembering what he said. And lock his answers in a drawer, unread, until a culprit's been identified, so there's no possibility of his views influencing the investigation."

"Yes, that would give you a very good idea of the value of graphology. A medium can fall back on *The spirits aren't talking to me* or *Someone at the seance is ruining the atmosphere* or *A ghost played a prank* or suchlike, whereas with a Scientific Graphologist, surely he should be right or wrong, no excuses." Hollis nodded slowly. "You'd need the right case, but I'd be very interested to see how that went."

"So would I. I've been chewing over how the blighter does it for weeks. It would be good to confirm for sure he's a fraud."

"And handy if he turns out to be a genius. I wonder if he'd agree to the test?"

Aaron thought about Joel Wildsmith, who grew that moustache on purpose. "I think he might, if it was a challenge. If he didn't, that would be telling in itself. Do you know, I'd blasted well give it a try, if I could find the right set-up."

Hollis took a ruminative sip of beer. "If he failed, that would be pretty good evidence of making money by false pretences for the future, wouldn't it? I might be able to help you with a case. Let me have a think."

Aaron toyed with the idea of letting Wildsmith know about Paul immediately, and decided against it. Going to see him risked looking eager in some way he didn't care to define, especially since he might be coming back if Hollis found a possible case to use as trial. Anyway, if Wildsmith had to worry a little longer, it would do him no harm and might cause him to reflect on the wisdom of making actionable claims about strangers.

He went back to work the next day, and was instantly

presented with a case that drove the graphologist from his thoughts.

"Body in the canal," he told Challice. She was looking rather drawn after yet another complaint of rape that had gone nowhere. He hated sexual offence cases: the shame and distress of the victims, the ugliness of the questions that had to be asked, and the frustrating difficulty of getting a conviction, still less a sentence that reflected the harm done.

DI Davis always put Challice on those cases. Aaron wondered if he realised how cruel that was. On darker days, he wondered if Davis knew it very well.

She deserved a bit of fresh air, he felt, which in this instance meant a corpse fished out of the Regent's Canal. "Chap's got a head wound so it needs looking into. Want to come with me?"

She beamed as though he'd asked her to dance. "I'd love to."

The body was one Gerald Marks, going by a battered card-case in his pocket and a laundry mark. He was middle-aged, and looked decidedly shop-soiled, although a night in the Thames would do that to you. His coat had also seen better days, but he had a very nice gold watch in his fob pocket.

"Which is still there," Aaron pointed out. "Wallet gone, watch left. If it was a robbery, it wasn't an efficient one."

The head wound was nasty, fracturing the back of the skull. "Could be a bludgeon, could be a paving stone. It was raining last night, so he could have slipped, and cracked his head. Not clear how he got into the canal, if that was the case."

The sodden body lay on the towpath. They were both

crouching by it in the mud, damply dusted by the relentless drizzle. The glamour of policing. Aaron looked around. "Maybe he tried to get up and fell in? I've seen people keep moving with worse injuries than this."

"But his wallet has gone, all the same," Challice said. "So, a robbery—or an accident, and a passer-by helped themselves to the wallet and shoved the body in?"

"Possible. Where was he found?" Aaron asked the uniformed constable who was hanging around, huddled under his rain-cape.

"Just where he lies, sir, only in the water. Close by the edge. A few of the boatmen fished him out with a hook."

"Cause of injury?" Challice suggested, with a slight tang of disappointment. "When they wave those hooked sticks around, there's a lot of force."

"According to the chap who found him, ma'am, his head was already smashed," the constable offered hopefully. Challice beamed at him. Clearly they both wanted a murder.

"We'll need to have the coroner's views on the head wound, and if he died from that or drowning," Aaron said. "We're not going to find any traces of his movements on the bank with all this rain and people fishing him out."

"Sorry, sir."

"Not at all, Constable." Aaron stood, wincing at the creak in his knees. "We'll need a trawl done for witnesses, and the coroner's report. Meanwhile, let's find out a little more about Mr. Marks."

The address on the business cards was close by, in Finsbury, a cramped dark building. There had been no keys on his person, but the building manager, who gave his name as Gillan, explained that he rented out his rooms as offices, and had spares.

"Mr. Marks dead," he observed, searching through a drawer. "There's a thing."

"You don't seem upset."

Mr. Gillan shrugged. He was a skinny man who Aaron suspected bought gin before food, his grey complexion limned with red capillaries. "Didn't see much of him. Didn't want to. Not a line of work I like."

"What did he do?"

"Stuck his nose into people's business, that's what," Mr. Gillan said. "No offence. He was a private detective."

"Was he indeed? Let's have a look at his room, then."

Marks' office was on the first floor, but didn't benefit from light or air, being a miserable dark space that was one dirty window away from being a broom cupboard. "Funny place to rent for a man with a nice gold watch," Challice remarked as they looked around.

"Nothing wrong with my premises, miss," Mr. Gillan said, the rebuke rather watered down by taking two goes at 'premises'.

"It all needs a jolly good scrub," Challice informed him severely.

"Excuse us, Mr. Gillan," Aaron said, and waited for the landlord to withdraw. "Challice, look at this."

He'd found a shelf of notebooks, identical cheap ones with thin ruled paper, each filled with the same handwriting and dated on the front. It crossed his mind, a fleeting thought, to wonder what Wildsmith might make of the hand.

"Marks' records," he said, pulling himself together. "This

should be useful. If..." He went to the far end of the row, checked the book, started working backwards, frowned. "They're all dated, but the last one I can find is three months ago. Have a look round for the recent ones, will you?"

They both looked. They went through the small room, the desk drawers, the piles and shelves and every scrap of space, and when they'd finished, Challice drew a long breath. "Nothing."

"No notebook or any other record dated from the last three months."

"Perhaps he hadn't had any cases recently. Or perhaps—"

Their eyes met. Aaron said, "Let's have another word with Mr. Gillan."

The landlord had refreshed himself while they were engaged in the office: the smell of gin was pungent.

"Did Mr. Marks have many clients?" Aaron asked him.

"Not so I saw," the landlord said without interest. "Not my affair."

"Was he busy in the last few weeks?"

"Dunno. Well, he must have earned something because he paid his back rent and this month's on time, no fuss, and that made a nice change."

"He'd made money. Any idea from whom?"

"How should I know?"

"Have you a home address for him?"

Gillan found a ledger with the required information. As Aaron copied it down, Challice said, "Was he working here yesterday?"

"Nah, didn't come in at all," Gillan said. "Just last night."

"He came here last night?" Aaron repeated. "What time?"

"I dunno. Midnight? Two?"

"Did you let him in?"

"Course not. He had keys."

Aaron and Challice glanced at one another. "Did you see Mr. Marks come in yourself?"

Dogged questioning elicited that Mr. Gillan slept in a small cubbyhole to one side of the entrance hall. He had been vaguely roused last night by the front door opening, and someone going up to the first floor who must have been Mr. Marks because the other office was unoccupied. Mr. Gillan had not thought it necessary to get up and check. The individual had gone upstairs, stayed there for an unspecified time, and left, not troubling anyone on the way in or out.

"What did you think he was doing in the middle of the night?" Aaron enquired, and got only a shrug. Irritated, he added, "Do you not feel it your job to protect tenants from burglars?"

"What burglar? He had a front-door key, didn't he?" Gillan said, taking offence. "Marks's office was locked when we came up, wasn't it? So what's the problem?"

"A private detective with a nasty head wound in the canal," Challice said, as they strode out of the stifling little building. "A new gold watch still on his person, and he'd been able to pay his rent recently. No keys on him, someone got into his office last night, and the records of his recent private detection are missing. *Ooh.*"

"Hold your horses," Aaron said. "We'll need a look at his home before we conclude the books are missing. And I'm not placing a lot of reliance on Gillan's testimony. I wouldn't like to put that fellow on the stand and have a defence brief demonstrate that he can't tell last night from last month."

"True," Challice agreed, deflating slightly. "You don't think he saw someone?"

"I'm reserving judgement till we see if Marks's notebooks and office keys are safely at home."

"Of course. But still..." she said with a tiny skip of excitement, and Aaron had to repress a smile. He remembered being a DC, feeling like that. It seemed rather a long time ago.

Mr. Marks had lived not far from his office, on Bunhill Row. The door was opened by a thin, tired woman. "Yes?"

"I'm Detective Sergeant Fowler, and this is Detective Constable Challice, ma'am."

Her expression clamped instantly shut, though he'd seen that often enough not to draw conclusions. "What is it?"

"Is this the residence of Mr. Gerald Marks?"

"Yes." She glanced between them. "He didn't come in last night. Has something happened?"

Her name was Mrs. Trotter. She insisted on tea, reminding Aaron of Wildsmith's almost resentful offer of the beverage, and waving away Challice's attempts to make it, and then took off her apron and sat, hands wrung together, face pale.

Marks had been with her for ten years, she said. He was a good tenant but times had been tight over the last couple of years. "He was short a few times, but I trusted him. He paid me on time for this month, and my back rent, too. He always did when he could."

"Had he a new case?" Aaron pressed. "A new client?"

"He didn't talk to me about his work. A private detective must keep things private, he used to say, and quite right too." She snapped her mouth shut illustratively.

"True. But unfortunately we do need to ask questions, so if you know anything—"

"Why?" she interrupted. "What happened to him? You said detectives. Was it—did someone—"

"We don't know exactly what happened yet. It might well have been an accident, but we have to make sure."

"Do you have any reason to suspect someone meant him harm?" Challice asked.

Mrs. Trotter drew back. "Well, he had a funny sort of business, didn't he? That's what he said. People hire you to ask questions other people don't want asked."

"Same as us," Challice remarked, with a winning smile.

"Not on Mr. Marks' saying," Mrs. Trotter retorted. "He said there was plenty of questions the police didn't want asked."

"What sort of questions?" Aaron asked.

"*I* don't know. It wasn't my business."

She was clamming up; he could feel it. "Of course he couldn't talk idly about his clients," he said, trying to sound approving. "Sounds like he knew his stuff. What sort of cases did he mostly do? I tend to think of private detectives as mostly lost dogs and divorces, but perhaps that's not fair."

Mrs. Trotter bristled a little, as he'd intended. "Indeed it is not. Mr. Marks worked on some very serious matters. Miscarriages of justice, even." She gave Aaron a significant look, which stung a touch. He hoped she had not recognised him from that dratted case in the papers; he still felt painfully self-conscious about the accusation.

"Really?" Challice chimed in. "Gosh, good for him. Was that recently?"

"No, it was not, or he wouldn't have talked about it," Mrs.

Trotter said severely. "It was the case of poor Sammy Beech. *If* you know his name."

It rang a bell, but Aaron couldn't immediately place it. He had a feeling that admitting ignorance would be taken as an affront. "What was Mr. Marks' involvement?"

"The family asked him to look into it, afterwards. They never believed what that man said of poor Sammy. Lot of lies," she said with clear challenge.

Aaron wasn't getting drawn into that. "I'd like to take a look at his room, if we may?"

Mrs. Trotter allowed it with a little reluctance. Marks had not lived with any more luxury than he'd died with; his room was sparse and worn, though clean, probably thanks to Mrs. Trotter. They didn't find money, or jewellery, or fine clothes to make sense of that gold watch. They also didn't find notebooks, papers, or anything relating to his work.

"So what do you think?" Challice asked as they made their way back to the station house.

"Right now, I don't think anything. I want to know what the coroner has to say. I want to know who used his keys last night, and where he got the money before he died. And I want to find his notebooks. I think Mr. Marks has a great deal more to tell us yet."

Chapter Six

Ten days later, Mr. Marks hadn't revealed any of his secrets. Aaron had plunged into the investigation like—well, like a corpse into a canal, but the uniformed officers hadn't turned up any witnesses to the death; no notebooks had been found; there was no indication where his flush of wealth had come from. The coroner's report was disappointingly non-committal too. Marks' injury had unquestionably killed him, but whether he had received it from a paving stone or a blunt instrument wielded by human hand could not be discerned. The coroner also reported that he was a heavy drinker who had consumed a fair amount of alcohol shortly before his death.

It was all rather frustrating, and Aaron was relieved for the change when he got the message from Hollis saying, *I've found a case for you.*

He felt positively nervous returning to see Wildsmith that evening. That was absurd. It had been weeks since the man had turned up at his flat: he'd probably forgotten about Aaron's existence. Or decided he was part of some kind of police conspiracy, one of the two.

He knocked, and could have sworn he heard an expletive from the other side of the door. Wildsmith answered after a moment. He was in his shirtsleeves, both rolled up to the elbow, despite the late November damp and chill.

"Good Lord. Detective Sergeant. Was I expecting you?"

"May I come in?"

"But of course." Wildsmith stepped back and gestured welcome.

There was a good fire going. "Not stingeing on coal, I see. Graphology paying well?"

Wildsmith lifted his left arm in reply. It was encased in leather straps from the elbow to the wrist, capped at the end by the holder of his split hook, which had a pencil clamped in it. Aaron had seen similar devices often, but usually just as the metal end poking out of a coat sleeve. Now he saw Wildsmith's forearm—pale flesh, a little soft, sprinkled with copper hair—strapped around with leather, and felt this was an indignity or an intimacy to which he had no right.

"This thing is blasted uncomfortable under every jacket I own," Wildsmith explained. "The sleeves are all too tight and the buckles catch, and it's such a flaming nuisance I sometimes throw caution to the wind and put the fire on. What can I do for you? Tea? Kettle's just on."

"You astonish me," Aaron said, and was a little too pleased to win a startled grin. "Yes, tea, please, if this is a convenient time for a chat."

"By all means." Wildsmith gestured at Aaron's usual chair—not *usual*, he'd only been here twice—cranked the device to drop the pencil, and went to the tap. His right arm, Aaron couldn't help observing, seemed significantly more muscular. Use, of course.

Aaron moved over to the table in a vague sort of way

rather than sitting at once, in order to glance at the sheets of paper there, covered in writing that looked a little childish in the determined yet uncontrolled shapes. "Practising?"

"Mmm. I spent ages trying to write with my right hand because everyone assured me that would be best, and I'm sick of it, so I need to get used to this thing."

"Why are you sick of it?"

"Because I'm left-handed," Wildsmith said with a snap. "*You* write with the wrong hand all the time, see how you like it. It reminds me of school. I want my left back, or at least the feeling of using my left."

Aaron flexed his own right hand. "I see."

"I came to that decision a while ago, in fact, but it's taken a year for me to get the hook, Government generosity to our wounded heroes being what it is. And now I have it, I don't actually *want* to get used to it, but needs must. I hope you don't object to me leaving it on? It's a sod to take off."

"Why would I object?"

"Some people might call it unsightly."

"Not in your own home, I hope."

"You'd be amazed." Wildsmith filled the teapot. "So to what do I owe this honour?"

"I've some news for you, and also a proposal."

Wildsmith spun around, right hand to his chest. "La, sir! You do me too much honour."

"Not that sort," Aaron said, unable to bite back a smile.

Wildsmith mimed a sad face, to absurd effect. "Shame. Go on, then."

"Firstly, I spoke to my cousin, Paul Napier-Fox. I advised him not to play the fool with the courts and said that I'd repeat what he told me if asked. If you get any further trouble from that quarter, let me know and I'll deal with him."

The mockery dropped away from Wildsmith's face on the instant. Aaron almost wished it wouldn't: he looked suddenly rather vulnerable. "Oh. That's a relief. It was good of you to take the trouble."

"Not at all. I spoke to Hollis too, and you needn't worry further there. It was a misunderstanding."

"Even better. Just milk, yes?"

"A splash." Aaron came up to take the mug of tea, rather than Wildsmith carrying it over. That put them close for a moment, close enough for him to see a hint of copper stubble, a look of weariness around the light eyes.

He retreated to his chair in haste, and let the other man sit before he went on. "And I went to Marylebone Station to ask about Constable Sefton."

He could all but see Wildsmith's hackles spring up. "Did you. And what did you conclude?"

"I didn't have to. He's been suspended for gross misconduct."

Wildsmith's eyes widened. "*Has* he. Has he really."

"Not related to your business. I mentioned it, without your name, to the officer dealing with the case, but—"

"Don't tell me. He didn't want to know."

"You could still make a complaint." Aaron hesitated, but had to add, "I don't know if it would do you much good."

"Of course not. It's my word against Sefton's, admission to indecent acts, blah blah, nobody cares."

"Yes," Aaron said. "I'm very sorry, but, yes."

Wildsmith let out a long silent *whew*. "But you asked. Which was good of you. And they're doing something about the swine, whatever their reasons, which is better. So I will chalk it up as a victory. Cheers." He held up his mug. Aaron startled himself by leaning over to clink it.

"Cheers. I'm sorry it's not more."

"Oh, well, my philosophy is to take your wins where you can get them. Thank you, Detective Sergeant. I do appreciate all that very much. And I am now madly curious to know about this proposal."

"It's...perhaps not a proposal. More of a challenge."

"I struggle to resist those," Wildsmith said. "As you know. Go on."

Aaron took a deep breath. "How would you feel about a blind test of your abilities?"

"Meaning?"

"I'd like you to look at some writing from a number of potential suspects in a case, and give me your opinion."

Wildsmith opened his mouth, then hesitated. "Is it a murder? A Molesworth thing?"

"I don't know."

"Sorry?"

"I don't know what the case is, or any of the people involved. And it's ongoing. Nobody knows who the culprit is, except himself. Or herself."

"Oh. So I can't draw any information out of you with my —" Wildsmith wiggled his fingers to indicate mystical powers. "And, what, you want me to look at a lot of suspects and pick the villain for you? Seriously?"

"I'd like you to give your opinion, which I won't pass on

to anyone until the case is resolved by normal means, and never if it isn't solved. This will not be part of the investigation process in any way. It's purely a test."

"For what purpose?"

"Satisfying my curiosity," Aaron said. "You've made remarkable claims and shown remarkable results. I'd like to see you repeat them in a controlled manner."

"Um." Wildsmith frowned. "Let me think about this. You've got samples of all the suspects' hands? Ones written after the crime?"

"I'll get them."

"Are you going to tell them what it's for?"

He certainly was not. Aaron quashed an ethical qualm. "There's no need for anyone to know, since they won't be used in the police investigation."

Wildsmith scowled. "They'd better not be."

"You don't trust your conclusions?"

"I'm not a nark, and I'm not doing your job for you."

"You're not being asked to; I dread to think what a defence lawyer might do with your involvement. I'm not working that case at all, and I won't pass your comments on to the man who is until it's resolved. That would be entirely wrong."

"I'd want that in writing," Wildsmith said. "Not that I doubt your word, but just in case."

"That's fair. So will you do it?"

Wildsmith made a face. "Mph. I feel like I'm taking rather a risk here."

"Why? If you can do as you claim..."

"It's possible that the writer's guilt or fear might shriek off the page. But it's also possible that I'd simply get a strong sense of a personality. Suppose one hand strikes me as cruel and violent, and another as sly and vicious. I take a punt and say it's the violent man, and you laugh at me because the case is a blackmail one. Meanwhile, my pick is beating his wife nightly."

Aaron hadn't thought of that. "Ah. Well, I suppose you'll need to write down all your conclusions—have them written," he added, as Wildsmith lofted his hook, "and give your probabilities."

"But not half a dozen, or you'll accuse me of hedging my bets, so I hope most of your suspects are reputable people. What if the real culprit isn't in your pool of suspects at all?"

"Then the test won't be valid. I'm not trying to trick you, Mr. Wildsmith. I just want to find out if you can do what you claim in conditions that make trickery impossible."

"I'm sure. I have to say, my experience suggests that if you decide to believe me, you'll see proof where it doesn't exist, and if you're determined not to, no proof will ever be enough."

"I'm a Detective Sergeant of CID. I'm reasonably good at assessing these matters."

"Hmph. And what happens as a result of this test?"

"In what sense?"

"Well, if I get it wrong, do you prosecute me for fraud? If I get it right, do you engage to defend me in the event of legal action?"

"Neither of those. Shall we say, we're making a bet?"

"We could," Wildsmith said. "What are the stakes?"

Aaron hadn't thought that far. "If you get it right, I agree you can do what you claim."

"And winning you round should be high enough stakes

for me?" It sounded challenging, but there was a slight grin lurking, and he cocked his head as he spoke.

"I'd have thought winning would be its own reward," Aaron said. "But I could throw in dinner."

Wildsmith froze. Aaron had just a second to wonder why the devil he'd said that, then the graphologist's mouth curved. "All right, but somewhere decent. None of your greasy spoons."

"Perish the thought." That wouldn't have sounded flirtatious if he'd said it to a fellow officer, therefore it hadn't sounded that way now. Aaron could feel the skin heating on his cheeks. He prayed it was the warm room.

"Dinner, then," Wildsmith said. "And if I were to lose? I'm not growing a moustache again, before you ask."

"I wouldn't want you to. If you lose, I have my scepticism confirmed. That will do for me."

Wildsmith gave him a squint-eyed look. "And this is not in any way official?"

"Absolutely not. This is my personal curiosity only. You are not entitled to call yourself a graphological consultant to the Metropolitan Police."

"All right. Let me think about it, and I'll let you know."

Aaron raised a brow. "I might have thought you'd leap at the chance to prove yourself."

"You'd be wrong, then," Wildsmith said. "I want to be sure I've thought the consequences through first. Well, here's one for starters: I'm not doing this for free. This will probably take a while and my time is a pound an hour."

"That's fair. Well, let me know, then."

Aaron rose. Wildsmith did too, started to extend his

hand for a shake, then pulled it back. "Actually, since this is unofficial...have you eaten?"

"Sorry?"

Wildsmith shrugged. "I've got more questions, and I'm starving. There's an A.B.C. just down the Pentonville Road."

"I thought you said no greasy spoons," Aaron said, stalling, because he'd felt a surge of panic. Going out for a meal with—

With someone, that was all. Not a suspect because Wildsmith had done nothing wrong; not a pal, because Aaron had no grounds to call him that. Just someone to share a meal with, instead of another solitary night at home, another omelette eaten with only the accompaniment of a book.

"I said no greasy spoons if *you're* paying," Wildsmith clarified. "Well?"

"I'm peckish myself," Aaron found himself saying. "Go on, then."

The A.B.C. was exactly like all the other A.B.C.s in London, which was to say rather downmarket compared to a Lyons Corner House, less clean than it might be, but warm and cheap. Wildsmith greeted the waitress by name, and was gestured to a table in a manner that suggested he was a regular.

"The bread's all probably stale by now but the pies are reliable," he advised Aaron.

Aaron glanced at the menu. "Can I trust the beef rissoles?"

Wildsmith rocked a hand. Aaron took that as a warning and went for the rump steak pie, Wildsmith for the macaroni cheese.

"Are you vegetarian?" Aaron asked.

"Me? No. Why would I be?"

"A lot of Spiritualists are.

"I'm not a Spiritualist."

"No, but you're—" He realised abruptly that this sentence wasn't taking him anywhere good. "Unusual?"

"Red-headed, left-handed, and queer," Wildsmith said, the words thankfully low enough to be lost in the chatter around him. "Is that what you mean?"

"Well—"

"I didn't choose to be any of the above. I didn't choose the graphology, come to that. I don't go out of my way to be different, I'm just going about my business as best I can. And I ordered macaroni cheese because I can eat it with one hand."

For God's sake. Aaron had watched him unstrap the prosthesis before they left, with a slightly uncomfortable feeling that had to do with intrusion, and the strange absence of the missing hand, and the look of leather straps on pale skin. He simply hadn't made the connection. "Sorry," he said.

"I don't actually mind you calling me a vegetarian," Wildsmith assured him. "I do object to being called a Spiritualist, because I'm neither a gullible idiot nor a crook. Whatever you may think."

"I don't believe you're either of those things."

"Then why the test?"

"If I was positive you were a crook, I wouldn't go to these

lengths," Aaron said. "I'm open to the possibility that you're unusually gifted."

"Oh. Really?"

"Possibility," Aaron repeated. "I am not inclined to believe without evidence, but I won't shut my eyes to what the evidence shows."

"Not a Spiritualist either, then."

"That's a little harsh," Aaron said. "A lot of Spiritualists aren't unduly gullible, or wilfully blind to the truth. It's a way to deal with grief."

"And it offers them hope: I know that. But seeing a medium who claims they can speak to your dead son is like me going to a doctor who promises to grow my hand back. Sometimes you just have to live with things."

He spoke with a sort of determined cheeriness that didn't really mask strong feeling. Aaron said, "May I ask what happened?"

"To my hand? Oh, funny story: I was shaving, someone startled me..."

"What?"

Wildsmith rolled his eyes. "Stray Jerry bullet, you berk."

"Where were you?"

"129 Field Ambulance. Flanders. Stretcher-bearer. I was waving for attention, and I got it. Took off most of the palm. There were a couple of carpal bones left, the ones at the base of the hand, and they thought they could save something but after a lot of faffing about—infection, whatnot—they gave up and removed the rest. It was relatively tidy as these things go and the forearm bones were undamaged. Could be worse."

Aaron didn't like to think how much time and pain the 'faffing about' had entailed. "I'm sorry."

"Worse things happen at sea. Well, you'd know: you were Navy. Where?"

"Grand Fleet, in the North Sea. Blockade work."

"How was it?"

"Cold and wet, mostly. After Jutland, Jerry didn't make much effort to break the blockade. We were twiddling our thumbs for the last couple of years. It had to be done, but..." He hadn't wanted to be in the thick of desperate fighting: he wasn't insane. But he had undeniably felt guilty about finding himself in a relatively uneventful post when others were enduring so much worse. "It did rather feel like sitting around, sometimes. In a cold, wet, stormy sort of way."

"They also serve who only sit and wait," Wildsmith said. "I'm no tactician, but you don't need to spend long at war to grasp the importance of supply lines. Talking of which, thanks, Aggie."

That was to the waitress, as she brought their food and two mugs of tea. The steak pie was surprisingly good. Wildsmith made rapid inroads into his macaroni cheese, which Aaron had always considered nursery food. That impression wasn't changed by seeing a grown man eat it with a spoon.

"Can you not use your device?" he asked. "To hold a knife, I mean?"

"I can, but I've been using it all day and I'm tired. Sometimes macaroni cheese is just easier."

"There's a good Italian place in Lisson Grove," Aaron found himself saying. "They do a dish called ravioli, if you know it? Little parcels with meat inside. You could eat that with only a fork."

"I'll have to win this bet then." Wildsmith glanced up as he said it, his pale brown eyes catching the light. They were still unsettling even with more acquaintance. You expected a man of his colouring to have green eyes, or blue, or dark brown; Wildsmith's were too light and too dark at once.

"I dare say I could spring for somewhere a little fancier, if you win," Aaron returned, because the thought of taking Joel Wildsmith to his little local place, just round the corner from his flat—

He needed to stop. "You said you had other questions," he remarked, and shoved a forkful of steak and pastry in his mouth as a means to stop himself talking further.

"Did I? Probably. Can't remember what they were. Oh, yes I can: why?"

Aaron still had a mouthful. "?"

"Why are you doing this? It can't just be curiosity, unless you're the most curious man alive. Are you trying to nail me for a fraud and hoping I'll betray myself? Testing whether I believe my own publicity? Trialling me as that graphological consultant you mentioned?"

"Not that last. I really do want to know the truth," Aaron said. "I found your results extremely impressive, and I want to know if you fooled me, I fooled myself, or you're remarkably gifted. It must be one of those, and I've been driving myself mad trying to work out which."

"Sorry to be occupying your thoughts," Wildsmith flipped back. "You should charge me rent."

Aaron had an urge to tell him *You're welcome, any time*, or some such damn fool thing. He forked up a bit of beef instead and chewed carefully.

"I suppose it's a policeman thing," Wildsmith added thoughtfully after a moment. "Wanting answers. Detective and all that."

"Mph. We don't usually get a mystery to solve, in the sense of some tidy arrangement with a limited set of suspects."

"You've never found a body in the library with a tropical fish stuffed down its throat?"

"When you're dealing with the average murderer, burglar, or racecourse terrorist, the only thing that goes down their throats is gin."

"How dreadfully lowering. Can I ask you about your work or would you rather not talk about it in your time off?"

"I don't mind." He didn't have much else to talk about. "Though I can't discuss ongoing cases."

"No, of course. But things like the gangs. The 'racecourse terrorists', as if there's a racecourse within miles of Pentonville."

"They travel," Aaron assured him. "The Sabini lot, who are the main players in this area along with the Yiddishers—"

"I know who the Sabinis are. I live here."

He said that rather sardonically, in a way that pricked Aaron's senses. "You've had problems with them?"

"Not me personally, but a friend has. And you see them in the street, in groups, which I dislike intensely, and the most awful stories go round. Maybe it's just gossip, but it feels like it's got worse recently."

"It is worse," Aaron said. "The London gangs have got

stronger since the war, no question. We don't yet have anything like the problems they have in the United States, and I hope we won't, but it's certainly something the police are aware of."

"I should hope so," Wildsmith said. "Is it true the Sabinis have an in with the Met?"

He didn't say it aggressively. It sounded for all the world like a real question rather than a sneer, but Aaron still felt as though he'd had a cup of cold water dashed in his face. "Are you referring to the case?"

"What case?"

"Mine. The one the other week."

"No?" Wildsmith said blankly.

"Did you read the reports?"

"No. I saw some guff about you in the Pictorial, but that's all. I don't follow the crime news."

Aaron felt his hackles subside a little. "One of the Brummagem Boys was on trial for killing one of the Sabini mob. His lawyer attempted to argue that G Division—the King's Cross police—were biased in favour of the Sabinis. Specifically, that I was, as the arresting officer. It's the kind of thing lawyers try sometimes."

"It's not nice having one's character impugned in court, is it?" Wildsmith remarked snidely, then lifted a hand in immediate apology. "No, sorry. That must have been horrible for you."

"It's part of the game."

"Still horrible, especially when one can't answer back. If it's any consolation, I don't believe for a second that you'd take bribes from a gang. Your hand reeks of honesty."

"Thank you," Aaron said, a second before realising he'd never actually admitted that he'd given Wildsmith his hand.

Bang like a barn door in the wind. Get someone to cut those laces for you before you pop. He could feel himself reddening. "So what *did* you mean?" he asked, almost aggressively. "About them having an in with the Met?"

"Only that everyone says it round here," Wildsmith said. "The word on the street, you know."

"That King's Cross nick is in the pay of Darby Sabini?"

"Well, that the police turn a blind eye. Warn them in advance of raids, don't do much about complaints. My friend, the one I mentioned, was very irate on the subject the other day. He's a pawnbroker. The Sabinis sent round some horrible thug demanding a weekly dole for 'protection', and threatened his wife pretty nastily when he told them to clear off. He ended up paying—as one would—and then went straight to the police."

"And?"

"They just fobbed him off, he said. Haven't done anything. His opinion is, and I quote, they're all on the take, and the Met's nothing but the biggest gang in London. He's not very happy."

"Dealing with protection rackets really isn't as easy as it might seem, largely because the perpetrators tend to be good at intimidating witnesses," Aaron said. "It takes a brave man to give evidence and stick to his story. As to bribery and corruption..." He paused, organising his thoughts, or perhaps his feelings. "It does happen. I don't know of it happening in King's Cross, or with the Sabini gang, but that doesn't mean it isn't. If the word on the street includes a name you can tell me—in strict confidence—I'll act on it."

"Really?" Wildsmith said, and then, "Yes. I dare say you would."

"I—we—would have to. Policing is a contract. The public agrees to give people like me the power to ask impertinent questions, give orders, or even deprive people of their liberty, under a strict set of laws and circumstances and restrictions that govern our behaviour. If we don't respect our part of the contract, the public can't be expected to respect theirs. And if the public decides that the police don't deserve to be obeyed, or that we don't serve a useful purpose—well, you considerably outnumber us. Corrupt police officers don't just harm individuals, they strike at the rule of law and the structure of society."

Wildsmith was looking at him, eyes wide, lips slightly parted. Aaron felt suddenly self-conscious. "You don't agree?"

"I agree entirely. I didn't think that was the Met's view. Don't you get dismissed for calling attention to your colleagues' wrongdoing?"

Aaron sent a malevolent thought in the direction of Sir William Horwood. "Our current Commissioner thinks he's defending the Force by refusing to hear a bad word against it, still less act on what he hears. It's not just morally wrong but tactically stupid. Look at my trial, the one I mentioned. If the man on the street believes that King's Cross is in the pay of the Sabinis, then so will the man in the jury box. So Dapper Melkin's brief felt it was a reasonable tactic to suggest undue influence, so that got reported in the papers, and now my reputation is stained, the newspaper-reading public has seen that idea floated about, and everyone's trust in the police is eroded a little more. It's a damn fool way to go on. Far better to cut out rot before it spreads."

"You feel passionately about this."

"Yes, I do."

"It suits you," Wildsmith said with a little, genuine smile, and Aaron felt the breath rush out of him at that. "They do all sorts of cakes and puddings here if you have a sweet tooth, but there's a pub on the corner. Can I buy you a pint? Tribute to an honest copper?"

There were a thousand reasons to say no. "Maybe just a quick one."

Chapter Seven

Joel brought the third round back from the bar. Fowler had offered to help, which was nice, Joel supposed, except that as a self-respecting Englishman he would need a lot fewer arms before he admitted he couldn't carry two pints.

It might have been a bit rash to suggest a third round. Or the first drink. Or, in fact, the meal. Possibly, and he wasn't going to rush to a decision on this one but *possibly* he was being a little reckless by behaving in a way that might be interpreted as flagrantly pursuing a Detective Sergeant. Some people might even call it near-suicidal stupidity.

On the other hand, Fowler had those liquid eyes, and when his mouth relaxed it was truly something special, and Joel had read his hand.

He responded differently to different hands, for reasons he couldn't even identify, still less explain. Sometimes he got a vague, surface sense of a few traits, sometimes a deeper feeling of understanding. Sometimes, even, it was a powerful emotional response, or a bone-deep certainty, as if he could taste or smell the person. He'd never been hit with a wave of desire until Fowler.

It was absurd. You couldn't get hot for handwriting. And yet he had, a response deep in the flesh, squeezing his lungs and tightening his groin. He'd sunk into the hand and felt all that discomfort and self-control to the point of pain and those bottled-up longings, and he'd wanted nothing more than to pop the writer's cork.

It had been a bit of a bitch to realise that the writer was the aforesaid Detective Sergeant but, Joel felt with the confidence of a man two pints in, nothing was insuperable.

He made his way through the groups of drinkers and talkers, and deposited Fowler's pint of bitter before taking his own from where his left arm clamped it to his side.

"Thanks," Fowler said. "This is the last one, though. I've work tomorrow."

"Absolutely. Can't interfere with the strong arm of the law."

"Long arm. Not strong."

Your arms look strong enough, Joel thought, though he managed to keep that one to himself. "So it is. I suppose I was thinking of strong-arming people into things."

"You usually seem to be," Fowler said, but without offence, which was good, because Joel hadn't precisely meant offence. He just tended to banter with bite, and all the more when he was nervous. "On the subject of arms..."

"Go on," Joel said, as permission seemed to be required.

"What did you mean, you don't want to get used to your prosthesis?"

"Sorry?"

"You said earlier that you didn't want to, but you were still practising, and—I realise it's none of my business. I just..." He paused a second. "I struggle to quite work you out."

Does that mean you want to work me out? Joel felt the tingle all over. Down, boy.

"Ask away," he said. "I'm very easy, really. A man of simple tastes."

Fowler narrowed his eyes and lips fractionally, as he

tended to do when Joel flirted. It still wasn't clear if he was disapproving or stopping himself from responding.

"Prosthesis," he reminded himself as much as Fowler. "Well. The thing is, they wouldn't give me one for ages. I still had my right hand, and since all right-handers seem to be convinced that left-handers just do it for our own perverse entertainment, apparently I was barely disabled at all. And, in fairness, there were plenty of people in more need than me, but I didn't ask to have my hand shot off and I do actually feel that the people responsible for the war should be responsible for the consequences. So I made a bit of a fuss and eventually got the hook affair, and it's awful. I hate it. A *hook*, like the villain in that bloody play with the flying children."

"It's not that bad. You wouldn't take your eye out if you scratched your nose."

"It feels that bad when it's strapped to me. And it's not *independent*. It holds things adequately, but it's a pain to open and close it, and it makes me feel ghastly. I don't want it."

"No," Fowler said. He was listening closely, a little frown between his brows. "I see that, but is there an alternative? If you can't learn to write with your right hand—and I take your word on that—what else is there?"

"A better prosthesis." Joel didn't usually talk about this, but then, people didn't usually ask. "There's a surgeon who's developed an artificial hand with articulated fingers, operated by arm muscle movements. I've seen a film. Chaps using them to hold teacups, and drink from them. One of them takes a matchbox from his pocket, and a match out of the box. It's not fast, of course, but it looks like a hand and it works independently. I want that."

"Good God. That's remarkable. How do you get one of those?"

"At vast cost. The inventor's a German—oh, the irony—so I'd probably have to go out there to have it fitted, and the devices are ferociously expensive. I'm never getting one from the Government, I can tell you that."

"So you're saving up for it," Fowler said. "Which is why you live in that rathole and do the graphology."

Joel would have taken exception to the description of his home as a rathole if it had been less accurate. "I don't know a better way to get the sort of money I need, except robbing a bank, which probably creates more problems than it solves."

"Professionally speaking, I would advise against it. Do you think—" He stopped.

"Do I think it will help?" Joel asked. "Do I think it will feel like a hand rather than another ungainly artificial thing strapped to my arm? Do I think it will make me whole again, or persuade other people that I am?"

"Of course you've thought about it."

Joel sighed. "I realise I might spend a fortune to get something that looks a bit more like a real hand and feels marginally less clunky, and discover I hate it just as much. I *know* that's possible. But I still want to try."

Fowler's dark eyes were fixed on his. Joel said, "What?"

"I don't know. I've done things because they feel like they might solve a problem, and then realised the problem is too big for any one thing to fix. You think it's the solution until you get there and it turns out it's just a plaster on a gaping wound." He grimaced. "But sometimes you simply need to know you've tried, and now and again, things work. I hope you get your hand, and I hope it gives you everything you want from it."

"Thank you," Joel said, a slight wobble in his voice.

"And that's why you're working so hard with the current device? Getting your arm stronger?"

"I should have been doing exercises for years. You know how it is. But now I'm putting some money away, it makes sense to get the arm back in shape, so I'll be ready."

"Sensible," Fowler said. "I suppose you've already had a lot of people assure you that there's no shame in a war wound."

"I have, yes. I've also had several people turn me down for jobs because why would they give themselves the mild inconvenience when there's so many two-handed people available?"

"Supporting our wounded heroes is one of many things that people feel passionately must be done, by somebody else."

"Ha," Joel said. "I realise I've got to get used to where I am. I don't want to be the bereaved person who insists there's still hope, and becomes prey to quackery at every turn. It's not going to grow back. But they *are* inventing all sorts of clever new devices—God knows there's no lack of a market—so I intend to try for something better than I've got. That's all."

"Good for you," Fowler said. "Damned good for you."

He extended his pint glass. Joel tapped it with his own. They both drank, Joel contemplating his glass furiously because he'd given away perhaps a bit more than he'd wanted to.

He hated his self-consciousness about his injury, so he

tried to act as if he didn't feel it, including refusing to wear a wooden hand to fill out the empty sleeve-end. He would gladly thump anyone who sneered at the hook, even while it gave him the horrors. He hadn't told anybody except his doctor about his plans to get hold of the German device, because *I want a working wooden hand* sounded like the stuff of fantasy.

And he'd just blurted it all out to Fowler. Prick.

They sat in the kind of silence you might expect when one party had just dumped a great lot of feelings on the table and the second party had no reason to care. Or at least that was how Joel felt, and he couldn't seem to find a way back into the conversation. They'd been doing fine before—two pints' worth of fine, chatting about this and that, sharing funny stories—and if his bloody hand had ruined it, he was going to kick himself for a week.

Then Fowler said, "So will you do it?"

"Do—?"

"The test." He paused, then added, "I wish you would."

"Because?" Joel said, and then, "Because you still don't trust me. Not 'still'. I mean, you don't trust me. It's always in the back of your mind that you think I'm a liar or a cheat or some kind of Svengali genius capable of setting up an elaborate deception scheme."

"Not the last one. I've discarded that possibility."

Joel eyed him malevolently. "I hope that was a compliment."

"Look, you're right," Fowler said. "I can't trust you, or I can't quite trust you, not because of you, but because of what you purport to do. I'd like to believe it's not a fraud, very much." That had a ring of truth, and more than truth. It sounded almost yearning, and Fowler paused for a second before he went on. "But as you said, believing things because one would like them to be true is a fool's game. So I hope you will do the test. I would like you to show me beyond all doubt that you really do have this remarkable gift, because then I will know how to think about you."

"And where does that take us?" Joel asked, and the words came out challenging. "If you decide you can trust me—what happens then, Mr. Detective Sergeant?"

Fowler gave a little inhalation, just audible. Their eyes were locked. "Then, I suppose, we could address the fact that you don't trust me."

Joel paused on that for a moment, and finally said, "It's not personal."

"You have reason to distrust the police. I grasp that."

I think you're all right, Joel wanted to say. *I really do. It's just the little voice at the back of my mind, the one that told me to keep low on the battlefield, reminding me how fucked I could be if you're not.*

He met Fowler's gaze, deliberately. He picked up his pint and drained it, gulping the beer down, then put it on the table with a decisive clink.

"Sod it," he said. "I'm in."

It felt a bit of an anticlimax that he then had to wait over a week to hear anything more.

It was fine. He worked hard on the writing, and found he was adjusting to the drag and weight and inflexibility of the hook to the point where his handwriting was looking almost respectable. He did a lot of arm exercises, and he saw a fair few clients. His bank balance ticked gently upwards. Not fast enough—it might be two or three years yet—but if he became more widely known he could perhaps increase his rates. Or even get a steady income. *Consultant to the Metropolitan Police* drifted across his mind a couple of times.

And then Fowler *finally* sent him a note, making a three-hour appointment, and Joel tried very hard not to feel excited.

There would be eight papers to look through. Fowler would attend and write down his impressions, which he guaranteed would not be shown to anyone until the case was concluded, or used for any purpose but the test. It was a very professional note, written by hand. Joel read it about six times, sinking into the black letters, feeling the maelstrom of Fowler's tensions and wants, and then gave up, rolled onto his bed, and put his right hand to urgent use. It still didn't feel as good as the left had, but if anyone did a prosthetic for that specific function, Joel hadn't heard about it.

He was undeniably nervous when Fowler arrived for their appointment on a dark grey Thursday afternoon. He hadn't bought a new shirt or anything stupid like that, but he might have got his hair cut, and had a decent shave while he was there. He wanted to look good, and he wanted to get this right.

Not just for Fowler either. If he was deluding himself and simply making up his responses to handwriting he should know. He probably wouldn't stop doing it, because what the blazes else was he to do, but he should know.

Fowler arrived right on time, of course. Joel couldn't prevent himself smiling. "Hello, Detective Sergeant."

"You really don't have to call me that. How are you?"

"Very well. Tea? Kettle's on."

"I'd be disappointed if it wasn't." Fowler looked around. "Suppose I sit at the table, to make notes?"

"And so I can't read your face?"

"You couldn't read my face if you tried, because I don't know anything for you to read. There are eight pieces of writing in this envelope. Some of them are from suspects in the case, and some are from uninvolved people. Each was marked with a number by the officer on the case; I don't know which is which. I propose that you assess each hand, and I'll take notes. When you've done, put the papers back in the envelope, and I'll put in my notes. We seal it, and both sign and date it across the seal, and it won't be opened unless or until the case is solved."

"Seems fair." Joel felt distinctly jangly now.

"We've done our best to make this watertight. Which means, if you get it right, it's going to be very hard to argue with your claims."

That was hardly terrifying at all. "I'll do my best not to disappoint you."

He brought over the tea. Fowler handed him the papers and prepared a notepad. Joel took out the sheaf, feeling his heart thump, and looked at the first, which had a circled 1 in the corner.

"Number one," he said after a while. Fowler had sat in absolute silence, not distracting him in the least except by existing, a dark masculine presence in the corner of his eye. "I can't see anything much here. I think this is a woman, and she feels a little nervous as she's writing. It's a hugely conscientious hand, rather joyless. Dutiful. I don't know if she's much fun to be around, but absolutely nothing in this gives me the sense of someone who'd commit a serious crime: I'm not sure she'd lower herself to shoplifting, even. This was written after the crime, yes?"

"All of them were written afterwards."

"I think, if she had done a bad thing, the thought would be overwhelming, even if she felt justified in it. She'd fret. I don't see anything like that."

Fowler was scribbling. "Is that it?"

"Yes, I think so. I am rather assuming this crime is big enough to make an impact, by the way."

"It's an ongoing investigation of a serious matter. Not shoplifting."

"Good. All right, number two." He let himself sink into the hand. "Well, he's none too bright, is he? Deeply unimaginative, no empathy. I can't imagine he's much fun to work for. I'd guess he shouts a lot, he feels like a bully. Would I expect criminal behaviour? Oof. I think if you put him into the army he'd be a perfectly good soldier, and if you put him into a gang of racecourse terrorists he'd be good at that too. I don't get any sense of guilt or fear here, but I don't know if that's because he's done nothing wrong, or if he has but he doesn't particularly think about it. He probably just goes along whatever path he's on, like a wind-up toy. If I had to sum him up in two words, it would be *No insight*. Which, I have to tell you, makes him a blasted bad fit for this sort of test because if he doesn't feel anything, I'm not going to feel it off him."

Fowler took it all down without comment. Joel waited for him to finish. He was feeling a lot more nervous now.

"Three," he said. "Oh. Oh, this...this is more interesting.

This person—not sure of the sex, going to say he—is very tense when he's writing this, but it's a curious sort of tension. I can't tell if he's afraid or exhilarated, but that's in the moment, because what he mostly is—it comes through every word—is resentful. Boiling with it. He's, oh, clenched up and furious and....you know, if he did something about it, I wouldn't be at all surprised. This is, I don't know, like a man turned down by a string of women, and if he's married at all, he chose her as a poor second and despises her for saying yes to him. Or he's been long overlooked for promotion—actually, that's much more like it, there's no sex drive here. Maybe even one of those church spinsters, if you know what I mean, someone who's directed all their energy into an organisation or a protegee and isn't getting the recognition they feel they deserve, and it's acid on the soul." He could really feel the personality now, the long-bridled, fermenting resentment. "This is a bitter, bitter person. I don't know if you could tell it to talk to them, they're all clenched up, but they're absolutely seething inside."

Fowler was watching him with those dark eyes. "Is this your pick?"

"It's certainly someone who's ripe for mischief, or rather spite, but I'd want to see the rest."

Number four was a lacklustre read: perfectly pleasant and worried a lot. Joel couldn't get anything more out of that. He made another round of tea before sitting back down to number five.

"Five. Hmph. This one's got a problem. Gambling, maybe, or...drink, perhaps, but the writing doesn't look shaky. Drugs? Might even be sex, I don't know, but he's not enjoying it much if it is. Again, I'm saying 'he' for convenience. He's ashamed, but he would be, and there's quite a lot of guilt and fear sloshing around, but I don't think they're new emotions to him at all. I'm honestly not getting much else outside the ruling compulsion. Mph. I wouldn't look at this and say he's definitely done something bad, but he's a person in the grip of addiction, and that can lead people to do bad things and not really think about it that much because the habit comes first. Ugh. I wish I knew what sort of crime this was, because honestly, two, three, and five are all capable of *something*."

Fowler wrote it all down. "Go on."

"Six... Oh, well, this is better. Oh, I like her. Her? Definitely her. This is someone...goodness, I bet she was Head Girl." In the corner of his eye, he saw Fowler's head twitch, as if he'd started to look up. "Full of enthusiasm and positivity and absolutely determined to do a jolly good job of things. Real salt of the earth stuff. A thoroughly nice person, probably so nice you barely notice the iron will." Fowler choked slightly. "Oh, definitely. Would she commit a crime? Quite possibly, if it needed doing. Beat a man to death with a lacrosse stick or a rolling pin, and then go straight to the police station to explain why it was a necessary and reasonable thing to have done. This isn't a mean soul."

That felt a bit better. He swigged tea and took up the next paper. "Seven. Oh."

"Wh—"

Joel flapped his arm for silence, glaring at the paper he held as the impressions coalesced. "Oh, no, I don't like this. I don't like this at all. I told you not to give me these people, for Christ's sake!"

"What is it?" Fowler demanded.

"This is bad. This is someone—absolutely no moral compass. Ruthless. Entirely ruthless. I would not put a lot past him. I think he would do extraordinarily bad things with open eyes. I think...shit. I think he might have blood on his hands." He stared at the uncaring loops of ink, awash with feelings he didn't like. "I really think he might. There's something so bad here, and he knows it, he's embraced it, he's relishing it, even, because it shows he's superior to everyone else."

"Superior?"

"It's how he feels. Whether he should..." Joel made himself take a step back, trying to look beyond the dark. "It's an educated hand, and he's a clever man. He might be doing pretty well in life. Well, it's probably easier if you're not encumbered with feelings—except self-interest and vanity, he's got plenty of those. Does it show? I don't know. He might seem a perfectly normal fellow, but behind the mask there's a sodding great void where a person should be. He does what he wants because what he wants is all that matters, and only he counts. That kind of superior. I don't like it." He shuddered. "Take a damn good look at this one. I don't know if he did your particular crime, but he's bloody well done *something*."

He stopped there. Fowler's pen scritched on a moment, taking it down. Joel waited for him to finish, and added, "And I did tell you not to bring me people like this."

"I don't know what the crime is," Fowler pointed out. "But I also didn't ask my colleague to avoid any specific type. I'm sorry. I didn't think of that."

His hand had gone to the back of his neck. Joel flapped the last paper. "Forget it."

Number eight read to be a thoroughly inoffensive sort of person who probably carried the collection plate in church, and knitted toys or mended children's bicycles as a hobby. It was something of a relief. Joel shuffled the papers together, put them back in the envelope, and tossed it onto the table. "Well, there you go."

"So, your conclusion?"

"Ugh. Two is very capable of doing bad things in a mindless sort of way, and five is an addict with all that entails. But three and seven are the ones that stand out. I'd say definitely seven except he's quite clever and he's got away with things before, so you might struggle to pin things on him. Three has the edge if it was poison pen letters or blackmail or forging a will, some sort of crime on paper, because of the personality. Is that hedging my bets too much?"

"It seems reasonable." Fowler put his own notes into the envelope, sealed it and signed across the flap. Joel signed in his turn. "That was certainly interesting."

"Let me know what happens, won't you? And I don't know if there's anything you can do about number seven, but look into him. Because I bet someone has complained about him, and I think you should take it seriously."

"Noted." Fowler hesitated. "I will let you know what we discover; I don't know when that might be. Well. Thanks."

"Will I see you before then?"

He had not meant to say that. Fowler froze in his tracks.

"Uh," Joel added. "I just—you know. If you fancy a pint? Or your Italian place sounded good. Not that— I just thought—" The words were propelling themselves out of his stupid mouth, apparently wanting him to sound like a needy idiot who courted policemen. "If you wanted."

"Well—ongoing case." Fowler raised the envelope as though Joel's words were arrows and the paper a shield. "Probably best not."

"No, of course. Find out I'm not a crook first."

"I didn't—"

"No, you're quite right. Silly question," Joel said. "Get the results and let me know as and when."

"I think that's best," Fowler said. "Thanks for doing this. Oh, the money is on the table."

I bet you say that to all the girls, Joel thought, but he'd fucked this up too much to say it. He glanced over and saw three pounds. "That's too much. It only took an hour."

"I booked three, so I paid for three. See you later." Fowler made a sharp exit. Joel stared at the closed door for a while and then walked over and banged his head on it, hard.

Chapter Eight

A week later, Aaron was still feeling like a bloody idiot in his spare time. It could be his new hobby.

He just suggested a pint, you could have gone was circling round in his brain, with *He all but suggested going to your place* and *Yes, he did, he wanted to* and *Job, career, reputation* hot on its heels. The only thing that shut the parade down briefly was *Wait till the results.* He'd never cared more about the results of an examination. He'd rarely cared more about the results of a case.

Which was stupid. Suppose numbers three or seven turned out to be the culprit and the graphologist was vindicated: that wouldn't make it safe for him to take Joel Wildsmith out to dinner, with his reckless smile, his sharp tongue, his gloriously scowling eyebrows, the indomitable, endlessly belligerent attitude and the vulnerability it hid. Because he had a conviction for indecent behaviour to go along with those things, and a decided problem with the police, and of all the men on whom Aaron might risk his career, his life—

All what men? There weren't any. He'd made bloody sure there weren't since he'd joined CID: at that point, illegal fumbles in dark streets or back rooms were far too weighted with catastrophic consequences. He'd experienced the humiliation of exposure at school, when Paul had caught him with another boy and made sure everyone heard about it. That had been bad enough; a CID sergeant arrested for indecency would be all over the papers. It would be career-ending.

Career-ending. The thought sat in his stomach like suet pudding, with a whole lot of other thoughts floating around it. *Maybe you oughtn't be a policeman if you can't obey the law* was one, and also *Why did you do all this if you're going to throw it away?*, and of course the throbbing, unexamined question that was always at the back of his mind, which he never looked at because if you didn't look, it might not be that bad.

You wouldn't have to get caught, a little voice wheedled. *A meal with a friend at a little place in Lisson Grove? Who's to know if he comes back to your flat after?*

Joel Wildsmith would know, that was who. And if he was indeed a fraud, a sufficiently clever one, it was entirely possible the approaches were aimed at trapping Aaron into a position where he couldn't denounce the fellow.

Aaron didn't really think Wildsmith was like that. He was also very aware that his thoughts were unfounded, unhelpful, and clouded by wanting, and it would be a lot easier if the many and worrying voices in his head would shut up for a bit.

So he set himself doggedly to work. At least it kept him busy.

The job was more frustrating than usual at the moment. Among his many other tasks, he'd looked into whether there had been a complaint about demands for protection money from a Pentonville pawnbroker, and been slapped down hard by Detective Inspector Davis, suggesting he do his own work before interfering in other people's.

That was partly due to the Gerald Marks investigation,

which was hopelessly mired. None of the leads that had seemed so enticing had gone anywhere. Marks's increased spending money had, it seemed, been paid in cash and there were no records of where it had come from. His notebooks still hadn't turned up, and nor had any recent client.

"Absolutely nothing, sir," Challice summarised. "I checked back with Mrs. Trotter, and I asked at his bank. He doesn't have a safety deposit box or anything lodged there."

"Well, it was a good idea."

"And..." She hesitated a fraction. "Sir, you remember Mrs. Trotter said he worked on a miscarriage of justice case? I looked it up."

Aaron had meant to do that, and forgotten. He kicked himself mentally. "What was it?"

"It was during the war—early seventeen. A man called Thaddeus Knight—wealthy art dealer—was beaten to death in the course of a robbery. He'd had a labourer, Sammy Beech, doing some work in his garden. A young chap, not bright, but everyone said he was a nice enough fellow." She made a face. "They found Beech dead drunk, with a bloodstained poker and a pile of cash under his bed. Beech had never been in trouble before, but there was just too much against him. He hanged."

It was a sad story, but not out of the ordinary. "Where's the problem?"

"The investigating officer had played cards with the victim a few times—in private homes, of course. He reported that at the outset of the case, but it was a very slight acquaintance, and neither owed the other money, and there was a war on and a shortage of manpower, so they left him in charge of the case. The defence barrister made quite a fuss about that in court. He said it was entirely inappropriate and the officer should have stood down, and that seems to be what the Beech family stuck on."

This was definitely ringing a bell. "Wait. The investigating officer—"

"The DDI, sir. It was Mr. Colthorne."

"Right," Aaron said. "Right. Was any substance found to the family's complaints?"

"None, sir. They spent a few years paying Marks and writing to the Home Secretary and so on, but the conviction was considered solid. The family gave up eventually, and left for Canada two years ago to start a new life. I asked Mr. Colthorne if he recalls anything about Marks—"

"You asked him that?"

"It seemed sensible," Challice said, looking a touch alarmed at his tone. "He might have remembered something. But he didn't know the name at all; he looked quite blank. Should I not have done?"

Aaron would have strongly preferred that she hadn't, but there was no point saying so now. They tossed around a few other ideas, but got nowhere. It was frustrating enough that Aaron took a long lunchbreak to walk off his annoyance.

When he got back, there was a message for him to call Sergeant Hollis.

"Done and dusted," Hollis said jovially. They'd gone to a quiet pub, not one frequented by coppers, where you could reliably get a seat and a bit of distance to talk. That meant the beer was awful, but swings and roundabouts.

"You got your man? Already?"

"It went very nicely. Found the money, got a full confession."

"Congratulations," Aaron said, tipping his glass in a casual manner that he hoped would conceal his tension. "So what was the case?"

"An embezzlement job, in a stockbroker's office."

"Embezzlement. Nothing violent?"

"Not at all. It was very niftily done, in fact. The missing money wasn't noticed for a while, and there were five clerks who would have been in a position to steal the funds. Tracks well covered. So, how shall we do this?"

"I have Wildsmith's impressions here," Aaron said, passing him the envelope. "I've kept it safe since our meeting. Do you want to check it's untouched?"

Hollis had a good look. "Not tampered with at either end. May I?" He opened the envelope, ripping across Aaron and Wildsmith's names. "Shall I read them all, or did he give a suspect?"

"He had several people who he thought were plausible candidates—"

"Ha. That's how these people work. Any number of guesses and you just hear the one you want to."

"True," Aaron said. "But he did specifically say, for a crime on paper, he'd point the finger at number three."

Hollis's mouth dropped open. He fished out a paper from his pocket and checked it. "Damnation. *Damn.*"

"He was right?"

"Spot on. Number three is an older man who'd been passed over for promotion for the third time, and decided the business owed him something for his years of service. Sour piece of work with a face like a wet weekend."

Aaron pointed wordlessly at the envelope. Hollis extracted the notes, found number three, read the paper with his brows rising steeply, and said, "What the devil."

"Yes."

"What the *devil.* No, wait. These people are jolly good at meaningful-sounding statements that could apply to anyone. Let me see the rest." He squinted at Aaron's notes. "One...yes, that's about right, very drab woman. Two is one of your ringers. I can't argue with three. Well."

"What about the rest?" Aaron made himself say.

Hollis went on through the notes. "Four—not much there, is there? Five. Oh, you're bloody joking."

"He was wrong?"

Hollis shook his head, in disbelief rather than disagreement. "He was absolutely right. Number five is up to his neck in debt on the horses. We wasted quite a lot of time assuming he was the guilty party because of it. How the *blazes*?"

They stared at each other for a moment, then Hollis shook his head and looked back at the notes. "Number six is another ringer. Seven— God almighty!"

"One of yours?" Aaron said hopefully.

"One of yours." Hollis's brows went up again as he read. "This is ripe stuff. He's calling number seven a murderer? Who is it?"

"I picked one sample out of a case file," Aaron said, his

voice horribly wooden in his own ears. "I expect that's the one."

"Ha! And is his read accurate?"

"It would be, yes."

"My God. And then number eight—oh for pity's sake. It says here he might do charitable work in his spare time. The fellow volunteers at an East End boys' club. For God's sake, Fowler, this is absurd. It's too much. Did we miss something? Could he have found out what case it was?"

"Not through me, since I didn't know. And I haven't mentioned this scheme of ours to anyone. Have you?"

"Not a living soul."

"I suppose he might have guessed I was doing this with you, and perhaps he could get hold of a list of everything you're working on from someone in your department—"

"I should damned well hope he could not," Hollis objected.

"But even if he could, he'd still need to pick the right case, get a list of the suspects *and* the ringers, get hold of samples of their hands to know who was who, discover enough about each of them to give these summaries, and then—"

"Work out that number three was the culprit, days before we did," Hollis finished for him. "That's where I stick. Stage magicians and mediums go to extraordinary lengths to get their effects, and I wouldn't put much past them. But to pull this off, this he'd have had to solve the blasted crime!"

"If he could do all that in the few days between you picking the case and me giving him the handwriting, he wouldn't be a shabby graphologist off the Pentonville Road," Aaron said. "He'd be running the Met."

They both contemplated that for a moment. Hollis took a long gulp of beer, and grimaced. "Hell's bells, Fowler. Is he the real thing?"

"Do you have a better explanation?"

"Not at the moment. Well, well, well. Do you suppose we could use him in court?"

"I wouldn't like to try it," Aaron said. "No professional qualification, and the defence would insist on proof. As well they should."

"Still, a useful man to have in the back pocket, as a consultant," Hollis mused. "Off the record."

Aaron had his doubts as to whether Wildsmith would do it. Then again, he needed the money, or at least wanted it. He didn't voice that to Hollis, and they talked a little longer about Wildsmith's accuracy, circling repeatedly back to any way he could have fixed it, concluding there simply wasn't one.

Aaron wasn't paying full attention. There were two thoughts occupying his mind to the exclusion of all else. One was that Joel Wildsmith was—impossibly, gloriously—the real thing. Not a liar or a manipulator or a fraud, but the bizarrely gifted, outrageously frank man he seemed.

The other was number seven.

"Well, this has been damned interesting," Hollis said at last. "More things in heaven and earth, and all that."

Aaron agreed with the sentiment. They finished their beers, and left the pub. Hollis walked off with a wave. Aaron went in the direction of the next pub that didn't look crowded, bought himself a half he didn't want, and sat at the table with the envelope in his hand.

He'd been assuming, or making himself assume, or

perhaps simply praying, that either the case was a murder and number seven the guilty party, or that Wildsmith would be proved to be fraudulent, deluded, wrong. Either of those outcomes would be better than this one, which was that a terrifyingly accurate graphologist had identified one of Aaron's colleagues as a moral imbecile and a probable murderer.

He'd told Hollis he'd taken number seven's sample from a file. He'd lied. In fact what he had done was to ask Challice for a sample of her handwriting, and have her copy out a passage from the novel she was reading at lunch. A few colleagues had demanded what they were up to, and Aaron had given them a cover story since he had not wanted to explain the test to his colleagues. Wildsmith called him honest, and he hoped he was, but he wasn't stupid.

So he'd claimed that his niece was enthused by a book on how to read handwriting, and had exhausted her own acquaintance. DI Davis had snorted, but DDI Colthorne had laughed and offered his services, and so Davis had done the same. And Aaron had put them in as the ringers, feeling a secret desire to get Wildsmith's opinion of his superiors. He'd thought it would be interesting, maybe even useful. That would teach him.

He knew which one was Challice's hand; he could guess number two, the unimaginative bully, was DI Davis. He did not want to face what that meant.

He wasn't usually a coward, but he still felt an urge not to check. To throw the envelope on the fire, pretend he never knew, keep his head down, let harm happen and make no effort to intervene.

No: that would not do. He could not ignore this, because

Joel Wildsmith had proved his gifts again and again, and if Aaron ignored this warning, he didn't deserve to keep his job.

So he opened the envelope, found the paper with a ringed 7 in the top corner and pulled it out, enough to confirm the very familiar hand.

"Hell," he said.

He headed straight to Pentonville without calling. Wildsmith might be out, or occupied, but Aaron couldn't wait. He couldn't sit alone at home tonight, and go into work tomorrow with this in his lap.

He arrived at about half past eight. Wildsmith's landlady made angry noises about late callers; Aaron made placatory ones and got himself allowed up. He knocked urgently on the door.

Wildsmith answered. He was wearing a frankly disreputable woollen cardigan over his shirtsleeves, and looked tousled and tired. "Oh," he said. "Hello. Was I expecting you?"

"May I come in?"

Wildsmith stepped back to let Aaron in. The bare room was familiar enough that he had an odd sense of finding safety. He still bolted the door after him.

He turned back from that to see Wildsmith looking rather startled. "Private conversation, is it?"

"Yes," Aaron said. "Please. I'm sorry it's late."

Wildsmith blinked. "Are you all right?"

"Not entirely. No."

"Sit. I'd offer you tea but you look more like neat gin."

"That—would be good, actually. Thanks."

Wildsmith had a bottle of Gordon's stashed. He poured two generous measures and handed Aaron a glass, and they took their usual seats, watching one another.

"So?" he said.

Aaron took a deep breath. "We got the results. The case, I mean. It's been solved."

"Oh. And?"

"It was an embezzlement case. The man who did it was number three. The one you named as the paper criminal, for the reasons you laid out. You got it exactly right. And you were right about number five too, he's a gambler, and number eight, who does good works. You were spot on with all of it."

"Oh," Wildsmith said again. "Well, that's good, isn't it? So you owe me dinner."

"Yes. Of course."

Wildsmith narrowed his eyes. "You know, I was anticipating feeling triumphant at this moment. Or maybe vindicated, or just to have slightly impressed you, but instead you seem to be in the grip of despair. Is it really that bad I'm not a fraud?"

Aaron tried to make himself sound more enthusiastic. "No, of course it's not. Congratulations. You've more than proved yourself. It still doesn't make any sense that you can do this, but you quite clearly can."

Wildsmith leaned back and steepled his hands, which was to say, he angled his right against the split hook. "You wanted to know if I was a liar, and you've proved to your own satisfaction that I'm not. So is this attitude of dismay because you no longer understand the world around you, or is it that you've run out of excuses not to trust me?"

It was a provocation Aaron didn't have the energy to deal with. He did try, but what came out of his mouth was, "I don't think I can trust anyone else."

Wildsmith's light eyes widened sharply. "Are you all right?"

"I— Just give me a moment, would you? Or, no, tell me something. When you make very specific assertions, as with my brother-in-law. You said that the rose bed was just an example, a lucky guess."

"It was."

"But with Paul's indiscretion, you said you knew. That you saw it."

"Not saw, felt. I had a very strong feeling."

"*How?* Where does it come from?"

Wildsmith gestured helplessly. "I have absolutely no idea. I try to put myself in the writer's shoes when I read hands, and sometimes I get quite vivid, definite impressions, and sometimes they're very strong. I don't know what gives me the clue, but I bet you have similar things in your field—policeman's instinct, or hunches, or whatever you call them. I think it's training oneself to note the tiny things that other people don't pay attention to."

"But you felt certain about Paul? That wasn't a wild guess that happened to land?"

Wildsmith exhaled. "Anything I say is a guess, in the sense that I can't know it to be true. But I didn't pull it out of my—out of the blue and it's not something I've ever said before. I had a very, very strong impression that he'd just fucked, and I really cannot tell you more. Why does it matter?"

"I just want a comparison," Aaron said. "Because when you said number seven—you remember hand number seven?—was probably a killer, how sure were you about that?"

Wildsmith didn't speak for a moment. Then he said, "Can I see it again?"

Aaron fished it out. Wildsmith looked at the paper in silence for what felt a painfully long time, and put it down. "I stand by it. There's the sense that he's superior, or untouchable, or above the normal run of humanity, and it goes with an absolute callousness. Sadistic, even. I'd be really astonished if he hasn't killed."

"We have had quite a large war," Aaron observed, a last throw of the dice.

"No, it's not that. Or at least, not just shooting at the other side. If it was in the war, it was killing unarmed prisoners, or civilians. He does things that are not allowed because it gives him pleasure, and because—well, why shouldn't he?"

"Hell."

"Is there any chance you could tell me what's going on? I mean, do you know who he is?"

"Yes."

"And you're not happy that I passed your test, because that suggests I'm right about him, and you don't like that at all."

"No."

Wildsmith hesitated. Then he leaned forward, and put his hand very gently on Aaron's knee.

"Look," he said. "I have no idea about this, but I do know

that you're a decent man. More than decent. I am absolutely sure you'll do the right thing if you can."

Aaron tried to ignore the warm touch of his hand. He ought to shift his knee, shake it off. He didn't. "I don't know what I can do. If I have the nerve to do it. I'm— Christ. The truth is, I'm afraid."

"This is sounding worse by the minute," Wildsmith said. "Do I want to know?"

"*I* didn't want to know," Aaron said, and the words rasped in his throat. "I'm sorry. You ought not be involved. I should go."

"No, stop. *Have* you involved me? I mean, does anyone other than you know about this experiment, or my conclusions?"

"Hollis. He was on the embezzlement case, but he doesn't know who the ringers were."

"The...?"

"There were five suspects. We felt one in five was too good odds for guessing so I got three other people to give me their writing. I didn't mention you."

"And number seven was one of those 'ringers', because if he was one of the suspects in Hollis's case, it wouldn't be your problem. And...I'm going to speculate you asked people at work... Oh fuck. Number seven's a copper? CID?"

Aaron really should not have come here. Wildsmith was too good a guesser. "This is not something to repeat."

"On the contrary," Wildsmith said. "It's bloody well something for you to repeat. It's not something *I'm* going to repeat because I've had quite enough trouble from the Met, thank you. Hollis isn't going to tell anyone about this, is he?"

"He doesn't know who the ringers were."

"But number seven knows he gave you a sample of his handwriting! And if word gets around about a particularly good-looking graphological genius—"

"Hollis isn't in CID. I only involved him because we'd already discussed you. I told everyone the samples were for my ten-year-old niece who's obsessed with graphology."

"Is she?"

"She's three and I hope she stays well away from the subject. Look, I won't involve you. I can't: nobody else would listen to 'A graphologist says so'. Don't worry."

"I *wasn't* worried, until you turned up and terrified me," Wildsmith pointed out. "Let me get this straight. You asked your colleagues to contribute simply to make up the numbers? You didn't suspect this man?"

"No. Or... No."

"Really? Because if your only reason to suspect him now is a ginger beer in a moth-eaten cardigan telling you he's a murderer on the basis of his handwriting—"

"I wouldn't put it like that."

"But here you are, looking sick as a dog, and I very much doubt that's simply faith in my powers. You think I'm right about number seven. You've got *reason* to think I'm right."

Aaron's head felt slightly fuzzy with the thrum of panic, the urgent desire to squash it all away. *Don't think about it, don't look.*

If he wasn't going to look, he should have gone back to Lisson Grove. He was here because Wildsmith's incisive gift had cut through to a truth, and he had to face that.

He took a deep breath. "If what you say is true, a number of other things make sense. It forms a picture. A damned ugly picture, but a coherent one."

"Is this man, number seven, clever?"

"Yes."

"Dangerous?"

"Perhaps," Aaron said, and had to add, "Yes."

"Hell and the devil," Wildsmith said. "So what are you going to do?"

Aaron knocked back a mouthful of gin. It was neat, oily, harsh on his throat. He never drank neat gin. "I'm going to look into it. There's nothing else to do, is there? I can't ignore it. He's in a position to do an astonishing amount of harm."

"Not just a constable then?"

"Don't ask any more. I mean that. I've said too much."

"Which is not your besetting sin," Wildsmith said. "You came here because you needed to talk to someone. If you want to keep doing that, you can."

Aaron's throat hurt, in the clenched way that suggested he was getting a cold, or going to cry, except he hadn't cried in a long time. "I don't think that's a good idea. You'd be best off staying entirely out of this."

"And what about you? Are you going to bring anyone else in? Tell anyone at work what's happening?"

"I don't *know* it's happening. That's the damned thing. I'll have to prove it from scratch, and looking into him is an unappealing prospect. Even raising it, if it gets back to him— Oh God, this is a nightmare."

"I'm sorry to have dropped this on you."

"Not your fault."

Wildsmith exhaled hard. Aaron caught the waft of gin. "I don't suppose I can do much, but if you'd care to take the night off—well, you're here already."

"What do you mean?"

"If you'd like to just sit here and drink gin for a while, feel free. Or tea? Or I think I have cocoa, and there's definitely toast. Well, it's currently bread, but it could become toast. And you could tell me all about it if that would help—strict confidence—or talk about something else, or sit in silence. Whatever makes you feel better."

Aaron stared at him. "Why?"

"Because you look like you need it? You've had what sounds like hell's own responsibility dumped on your shoulders out of nowhere, you seem quite upset, and if I were you, I wouldn't want to be alone right now. I've been alone when I didn't want to be, and I didn't like it. So if it helps, you're welcome to be not alone with me."

Aaron shut his eyes. He'd found Wildsmith by turn bewildering, provocative, alarming, infuriating, arousing. He thought this kindness might be the most devastating facet yet.

"Thank you," he managed. "But you missed something. I am upset and afraid and alone, but I'm also angry. I am bloody angry." He felt the truth of it rising as he spoke. "This isn't right. It is not how it should be. That man took an oath, and he takes a salary, and if he's a cuckoo in the nest, I am damned well going to deal with him, starting tomorrow."

"Good for you," Wildsmith said forcibly. "Oh, good for you."

He held out his glass. Aaron clinked it with his own, the proxy touch sending the tiniest shudder up his arm.

"And you needn't apologise," he said. "I knew something was wrong, and I haven't been facing it. If you've identified the source of the rot, I'm grateful."

Wildsmith winced. "Does it make sense that I

simultaneously bloody hope I'm right, and bloody hope I'm wrong?"

"I will be looking into it properly," Aaron assured him. "I'm not just going to take your word for it. But I've yet to see you be wrong."

"Stick around, boyo."

"About graphology."

"I'll grant you that. So, Detective Sergeant. *Does* this mean you've concluded you can trust me?"

"I don't think I have a choice," Aaron said. "If you've managed to do this by fraud, you're so much cleverer than me that I wouldn't stand a chance anyway."

"I'd prefer you to say that as if you think it's possible."

"I find it easier to believe in the graphology."

"*Ooh.*"

Wildsmith grinned at him, the familiar spark of mischief glinting in his eyes. Aaron found he was smiling back. As if his indomitable attitude was contagious; as if the crushing weight of fear and responsibility was something he could leave outside Wildsmith's door, just tonight.

As if...

"I do think I can trust you," he said. "That still leaves the question of whether you might be able to trust me."

The words landed in silence. Not uncomfortable, more a quivering awareness that he'd taken a step forward. A moment of recalibration.

Wildsmith's eyes didn't leave his face. "We could put that to the test too, Detective Sergeant. If you wanted. Though if you'd prefer gin and toast—"

"What test do you have in mind?"

Wildsmith took a deep breath. "I could make an indecent approach and see if you arrest me?"

Aaron's heart was thundering. This was terrifying and dangerous and stupid, but so was everything else in his life. He'd been afraid and despairing, and now he wasn't alone. And Wildsmith was lovely.

"Go on, then," he said.

Chapter Nine

Joel wasn't entirely sure how to do this.

It was probably the worst-timed come-on he'd ever given and certainly the most reckless. He could have just left the offer of tea and sympathy on the table. Fowler had looked shocked, lost and hurting, but he was a big boy, he'd manage.

Only, there was that fizzing spark between them. And Fowler had harked back to that crackling moment in the pub, and God damn it, Joel lived on his intuition. He might as well stand on it.

He put down his glass and rose. Fowler looked at him, confused, then stood too. Joel stepped closer.

"Hello," he said softly. "My name's Joel. You've got gorgeous eyes."

"Aaron."

"Nice name."

Joel reached up, slowly enough that Fowler, Aaron, could back away, which he didn't. He slid two fingers over his cheekbone, down his jaw, down his neck. Felt as well as saw the convulsive swallow.

"Am I in trouble yet?"

"Depends on the magistrate," Aaron said. His voice sounded a bit constricted.

Joel spread his fingers, running his hand slowly inside Aaron's jacket, down his shirt, feeling firm flesh and muscle underneath. All the way down to the jut of hipbone. "Still legally sound?"

"Becoming questionable."

Joel slid his hand round the curve of the policeman's arse. God, he wished he had two hands still: Aaron's arse deserved them. He rested his left wrist on Aaron's hip anyway, and stroked and squeezed with his right, fingers running over cloth warmed by body heat. "Where does groping your arse come in the statute book?"

"Depends on intent."

"Intend this," Joel said, and pulled him in, stepping closer as he did it, bodies colliding. He wrapped his left arm around Aaron's waist, irritatingly aware of not wanting to catch him with the hook, and felt Aaron's hands close on his back, pressing him closer. They stared at each other for a fraction of a second, and then Joel kissed him.

He felt Aaron's lips part in a tiny gasp. Then his hands tightened, and he was kissing Joel ferociously, desperately. Joel grabbed his shoulder, hanging on for dear life as he wrapped a leg around Aaron's thigh. Aaron's fingers were digging in, his lips and tongue were urgent, his substantial erection hard against Joel's stomach. They were both gasping pleasure and relief and this was fucking glorious. He'd *known* it would be glorious.

He moved his arm up unthinkingly, wanting to span more of Aaron's broad back, and caught the sodding bastard hook in his coat.

"Fuck!" he said in Aaron's mouth.

Aaron jerked his head away. "What—"

"Sorry." He tugged unavailingly, feeling his cheeks heat. "Sorry, sorry. It's this damned thing. I forgot about it."

"It's all right."

"It's not. It's a bloody pain."

Aaron put a hand to his chin, tipping it up so Joel met his eyes, dark and deep. "It is *all right*, Joel. If you forgot about it, I take that as a significant compliment."

His voice was dark and deep too, and Joel's name sounded good in it. Joel breathed out. "You…could do that. But I'm still caught in your jacket."

"Hold still." Aaron shrugged it off his shoulders, loosening the tension so between them Joel could get the hook out.

"Thanks," he said. "You know, if that's half off anyway…"

Aaron regarded him for a second, then shook the jacket past his elbows and tossed it onto a chair. He looked good in his shirtsleeves. He'd look even better out of them, in Joel's opinion.

"You could very usefully shed the cardigan," Aaron observed.

Joel had forgotten he was wearing the ghastly thing. Shit. "Probably for the best, yes. It may have moths."

"It looks like it has moths."

"They might have moved out in disgust." Joel worked his way out of it. "Uh. How do you feel about the prosthetic?"

"If you want it on, keep it on. If you want it off, take it off."

Joel unbuttoned his cuffs, pushed the sleeve back, glared at the stupid thing. He really wanted a word with whoever had invented a prosthetic whose straps were fiddly for the one-handed. "I just need to do the buckles."

"May I help?"

Joel considered, not sure how he felt about that. Then he extended his arm.

Aaron moved over and ran his hand lightly over the pale, soft, freckled skin, tracing the edges of the straps where they touched the skin. Joel shivered, and his hand stilled instantly. "Is that—"

"Fine. It's good."

Aaron's fingers moved again. He had big hands, capable ones. He eased the first strap very gently through the buckle, a slow unfastening. He eased the strap loose, sliding a finger underneath it, and Joel let out an involuntary whimper.

"Joel?"

"No, that's—that's good. Definitely."

There was nothing erotic about the prosthetic. There was everything erotic about Aaron's silent concentration, his hands on Joel's skin, carefully tending to every strap and buckle in turn. Joel breathed through it, enjoying each loosening, and found himself almost sorry there were only four.

He pulled the prosthetic's cup off his stump, and tossed it onto the table. He didn't quite want to see whether Aaron was looking at the stump or avoiding doing so.

"Better?"

"Less likely to snag, anyway." He pushed the rucked-up shirtsleeve down again. "I might keep my shirt on, though. For now."

Aaron cupped the back of his head, tugging him over so they were body to body again. "Whatever makes you comfortable."

"On which subject," Joel said, slipping his hand round

Aaron's arse again, tilting his hips. "Shall we both get rather more comfortable?"

He felt breath ruffle his hair. "I would like that, but—ugh. I think you probably realise I don't have a lot of experience. Certainly not as much as you."

"Are you insinuating something, Detective Sergeant?" Joel enquired, mock-huffily.

"Habitual bad character?"

"Yeah, fair enough." He very much wanted to pop Aaron Fowler's cork for him. The question was how to go about that, and he suspected Aaron wouldn't be much use at saying what he wanted, if he even knew himself.

Then again, those careful hands on the buckles...

"Well," he said. "Turnabout is fair play, right?"

"Yes?" Aaron said cautiously.

"Then I think I deserve a policeman sucking my cock."

Aaron inhaled sharply. There was a silence long enough for Joel to conclude without reservation that he'd got it horrifically wrong. Then Aaron's hands dropped to Joel's waistband, one on the button, one splaying over his erection, and he nearly collapsed in relief.

"I dare say you're entitled to that," Aaron said. "In a spirit of justice." He moved the braces off Joel's shoulders with his right hand, one at a time, keeping the other firmly pressed against Joel's prick. "God. Here?"

Joel propped his arse against the table. "Right here."

Aaron shut his eyes. Then he went to his knees, and Joel thought he might come there and then.

He reached out, running his hand lightly over Aaron's face. The shudder he got made him do it again, then more firmly, sliding his fingers over ear and jaw and finally lips, which parted for him. He slipped the end of his finger in, just a little, and felt the cautious touch of Aaron's tongue.

"Oh Jesus," he said. "You're going to be wonderful."

Aaron made a noise, a little moan. Joel was finding it hard to think. He suspected that breathing and staying upright were about to pose their own challenges.

"Touch me," he rasped.

Aaron moved silently, easing the cloth of Joel's opened trousers out of the way, loosening his drawers and pushing them down, letting his hard-on loose. He exhaled, the breath ruffling Joel's groin, and ran a very light finger across a tangle of hair. "Red."

"The carpet matches the curtains."

"It's beautiful."

That wasn't what most people said about ginger pubic hair, but whatever smart-alec reply Joel might have made was lost as Aaron gently circled his prick with a thumb and finger. "God!"

"Tell me," Aaron said, very softly. "Please."

"Suck me. I want your mouth on me."

He felt the tentative flick of a tongue, the light slide of lips, and Aaron took him in his mouth.

Joel had had his prick sucked as often as the next man, and probably quite a lot more than the man in front of him. Aaron was not a rank amateur, this wasn't his first, but he was clearly no expert either.

And he didn't have to be, because this was lovely. He was kneeling, sucking Joel, hand and mouth moving with more confidence as he found a rhythm. Serving him, and moaning as he did it, little pleading sounds Joel was sure he didn't know he was making.

He was loving it. Joel wished his hair was longer: he wanted to grab a handful.

"Perfect," he said. "Fuck, yes. God, you're good on your knees. Can you take a little more?"

A fractional pause. Then Aaron leaned in, and Joel's breath rushed out. "Christ. Oh, you're good, you're so fucking good. Just the way I like it." He slid his hand to the back of Aaron's head. Not exactly pushing, just a little bit of firmness, and Aaron panted around his prick and took him that tiny bit deeper, and Joel was hanging on by his fingernails now. "Jesus Christ. Lovely. Bit harder— oh, fuck, going to come, move if you don't want—I'm not joking, Aaron, oh *shit*—"

He came. Hard, compulsively, hips jerking with the relief and release, right down Detective Sergeant Fowler's throat.

Joel sagged, releasing Aaron's head to get a grip on the supportive table. Aaron's mouth was still round his prick. He stayed there for a few seconds, then pulled off, and Joel saw his eyes dart.

"Sink," he said helpfully.

Aaron hurried over, spat, and rinsed his mouth. "Well," he said, after a second. "I'm afraid that is an unquestionable offence of indecent behaviour. It's a shame I just destroyed the evidence."

The laugh exploded out of Joel. He gathered up his trousers and walked over, meeting Aaron half way, and pulled his face down for an open-mouthed kiss, tasting himself.

"That was fucking amazing," he said. "Thank you."

"My pleasure."

Joel rather thought it had been, and a nudge of a thigh

indicated that Aaron was indeed sporting a substantial bit of stiff. They also serve who only stand and get sucked off, he decided.

"Well, now." He slid his hand down, and Aaron tensed so hard he could feel it. "Aaron?"

"Uh." Aaron sounded a bit strangled. "If you touch me, I'm not going to last."

Joel just bet he wasn't. Poor bastard probably hadn't had his prick felt in years. "Don't worry about it. In fact, leave that to me. Back."

He steered Aaron backwards to his single bed. "Unbutton your shirt for me?"

Aaron grabbed for the first button. Joel said, "No, for *me*. Slowly. I want to watch you."

Aaron's eyes widened. His hand stilled, then he carefully eased the button through. Careful, thorough, exactly as Joel wanted.

"Jesus," he said. "Perfect. Keep doing that."

Button after button, revealing a tantalising glimpse of dark hair at the neck of his undershirt. Joel licked his lips, making sure Aaron saw him do it. "Take those off."

Aaron pulled down his braces, pulled off the shirt, made to drag off the vest. He tugged it over his head slowly, so Joel got a good look at his belly and chest, the dark tangles of hair, the movement of muscles.

And there he was, bare to the waist, waiting.

Joel was already hard again. He stepped forward and ran his hand up Aaron's stomach, through the wiry hair, feeling his muscles spasm.

"On the bed," he suggested.

Aaron sat, and kicked his shoes off, which was very polite

of him, then lay back. He looked like a man in a dream. Judging by his visibly straining prick, it was the kind of dream that left you wanting new sheets.

"Maybe you should unbutton," Joel suggested. "Don't touch it. Just, you know, get it clear for me."

Aaron's eyes narrowed a fraction, though his hand moved obediently. "What, exactly, are we doing?"

"Well, you said you'd come as soon as I touch your cock," Joel said. "So I thought I wouldn't do that quite yet."

"Of course," Aaron said on a breath. He unfastened his trousers, pushed at his drawers, released himself. He had a substantial prick in a nest of thick black hair, the end glistening wet.

"God, you're ready," Joel said. "I love it. Shove up."

Aaron moved, not that it left much space. Still, Joel got a knee on the bed, and bent forward. He ran his fingers delicately over Aaron's chest, flicked a nipple, heard him inhale.

Nice. He dallied over the nipple a little, rolling it in his fingers, then moved to the other. Aaron's breath was coming short. Joel skimmed his pectoral muscles, which were impressive, then traced a line up, over his powerful shoulders, up his neck which was rigid with tension, but, he thought, in a good way. He brushed his thumb over Aaron's lips, nudged it between them, felt him suck at it.

"Oh, damn, you're good," he said softly.

It wasn't what Aaron was doing: it was simply what he was. The man was trembling with desire, stiff and aching with it. Those beautiful eyes, the magnificent body, all of it being offered up to him.

He moved the thumb gently in, pushing Aaron's lips

apart because they looked good like that, wet and open. Then he shifted down to the floor so he could get his mouth to Aaron's nipple.

"Jesus," Aaron said thickly, around his thumb. "Joel."

Joel sucked a little harder. Dragged his hand down to get hold of the other nipple, working them both in turn, moved his mouth down to trail his tongue over Aaron's belly, until Aaron was writhing under him.

He pulled his mouth off at last, and shifted round to seat himself on Aaron's powerful thighs, looking down at his painfully erect prick, slick with moisture where he was leaking like a Government department. A drop had fallen onto his belly, but was still connected with a line of glimmering spiderweb. It was beautiful.

"Fuck me," he said. "To be clear, I'm actually going to be quite disappointed in myself if you *don't* blow when I touch you."

Aaron made a sound that might have been a laugh or a gasp of agony. Joel looked at him a second longer, then ran his hand up between Aaron's thighs, over his balls, up his shaft.

And that was all it took. Aaron convulsed, hips up and head back, gasping aloud, spending like a sailor in a spurt of white pleasure. Joel gave a crack of gleeful laughter. "Fuck. *Yes.*" He held on, making sure he'd milked every drop, until Aaron made a pleading noise and he reluctantly let go.

Aaron looked like he'd been hit with a brick. Joel sat back on his thighs, watching, until he blinked his eyes open.

"Great God," he said. "God. That—"

"I enjoyed every second of that," Joel said. "Particularly the last few. I think you've got spunk on your face."

"I think I might have got it on the wall," Aaron said. "Christ. Uh, would you...?" He moved his arm, just slightly, but enough that Joel read, *Come here.*

"One minute." Joel fished out a handkerchief and tossed it to him, while he rapidly unbuttoned his own shirt, because it was clean on this morning and he didn't need jism stains. He pushed it out of the way and lay down, mostly on Aaron because there was a lot of him and not much bed, and felt a strong arm close over his shoulders.

It felt so good. Joel didn't go short of encounters, but he couldn't remember the last time he d...'cuddled' wasn't really a word he could associate with Aaron somehow, but he couldn't think of a suitable alternative. Cuddled. Fine. He snuggled up into the hold.

"That was marvellous," Aaron said into his hair. "All of it."

"Wasn't it. I did say you'd bang like a barn door in the wind."

"That was you. All you."

"The devil it was. I'm giving it two weeks of practice before you're fucking me blind."

That met with a ringing silence. Joel felt his stomach plunge. "Oh. Right. Sorry."

"What?" Aaron asked, sounding slightly alarmed.

"Nothing. I just thought we might do this again, if you wanted, but—" But of course Detective Sergeant Fowler wouldn't want to be running an illegal love life on the side. Naturally not.

Which was fine. Joel had come on to Aaron in the first place, not the other way around, and he hadn't suggested anything more than a fuck, so he had no reason to expect it.

They'd had fun. It was fine. He'd just thought they might have had fun again, that was all. "Don't worry about it."

Aaron didn't reply for a second. Finally he said, carefully, "Would you want to do it again?"

Joel shrugged, feeling Aaron's arm shift over him. "If you happen to be passing."

"I wish I might be. That was the most—oh, the most generous night I've ever spent. You're astonishing. But...you know my job."

"Of course I do. I did."

"That's mine to worry about," Aaron added quickly. "Not your concern. But it doesn't make anything easier, I'm about to be in a devil of a mess, and I don't think there's any way I can have something that lasts longer than an evening."

"Of course not."

"I'm sorry. I didn't consider—"

"Nothing to consider," Joel said before this got even more embarrassing. "I made a pass, not a proposal. If you want to do this again, you know where I live, and if you don't, no hard feelings."

"Right."

Well, Joel had managed to ruin a perfectly lovely interlude very effectively. He glared at his side view of Aaron's chest.

"I'm sorry," Aaron said again. "Do you want me to go?"

He did, actually. He wanted Aaron to piss off and leave him alone with his humiliation at having made and voiced a silly assumption. And Aaron doubtless knew it because the tension was back in his tone, and Joel could tell him to piss off now and he'd leave and never come back. And then at least Joel would be able to tell himself he'd told Aaron to piss off, rather than being rejected, which would make all the difference.

Grow up, you ridiculous child.

"Ah, not yet," he said. "I'm too comfortable. You make a good pillow."

"Pillow?"

"A very manly sort of pillow. Full of muscles. It's like lying on a sack of walnuts, actually; not comfortable at all."

"All right, all right," Aaron muttered, and Joel felt him relax a fraction. "You're remarkably easygoing."

"No, I'm not. I'm a stroppy bitch."

"Also that. I meant—well, thank you for understanding my position."

"Oh, well. Better to take what you can get and enjoy it than sulk because there's not more."

Aaron's arm tightened. "That's not right."

"It's how it is. You know that as well as I do, Mr. Detective Sergeant."

"Yes." Pause. "I suppose you think I'm hell's own hypocrite."

Joel attempted a shrug. "You're hardly the only one. I know a lad who services a High Court Judge weekly. He dresses up in a garter belt and stockings—the judge, not the lad—and gets spanked. Then he sods off back to the Bench and sentences people."

Aaron exhaled long and hard. "It's contemptible. I know."

"A bit, but what's the option? And anyway, this country runs on hypocrisy like a motor-car on petrol. I don't see why you have to be better than anyone else."

"Because I've taken on a job that involves enforcing the

law on other people. You can't justifiably do that and break them in your spare time."

"Bad laws *ought* to be broken," Joel said. "First, because obeying bad laws is a mug's game, and second, because if nobody breaks them, why would anyone see the need to change them?"

"Change?"

"If enough people say *I'm not doing it your way*, they'll sodding have to change it, won't they? It's like you said about the police. If people stop agreeing to be ruled, the authorities have a problem."

"That's true, but—"

"But until it's changed, we have to live with it, one way or another," Joel went on over him. "Just like all the other stuff we live with because that's better than the alternative. So you fight it, or obey it, or try to fit your life round it by whatever means necessary. Go become Chief Superintendent and welcome, if you can do it without squashing yourself flat."

Aaron snorted. "You're a very practical man, considering how you make a living."

"The important part of that sentence is 'you make a living.'"

"Fair. And I take your point, though I don't know if I agree."

"You must agree, because you're doing it."

"Tonight," Aaron said flatly. "This is the first time in five years."

"You're sodding joking."

Aaron gave a mirthless laugh. "You must have noticed."

"Christ. Or do you not mind going without?"

"Yes, I mind," Aaron said through his teeth. "I mind a

great deal. I minded so much that, since you started your relentless campaign of flirtation and provocation and being too damned lovely in a built-up area, I haven't been able to get my mind off you. And now this."

"Oh."

"The point is—that's how I came to an accommodation, in my own head. And I've made a mockery of it tonight."

Shit and derision. "Look, this is between us," Joel said. "It's nobody else's business, and you don't have to feel bad about it if I don't. Which I don't. If anything, I feel quite flattered you broke your duck with me."

"Broke— I was not unable to find anyone, thank you. I *chose* not to."

"If you say so," Joel said with heavy scepticism. Aaron started to respond, and turned it into an exasperated noise. Joel grinned into his chest.

"Anyway," Aaron said. "It's not something I can repeat. Once in a blue moon is one thing, but I don't think I can reasonably have more."

"Right. Understood. I'm sorry, though."

"So am I. And deeply grateful for tonight. I was feeling very bleak and you made all the difference."

He sounded so aching, so alone. "I mean, we could still meet one another," Joel said. "No laws against that. In fact, we have to, because you owe me dinner, remember?"

"Oh. Yes, I do."

He didn't sound excited. "Not if you don't want. Don't worry about it."

"Nonsense. It was a bet, and you won fair and square, and as you say, there's nothing questionable about meeting in a public place. Any preferences?"

Joel didn't care about expensive meals, and didn't own the kind of clothes you needed to eat them. He wanted to go to the little Italian restaurant in Lisson Grove that served ravioli and was near Aaron's flat. "I'll leave it to you. Whenever, no hurry. Nothing fancy." He'd have to wear the hook and use a knife at a fancy place, and people always looked, or at least he always felt as if they were looking.

Aaron considered for a moment. "Do you like Indian food?"

"I've had kedgeree?" Joel said dubiously. "And my old landlady did a thing she *said* was beef curry, but frankly—"

"You haven't had Indian food. There's an excellent place in Gerrard Street. It's almost entirely frequented by Indians, and a fair few of them eat with their right hands only, so all the food is prepared with that in mind. I thought perhaps—"

"Yes," Joel said. "Let's go there."

"I'll arrange a time shortly." Aaron sighed. "I really should go now. That was a wonderful evening. And I don't think I said nearly enough as to how outstandingly impressive your results were. You were astonishingly accurate and you deserved a great deal more applause than I gave you. I would very much like to call on your abilities again."

"Any time," Joel said. "Usual rates. You know where to find me."

Aaron's arm tightened. Joel felt a whisper of movement, as though his lips had brushed Joel's hair. "I won't forget."

Chapter Ten

"It's not good enough, Fowler."

Aaron stared at the wall of DDI Colthorne's office, trying not to react. It wasn't easy. The DDI's tone was very much 'more in sorrow than in anger', but Aaron couldn't help feeling the kindly tone as a taunt.

He'd have been thrumming with tension anyway. This was the Divisional Detective Inspector hauling him over the coals, and rightly so, while DI Davis watched the whole thing with an unpleasant smile. It would have been bad even if he hadn't been so horribly conscious of Joel's words.

I think he would do extraordinarily bad things with open eyes. I think he might have blood on his hands.

Colthorne shook his head, a responsible man sadly disappointed. "You have achieved very little in the past weeks. You've ignored other jobs and wasted your time and the public's on a case that I cannot see is more than an accidental death. What are you playing at?"

Aaron might have asked himself the same. He'd spent the last fortnight, since that catastrophic, wonderful evening with Joel, in surreptitious efforts to observe his superior, as well as pursuing the Marks case, and looking back at the Sammy Beech trial. He'd let other things slide; he'd asked questions that must have seemed meaningless; he'd probably appeared shifty to his colleagues, because he was concealing something huge and the discomfort of it doubtless showed in everything he did.

And he'd achieved damn all. He hadn't found anything to back up Joel's intuition on Colthorne's handwriting, and every futile day and sleepless night was chipping away at his confidence. Maybe he was a gullible fool, taking the word of a fraud or a fantasist and destroying his career over a chimera. Maybe Marks's death was really an accident, or a killing that had nothing to do with the DDI, and Sammy Beech's name had cropped up by sheer chance, and if favours were being done to gangs it was at a lower level, and all his unnerving feelings of being cast in a role he didn't want were just his own awkwardness.

He'd felt a soul-chilling certainty when he'd seen Colthorne's hand labelled with that lethal seven. He needed to hold on to that.

He stiffened his spine, literally and metaphorically. "Sir, there are a number of suspicious circumstances in the Marks death—"

"The man was drunk, the night dark, the path slippery, the injury consistent with a fall, and the body not robbed. What is suspicious here? Have you witnesses?"

"No, sir."

"Then what are these circumstances?"

"According to the doorman at his office, someone came in—with keys—on the night of the murder and went up to the first floor, where Marks's office is. Marks's keys haven't been found. And his notebooks for the last three months are missing, meaning we can't establish the cases he was working on when he was killed, or where his recent flush of wealth came from. That all seems highly suggestive, sir."

Colthorne tipped his head. "As far as it goes, but it isn't

going far enough. Have you any reason to suppose the man who came in wasn't Marks himself?"

"The medical examiner believes he went in the water some time between ten and midnight. The doorman thought that the man who came in did so between midnight and two."

"Where is this office?"

"Macclesfield Road."

"That's minutes from the canal, and you know how loose medical timings can be, especially with a body in the water. Not to mention that keys can fall out of pockets. I suppose you haven't had the canal dragged?"

"No, sir. DI Davis indicated the expense wouldn't be approved."

"Not without more grounds. Where have you looked for these missing papers?"

"We've searched his home and looked into whether he had a safe deposit box or kept anything at his bank. He didn't."

"Who did he talk to? Friends, family? Does anyone know what he was working on?"

"Not that we've yet found. He was a loner, and kept his business confidential."

The DDI leaned back and steepled his hands. "Look, Fowler, I can see why you wanted to look twice at this, quite apart from pot-hunting."

"From what, sir?"

"Oh, don't be coy. We all like to have our picture in the newspapers, and once you have a taste of fame, it's very tempting to pursue more. Well, you have quite the publicity-hungry family, don't you?"

"Sir—"

"But the Met isn't here to bolster your public profile," Colthorne said over his objection, "and we don't need your egoism getting in the way of your job."

The injustice of that was a slap. Aaron inhaled involuntarily to protest, met Colthorne's eyes, saw nothing but mild amusement.

Behind the mask there's a sodding great void where a person should be.

"You can't make up a murder from lost keys," Colthorne went on. "By the way, I knew Marks slightly. Were you aware of that, Fowler?"

It was a simple question, simply asked. It felt menacing all the same, and Aaron had an instinctive urge to deny everything, but that would put Challice in hot water. "I believe so, sir."

"Mmm. He approached me over an old case, one where the guilty man's family felt justice had not been done. He didn't make a good impression, I must say. He was all too clearly a drinker, and in my view he was milking the Beech family for what he could get. That conviction was one of the surest of my career and I rather resent the attacks on my character that resulted."

"Sir."

"I understand the Beeches have given up their efforts to get him cleared?"

"They've emigrated, sir."

"Good. Good. A new start. I do despise charlatans like Marks who whip up grudges. I don't suppose any of us would look marvellous if someone set out to dissect every act and motive and mistake of our lives." His eyes locked with Aaron's. "Do you, Fowler? Would your character survive close examination—from an uncharitable perspective?"

Aaron's throat felt thick. "No, sir."

Colthorne gave it a long few seconds, then clicked his tongue. "Well. Marks met a bad end, and if it was foul play it must be dealt with, but on the face of things, it seems to me that you've a bee in your bonnet. From now on you will report directly to me regarding any further lines of enquiry on the Marks case, and I will tell you if I think your theories have merit."

He sounded so reasonable. Aaron said, "Sir."

"I want you to pull yourself together, Fowler. You're a good officer, but you've been erratic. There are questions being asked about your commitment and your attitude. I want to see you succeed, and I am going to put you to work accordingly."

"On what, sir?"

"There's talk of another canal workers' strike. Trouble in the Midlands, mostly, but you'll know that the Watermen's Society joined that new amalgamated union—"

"The Transport and General Workers' Union, sir."

"And we know what that means. One out, all out, and union organisers putting pressure on decent working men. A lot of Reds trying to bring the country to a standstill. That's where we need to have our focus right now, not drunken accidents. I want you on the canals, Fowler. You've got the inside knowledge, the connections. Find out what's going on. We'll make them toe the line, and come down on them like a ton of bricks if they cross it."

"You want me to investigate union activity, sir," Aaron repeated in a voice that didn't quite sound his.

"Investigate it, and put a stop to it. Someone will be going too far; they always do, and then we can nail the lot of them. Let's see you put some work in, Fowler. And—I will tell you frankly, there are questions as to where your loyalties lie, and we can't have that." He smiled. "So show me."

Aaron said, "Yes, sir." He repeated "Yes, sir," at every suitable point in the subsequent briefing until Davis asked him if he had any more questions, to which he replied, "No, sir."

Then he got out of there, went straight to his desk, dialled 190 for the Central Telegraph Office, and sent a telegram to 22 Great Percy Street. It read: WILDSMITH SHAFIS RESTAURANT GERRARD ST 7PM.

At ten past seven that evening, the wave of fury had ebbed somewhat and Aaron was sitting alone in Shafi's, wondering if Joel would arrive, and whether he wanted him to.

He still didn't know how to feel about that damned stupid perfect evening, except for 'guilty'. He'd felt Joel flinch and withdraw when he'd turned down his offer, or assumption, and hated himself for it. Joel had been so generous, so easy, so warm; he had deserved more. Aaron had wanted to give more, to bury his face in the pale neck and beg to stay as long as Joel would have him.

That couldn't happen, for more reasons than he wanted to consider at this moment. And this was the worst possible time to be continually distracted by illicit desires, by memories of the taste of skin or the sound of moaning, by the overwhelming urge to talk to someone who cared.

Joel *didn't* care, he reminded himself. He couldn't, because they barely knew one another. Yes, they'd fucked, but then, he'd fucked an undercover constable in a public lavatory: he wasn't like Aaron, holding back from the sins of the flesh until it felt like that flesh had turned to stone. Aaron wouldn't find the answer to anything in his arms, unless he counted the question, 'How can I most quickly ruin my career?'

But all that aside, Aaron owed Joel a meal, and he wanted to see him. He'd wanted to see him so much that he'd delayed and delayed what he owed, until fury had driven him to send the telegram.

Perhaps he'd delayed so long that Joel had thrown his telegram in the waste-paper bin. Perhaps that was for the best. He usually ate alone anyway, and he came to Shafi's often enough that he was on excellent terms with the owners. Rahim Mohammed was on the floor tonight, with his brother in the kitchen.

"You ready to order, Mr. Fowler?" Rahim asked. He was a forward-thinking young man who'd come to England to study, recoiled in horror at the food, and seen a gap in the market for feeding his equally appalled compatriots. Business was thriving.

"I'm hoping a friend will join me, so I'll wait a few more minutes, if I may."

"Something to nibble on," Rahim decreed, and waved at the overworked waiter. "You're well, Mr. Fowler?"

Aaron agreed he was, and asked after the family. They chatted for a couple of moments, until the doorbell jangled and Rahim looked over. "Is that your friend?"

It wasn't a great deductive leap, since most of the

clientele here was Indian, and the few other white faces belonged to regulars. "It is, yes." Aaron raised a hand.

Joel's cheeks were pinked from the cold, and he had a slightly wary look on his face which flickered into a smile as he saw Aaron, then dropped away almost immediately.

If he wanted to change his mind and leave, he didn't stand a chance. Rahim scooped him up with an enthusiastic cry of "Mr. Fowler's friend!" relieving him of coat, hat, and umbrella like a top-class pickpocket.

"Goodness," Joel said, sitting down since he wasn't being given a choice. "They seem to like you here."

"I come a lot. The food is excellent and it's very peaceful."

Joel glanced round at approximately fifty Indians talking at full volume in multiple languages. "It is?"

"Well, I find it so. Everyone here is entirely concerned with their own business, and nobody gives a damn about me. Whereas there's quite a few restaurants where a CID man walks in and half the clientele leaves."

"And who could blame them. It seems nice, anyway. Smells marvellous. Is the food very hot? My landlady's beef curry was a painful experience."

"I don't find it particularly hot. I believe the food is the type served in North India where it's less hot than in the south, but ask Rahim. Are you averse to spices?"

"I was averse to that beef curry, but I'll reserve judgement till I've eaten the real thing. You order."

Aaron did so for them both, requesting a couple of bottles of Bass. He waited until those arrived, along with a plate of fried battered vegetables and some pickles and chutneys, before saying, "Thank you for coming. I wasn't sure you would."

"No, nor was I," Joel said. "Actually I'd concluded some days ago that you were welshing on me, and had decided to tell you where to stick your dinner if you did ever trouble to get in touch."

"Oh."

"Then I thought, perhaps you'd fallen under an omnibus and were lying in a hospital bed. Clearly you aren't, which is disappointing on the face of it. But since you telegraphed, and you owe me a meal, I thought I'd give you a chance to tell me how terribly busy you've been and why it was completely impossible to fulfil your obligations in a timely fashion."

"You don't hold back, do you?" Aaron said.

"Not usually. Do we eat these?"

"It's the usual practice. Try them with the green sauce."

Joel did. His eyes widened. "God. That's delicious."

"Try the others."

Joel launched into the chutneys. "I might forgive you if it's all this good," he said after a few moments. "So *have* you been terribly busy?"

"I've been having hell's own time," Aaron said, and he didn't manage to match Joel's light tone at all.

Joel paused, fork in hand. "The thing you talked about?"

"Yes."

"Not good?"

"Not good at all. It's— Never mind. I didn't invite you here to listen to me complain."

"All right, but, since you raise it, why did you invite me?" Joel said. "Settling your debts? Because I'd resigned myself to our last meeting *being* our last meeting, and I'm intrigued what you're hoping for now."

"I don't have an ulterior motive, if that's what you mean," Aaron said stiffly.

"Ulterior motive? God above. I'm not a fainting lady from the nineteenth century."

Aaron inhaled deeply. "I don't expect anything from you. My situation hasn't changed. I owed you a meal, that's all."

"That's all. Right. Glad I bothered."

Joel could be making this easy and pleasant if he wanted to. *For God's sake*, Aaron wanted to say, *I invited you, is that not enough of an olive branch?*

Maybe it wasn't.

"I owed you a meal," he repeated, "and I wanted your company."

"Did you."

"I've had a bloody awful couple of weeks which, yes, have been terribly busy too. I'm sick to the back teeth of a lot of things, and I thought it would be good to see you. A lot better than anything else I've been doing. I'm sorry it took me so long."

"Better." Joel leaned back as Rahim and the waiter arrived, bearing a small banquet between them. "Good Lord. Are you particularly hungry?"

"I've seen you eat," Aaron pointed out. "We'll finish it, don't worry."

The food was as good as ever. Joel dug gleefully into an aromatic slow-cooked mutton dish, made indescribable noises over the curd with spinach, and had a religious experience with the fish, which was served whole and rubbed red with spices, then fried till the skin was crisp perfection and the flesh flaked effortlessly off the bone. Aaron ate with quieter enjoyment, watching him.

He'd never taken a man out for a meal before. Well, of course he had: colleagues, old friends. But he'd never taken a man for dinner as others might take a girl.

He wasn't doing that now, of course. His situation hadn't changed and he wouldn't be going back to Pentonville Road with Joel. He was just eating with him, watching his eyes light up at flavours, enjoying his pleasure.

Joel cleared his first plateful like a starving wolf and leaned back. "I am taking a breather, and then I'm going to eat literally everything else and not move for days," he said. "Amazing. Consider yourself forgiven."

"Good to know."

"Do you want to talk about it?"

Aaron hesitated. "About what?"

"The hell's own time you've been having. Whatever it is that made you so explosively annoyed that you felt compelled to arrange this dinner at a few hours' notice, presumably as a 'go-to-the-devil' gesture to someone. We don't have to talk about it, of course. I'd be perfectly happy with witty banter, or simply stuffing my face. But if you want to..." He let that hang.

Aaron did want to talk about it, all of it. He wished he could.

"There has been quite a lot," he said carefully. "The business we discussed last time—I won't talk about that. A frustrating case, too. But then, today, my superior told me I'm being put on a new job." He had to force the word out. "Unions."

"Unions?"

"There's a possible strike being fomented. It's our role to keep an eye on the organisers to make sure it's all being done legally."

"Hang around in an intimidating way, breathe down people's necks, make heavy-handed threats, pretend the organisers are in the direct pay of Moscow, and bring the hobnailed boot of the law down on anyone you can at the shade of an excuse?"

Aaron blinked at him. Joel shrugged. "I did a bit of work on a left-wing newspaper. You know what I mean, though."

"Yes. And...yes, that's my superior's intent. I have no problem with ensuring the law is observed, but that's not what he's asked for."

"And that's a problem? I mean, joking apart, you're in the Met. Isn't that what you do?"

He didn't know, Aaron reminded himself, couldn't know how much that simple syllogism hurt. *You're in the Met, the Met breaks unions, that's what you do. Who you are.*

He took a deep breath. "My father was a union organiser. Quite well known. His name was Terry Fowler."

Joel blinked. "Terry—you don't mean Firebrand Fowler? Oh good God, you do. How on earth are you in the police? No, wait. How are you related to Paul Napier-Fox if you're Firebrand Fowler's son?"

"He's my father but I'm not his son. That's rather the point."

Joel raised a finger for a pause, and carefully eased more fish off the bone. He added rice and more saag paneer to his plate, plus a dollop of pickle. "Right, I'm ready. Enlighten me."

"My mother was a Napier-Fox. Wealthy upper-crust

family, high society, a Bright Young Person before her time. She went to Italy to study art one summer when she was nineteen, and married an Italian painter on a whim."

Joel's eyes flicked over his face. "Ah."

"The family got the marriage annulled without much difficulty, but it was already too late. She was packed off to an aunt's house in the Midlands for a year to have the baby, regain her figure, return, marry, pretend it had never happened. I've never known what they intended to do with me. A childless family, an orphanage, the doorway of a police station?"

"Lovely."

"But instead she met Terry Fowler. The family, the Napier-Foxes, were livid. She was told she'd be cut off without a penny, but she didn't care and nor did my father. He married her, knowing she had nothing and with another man's child in her belly."

"Gosh. He must have loved her very much," Joel said. "Or been a very good man. Or both."

"Oh, he was a good man," Aaron said. "An excellent man. He was willing to take on a child that wasn't his. He let everyone—her, me, everyone we ever spoke to—know how he had taken on this child that wasn't his, all the time. I never had a chance to forget how good he was about that."

"Oh."

"It was what he did. He sacrificed himself—for the Cause mostly, but for anything else he could see going, and he never asked for anything in return, despite all he'd done for you. I was always, unchangeably, drowningly, in his debt."

"Oh God," Joel said. "I'm so sorry."

"My mother got back in touch with her family when I

was around seven, and insisted on me and Sarah, my sister, spending time with them. My father hated that. Well, so did I: they were mostly dreadful to us. Paul's mother was particularly vile, and he was a shocking bully, but I rather liked my grandmother: she was a fierce, proud old woman. She detested my father. She paid for my schooling, Harrow. I didn't like it—Paul was there too, and made it very clear I oughtn't be—and my father loathed the very idea, but Mother put her foot down."

"It sounds like you couldn't please anyone."

"No," Aaron said. "I couldn't. Too common for the Napier-Foxes, too stuck-up for the Fowlers, and too visibly foreign for my father to forget, even for a second, what a good thing he'd done in taking me on."

"Shit."

"Mother died when I was thirteen. Grandmama died a few years after, and left me a generous legacy. She left Sarah nothing: she said that since her father despised the Napier-Fox family so greatly, he wouldn't want them funding his child."

"Oof."

"It was spiteful. But she had outlived her daughter and missed the greater part of her life, and I suppose she preferred spite to regret. Happy families. Anyway, my father made it clear that he didn't want a penny of my legacy. He had provided for me all my life, another man's child, without ever asking for anything and he didn't expect any return for it now. So I told him that was an admirable attitude, and by the way, I was joining the Met."

"Just as a slap at him?"

"No," Aaron said. "Or, not only. I really did want to do something useful."

"To sacrifice yourself thanklessly for others?" Joel suggested.

"Ouch. No, I truly wanted to serve. I believe in service, and I believe there ought to be law and justice, and someone has to make that happen. I thought the police was the answer to everything that felt wrong. But also, yes. I knew very well my father would be furious, and indeed he was. He never spoke to me again."

"Actually never spoke?"

"I last saw him at my sister's wedding. I said hello, and he turned and walked away. He died earlier this year. I told Sarah that I would come to see him if he wanted me to, but he refused. He didn't want to set eyes on me."

Joel put his fork down and reached across the table, covering Aaron's hand with his own. "I'm so sorry. I really am."

Aaron wanted to cap Joel's hand with his own, or to turn his and interlace their fingers, but he was very conscious of the public place. "It's nothing. Or, at least, it's done. He wasn't a bad man."

"He sounds bloody awful."

"No, truly. He never expressed a regret about taking me on. He gave us everything he could. When I was seven or so, a group of bigger boys was bullying me, and he came out and gave them what for, then laid into their fathers too when they came round. Absolutely furious, defending me to the hilt. My father looking out for me. I felt so safe in that moment." He sighed. "And then he shouted, 'Don't you touch my wife's boy,' so there we were."

"Defeat from the jaws of victory." Joel kept his hand on Aaron's a moment longer, then pulled it away, leaving Aaron's skin bereft. "If not bloody awful, at least bloody difficult?"

"Definitely that. My mother said that he only knew how to love in the abstract. He loved 'the people' or 'the workers', and he loved the idea of taking on a fallen woman and her child. And he worked damned hard for us all, did his best, and sacrificed a great deal. There's plenty who consider him something close to a saint, although they're largely people who didn't know him."

"Ha."

"But they knew what he did, and what you do is surely what counts, in the end," Aaron said. "And I don't expect any saints are easy to live with. It's asking a lot of anyone to do so much and be cheerful about it."

"Then he perhaps should have done less, better," Joel said tartly. "Or stuck to labour disputes rather than raising children. I don't have a great deal of time for grown men who can't manage their own moods."

"You're not without a temper yourself," Aaron felt compelled to observe.

"Oh, I am—I mentioned this, I think?—a stroppy bitch, but I try not to ask other people to soothe my feelings for me. I also don't look after orphaned children or fight for workers' rights, so perhaps I've no room to criticise those who do. I'm quite prepared to agree your father was a better person than me. But he sounds like a prick."

Terry Fowler had loomed very large through Aaron's life: a hero to some, a bogeyman to others, a constant presence for good or ill. Everyone had strong opinions on him; Aaron did himself. 'Prick' was a welcome deflation.

"Maybe a bit of one," he said, and couldn't help a smile, and Joel smiled back.

"You call him father," Joel went on after a comfortable moment broken only by a last attack on the skeleton of the fish. "Not stepfather?"

"He insisted on Father. I wanted to change that at one point but Sarah was about six then, and got very upset at me not being her real brother. So I left it. And I didn't change my name for the same reason when my grandmother suggested I should—not that I greatly wanted to be a Napier-Fox either, and Lord knows the rest of the family would have objected. Fowler is my name now, however I got it."

"Do you know your, uh, original father?"

"Never met him. He knew my mother was pregnant when the family paid him off, but he never sought us out. And he was forty-eight when he married a nineteen-year-old, so I've no great desire to make his acquaintance. I really don't know what I'd say to him."

"Was there something you wanted to say to your father?"

That hit home. Aaron stared at the wreckage of the fish between them. "I would have liked to thank him. To tell him I really was, am, grateful. I think if I could have done that, it would be easier to remember him for what he did well instead of dwelling on what he failed at. But he didn't want to see me. I had gone over to the enemy and that was that."

"Not a man for compromise. I suppose saints aren't. And now they, the Met, want you to work on unions," Joel said. "Does your boss know who your father was?"

"Oh, yes."

"Is the idea that you'll be excessively keen to stamp out union activity because of him?"

"No. No, I don't think they can think that."

Joel put his fork down. "Aaron. For want of a better way to put it, what the bloody hell? Without knowing how the Met or CID normally conducts itself—"

"It's not normal," Aaron said, although his mind flickered to Helen Challice weeping in a dark room, sobbing, *It's again and again every day and I can't bear it,* into his shoulder. "Or at least, it's extremely hostile."

Joel was searching his face, light eyes flickering. "If I were to ask you if this is related to the other thing we talked about—"

"Best not."

"Right." Joel sat back. "Well, this sounds absolutely awful."

"It is rather." He smiled on the words, as one had to, and knew that it didn't look right.

Joel puffed out his cheeks. "Look, I couldn't eat another bite. I don't suppose you'd care to walk this off?"

"Where to?"

"Home. That is, that's where I'm going and you could come in that direction. You could come with me as far as you'd like to go." His eyes locked on Aaron's. "Why don't we find out how far that is?"

Aaron's heart was thumping. He ought not. It would be wildly reckless to go back to Joel's room, to be there late into the evening, again. But he was angry and tired, and he didn't want the evening to end. Even if he could just speak to Joel a little longer, that would be a bright light in a long, dark time.

"I'd like that," he said.

Chapter Eleven

The maitre d', or whatever you might call that in an Indian rather than French restaurant, asked Aaron for a private word as he paid the bill. Aaron went with him, and was a good five minutes in the back room. Joel wondered what it was about, but not very hard. He was preoccupied.

He'd been decidedly unimpressed by Aaron's failure to contact him as promised, and as the days passed, he'd had to face the fact that he was not just feeling snubbed, and welshed on, but disappointed. Their night together had been something out of the ordinary. Aaron's need, and restraint, and how he'd finally surrendered himself, putting himself entirely in Joel's hands. Hand.

And it wasn't just that he did indeed bang like a barn door in the wind. It was the rawness when he spoke, as though he never told anyone anything and didn't know how to do it. It was the inexplicable feeling that he trusted Joel, and Joel could trust him.

Met fucking Police. Joel must be off his chump.

And yet here he was now, waiting for a man with a laundry list of problems who'd ignored him for weeks and then sent a telegram ordering his presence, and who was even now in the back room with a doe-eyed and handsome restaurant proprietor doing God knows what. That said, Joel would fuck for this food, so he couldn't argue that one.

So he waited until Aaron emerged—looking, it had to be

said, grim-faced rather than sexually replete—and they thanked the proprietor and headed out into Soho.

The night was bright with lights despite the darkness and faint prickle of moisture in the air. It was not yet nine o'clock. Joel didn't want to ingest anything else for several days, but he suggested, "Want to stop for a drink?"

"Not in Soho, I was stationed here for a while. Do you want one?"

"I'd rather walk the food off, if you're all right with that."

"Absolutely. How have you been?" Aaron asked, somewhat abruptly. "I am aware I've just talked about myself."

"You have more going on. I've been fine. Nothing new. Clients. Saving up."

"No trouble from Paul?"

"Not a peep." Joel felt slightly bad now about mocking his relationship with his cousin. "It's been terribly boring."

"Be careful what you wish for," Aaron muttered. "What about your family? Since you know about mine."

"I don't have one. My father didn't care for how I am, my brother was the same but more so, and my mother and sister weren't going to put themselves in the firing line for my sake. I shook the dust off my feet a long time ago. Well, they strongly encouraged me to shake it off, but whatever."

"You've never gone back?"

"Why would I do that?"

"I don't know," Aaron said. "Maybe it's easier as a grown man, or at least different."

"Perhaps my brother has matured into a thoughtful man who regrets his bullying ways, and my mother wants nothing more than to see her lost son once again. That's possible, right?"

"Yes, surely."

"Then it wouldn't be hard for them to find me and say so. There's not a lot of Joel Wildsmiths in the world; they could send their letters of regret and reconciliation to me at any time. Only, they haven't, so I'm going to assume nothing's changed, and not trouble to put myself through finding out for certain."

"Right," Aaron said. "Fair. I'm sorry it was like that. My father wasn't easy and my mother had regrets, but my sister would fight tigers for me and that made a huge difference."

"You sound like you're very fond of her too," Joel said, needing to shift the subject. "And a niece, was it?"

"That's right. Violet is three, and shaping up to become a force of nature like her mother. Roger, Sarah's husband, is the most placid man alive, and needs to be."

Prodded further, Aaron told a couple of stories about his niece and sister—inconsequential stuff, just the trivial web of incident and amusement that made up family life, but told with immense warmth and clear fondness. Joel listened and laughed, and wondered how a man with so much love to give could be so lonely.

Well, he knew how. Aaron had told him.

They had walked up Charing Cross Road. By silent consent they swung right along New Oxford Street, dodging the crowds, heading towards Holborn.

"Is it more comfortable here?" Joel asked. "Out of Soho, I mean."

"At least before we get into King's Cross and Clerkenwell."

"You probably see the streets entirely differently, don't you? For me it's just another bit of London, and for you it's a place of crimes and gangs and murders and, uh, traffic offences."

"It's not that bad. But you get to know a lot of faces, I will grant."

"And people know yours. I like to be anonymous in the crowd: it's why I came to London."

They walked up Theobald's Row, feet in comfortable synchronisation. Joel was beginning to feel slightly less bloated.

"That was a magnificent meal, in case I didn't make that clear," he said. "Debt paid in full. What were you talking to the owner johnny about? You looked rather annoyed."

Aaron exhaled. "A small annoyance. Nothing to concern you."

Well, that was him told. "I beg your pardon. Didn't mean to interfere in your private business."

"No, it was a fair question. I just can't tell you the answer."

It wasn't Joel's affair and in truth he didn't care; he'd just been making conversation. But the response was yet another *Thus far and no further* from Aaron, and it reminded Joel abruptly that he'd been a whisker from dropping the telegram into the waste-paper basket.

"So are you planning to come up?" he asked abruptly.

"Up?"

"To mine." He'd made the invitation earlier, as he kept making all the running. He needed to hear something back, even just a clear *Yes, please*.

Pause. Then Aaron said, "I don't think so."

"Right." That was a bucket of icy water. "Right. Of course. Entirely up to you. Just out of interest, what was the fucking point of this, then?"

"Point of what?" Aaron asked, and it was such an obvious bit of stalling that Joel's temper exploded.

"Come off it. You didn't invite me to dinner because you wanted company, still less walk up this way when you live in Lisson Grove."

"You have no idea how much I wanted company."

"Right, of course. So naturally you called me, a man with whom you have had frequent interesting conversations."

"Yes," Aaron said. "I enjoy talking to you, and I owed you dinner, so—"

"The funny thing is, I read your hand and saw a painfully honest man," Joel said. "And yet on this subject, you lie like stink."

Aaron gave the harsh exhale of exasperation. "I don't know what you want me to say."

"Well, 'Last time was wonderful, shall we do it again?' would be nice, and 'I'm too much a coward to ask for what I want' would be truthful, and 'I'd rather be celibate forever than fuck you again' would at least put an end to this farrago. I'd just like you to make up your mind what you want and stick to it, that's all, because this pissing around is—" *Painful*, he wanted to say. *Gutting. Leaving me lonelier than just being alone would.* "Fucking annoying."

"It's not about what I want, because what I want and what I can have are extremely different things," Aaron's voice rasped. "It would be too great a risk for us both."

"Then why did you summon me for this evening in the first place?"

"I told you! Why is that so hard to believe? Don't you think you have any other worth in life than—than—"

"Fucking? Yes, I do. I've got plenty of worth. I'm dripping in worth, me in my shitty flat with my made-up job and my missing hand, because at least *I* have the guts to know what I want and try for it, and that's more than you do, Detective Sergeant!"

"Christ, don't start that again. And why the devil are you so offended?" Aaron demanded, in one of those voices that combined shouting and whispering to strangulated effect. "Why is it such an affront to have someone seek you out for your company, not your—services?"

"Services? Fuck you!"

"You know what I mean."

"You might find out what you mean yourself, if you had the balls to say it," Joel informed him. He felt rather sick, and it wasn't the overeating.

He *didn't* think he was only worth fucking. He had plenty of friends, and a job of sorts, and a whole life he'd built all by himself in a world that kept taking things away from him. If he didn't have healthy self-esteem, he at least had enough front that nobody else could tell the difference.

That wasn't the problem. The problem was his response to Aaron's hand, and how much he wanted the policeman to look at him with those dark eyes lit by desire, and that when Aaron's telegram had arrived, he'd stupidly, irrationally *hoped*, because all his hard-won experience of life, all his common sense, hadn't been enough to stop him believing deep down that this, between them, was something special.

So he'd offered, and Aaron had turned him down flat, and now he felt like a self-deluding fool, begging for crumbs, *again*. He should have known it was all going to end in tears; everything did, but he had thought they might have fun on the way.

"Fuck you," he said again, since it summarised his thoughts so neatly. "We're not friends, I don't know the rules to the game you're playing, and I'm tired of it."

"Joel!" Aaron said. "Will you just listen?"

"To what?"

Aaron grabbed his arm. Joel wrenched it away. "Look, I'm sorry. I just wanted to see you, and that was selfish of me. And yes, I wish to God I could have more than just a meal with you, but I can't. And that's not because of you in any way."

Why is it, then? Joel wanted to ask, but that way madness lay. He was not going to lay himself open to another rejection. He was going to extricate himself from this hot-and-cold nonsense with a man he barely knew, and stay well out of whatever trouble Aaron was in. He had money to earn.

"Whatever," he said. "It's been fun, lovely meal, but I'm freezing so I'm going to keep walking. Don't come with me."

"Goodbye," Aaron said quietly, and the soft finality of that stayed with Joel as he stamped furiously away, cursing himself, and men who didn't know what they wanted, and whatever was squatting on Aaron's shoulders, and himself again. Mooning like this over a man he'd fucked once: ridiculous. It would make a funny story in a few weeks' time.

He marched up Gray's Inn Road. The south end was lawyer territory; as you went further north towards King's Cross the area became dangerous in different ways. He kept an eye out as he walked, alert for lone men doing nothing much, or the occasional flare of light that was huddled smokers, waiting in doorways for whatever it was they waited for. Victims, companions, the morning, or maybe just an end to the persistent, pervasive winter drizzle. In their dreams.

Joel's footsteps echoed flatly on the wet pavements. Gray's Inn Road could feel very long on a rainy night. Cold, too. His hand was bare because getting a glove on one-handed involved holding it with his teeth and he hadn't wanted to do that in front of Aaron. He couldn't be bothered to stop and go through the palaver now, but he wished he had done it earlier because his fingers were icy. Good thing he didn't have two hands, or he'd be freezing.

His stump hurt too. It still ached now and then; probably it always would. He didn't get phantom hand sensations any more, thank God, just firing nerves and a dull pain in the cold, but there was plenty to resent, all the same.

He passed the Royal Free Hospital with the glower he always gave hospitals on principle. Nearly there now, which was good because he was itching to be home, even if his bedsit scarcely deserved the name. He wanted to be inside, away from the cold and damp and dark and the sense of people watching him.

He wasn't quite sure where that last thought came from. It came, though, and he felt himself straighten as his muscles tensed in response.

He didn't ignore it, because his instincts paid his bills and had carried him safely through three years of war, before he got careless. He sped up a little, heart thumping, eyes darting. Couldn't see anyone. There were feet behind him, but well behind. Might be nothing. Lots of people would be walking to the railway station, even at this hour.

He turned down Acton Street, ears straining for feet behind him, and crossed over Percy Circus, and now he was pretty sure he wasn't being followed at all. What a drama out of nothing. He'd laugh at himself as soon as he was inside.

A handful of yards past the roundabout, number 22 right there, and a man just a few steps further along. He was leaning against the railings, smoking a cigarette, cap pulled down low, and he'd turned his head to watch Joel approach.

Joel's keys were in his overcoat pocket. He closed his hand round them, slotting them between his fingers, with a tiny anticipatory pulse of nausea at the idea of punching someone with them. Breaking his fingers, or the metal tearing them, anything that might damage his remaining hand—

Calm down, he told himself. He kept his pace steady, and the man kept his gaze steady too, watching Joel and making no effort to hide it. Joel pretended not to see. He climbed the steps with his spine clamped tight, his skin prickling, poised to whip round at the slightest sound of movement.

None came. Nothing at all. He unlocked the front door with a shaky hand, which was absurd. He was panicking over nothing, over a man who was loitering in the drizzle for his own reasons and would probably have watched any passer-by—

He glanced down, and the man looked directly up at him, meeting his eyes. He kept looking, without speech or movement, until Joel closed the door.

He did not sleep well that night.

A few days later Joel was still feeling fairly wretched about all of it.

For one thing, he'd been unreasonable and he knew it. Aaron's back-and-forthing, his cowardice even, was a perfectly good reason to give him short shrift, and if Joel had said as much in a sensible way, he'd have nothing to feel bad about. As it was, he'd flown off the handle when Aaron had declined sex, and that was shitty, even if it wasn't what he'd actually meant. He ought to apologise, if only for that part.

He wasn't going to, obviously, certainly not in the absence of any apology from Aaron for all the pissing about. He'd do much better to forget the whole thing, since his stupid hopes and nonsensical feelings had worked him up into a state where he'd not only embarrassed himself making unwanted demands, but talked himself into being terrified of a few footsteps and a loiterer.

That was Aaron's fault too, of course, him and his vague allusions to risks and dangers and dodgy colleagues. Not Joel's problem, and he was going to stay well away. Any further telegrams—not that there would be any, nor was he hoping for one—were going straight into the waste-paper basket.

"Pick yourself up, Wildsmith," he said aloud. He'd done it before, in far worse circumstances. When you'd lost your family, such as it was, and your dominant hand, and your liberty, you learned to shake off minor losses such as a casual one-night lover who didn't matter anyway. He just wished he had a few more clients to keep him busy while he did the shaking off, because right now the afternoon was stretching very emptily in front of him.

Fine. He'd meant to refresh the classified advertisement he put in the papers anyway, so he'd do it now. He'd pay for more space, enough for a testimonial or two, maybe get someone to lay it out with a few decorative flourishes. He could afford to invest a little more in finding new clients.

He was just drafting the text when somebody knocked.

Landlady, probably. It wouldn't be a telegram boy and it certainly wouldn't be Aaron. It was the middle of the day, and he wasn't thinking about Aaron.

He went to the door and opened it to see an unfamiliar man in a check coat. It wasn't a nice coat, but he didn't look like a terribly nice man. The cold eyes, broken nose, and mangled mess of one ear might be clues.

"Hello?" Joel said.

"Joel Wildsmith, graphologist?" the man asked. He didn't say it nicely.

"That's right. Who are you?"

"Mind if I come in?" The man had already started moving. Joel stepped back. He had the distinct feeling that if he didn't, he'd be pushed.

"I don't think we have an appointment," he said warily. "Who are you?"

The man was looking around. His cheeks had the broken blood vessels of a drinker, or a fighter, or a rough life, or all three. "Nice place, Mr. Wildsmith. Graphologist? What's that, then?"

"I analyse handwriting. Again, who are you?"

"You can call me Mr. Twigg."

"And...do you want some handwriting analysed?" Joel

wondered if Mr. Twigg actually wanted something read to him. He didn't look like he'd paid a lot of attention in school, somehow.

"Nah, nah. Save it for the suckers."

"Then what can I do for you?"

"Now you're talking," Mr. Twigg said. "Only, it's not for me. See, I work for a fellow named Darby Sabini, if you know the name?"

Joel's mouth dried. "The gentleman who..." He couldn't think of a polite way to express *leads the biggest gang round here*. "Runs things in Clerkenwell?"

"Very good. So I dare say you know Darby and the boys keep an eye on the area. Make sure things run smoothly for small businesses like yourself."

"I don't have a business. I just read handwriting."

"And get paid for it, right? Everyone's got to make a living. So what Darby wants is a small monthly payment to cover his costs, so you can keep on making a living."

Joel didn't bother to ask what costs, or what Darby Sabini would actually do for his money. He knew what this was, and Mr. Twigg knew he knew.

"How much?" he said.

"Pound a week sounds fair."

"What?" Joel yelped. "Are you serious?"

"Dead serious. Here you are, no overheads, getting paid for reading, you can spare it."

Most clients took less than half an hour, and sometimes Joel only had four or five clients in the week. "That's too much," he said.

Mr. Twigg's eyes snapped to his. "Did I ask what you thought?"

"I don't make that much money! I don't know what you imagine—"

"I don't imagine. Never have. I bet you're an imaginative sort, graphologist and all that. You got a good imagination?"

"Look, Mr. Twigg—"

"You got a good imagination?"

Clearly he had to answer. "I suppose so."

"I bet you do. " Mr. Twigg gestured at Joel's left sleeve. "I expect you're always imagining stuff about that. What if you lost the other hand. What if someone took a brick to your fingers, smashed 'em flat. One by one." He made a sharp, violent, downward gesture. Joel flinched. "I bet a man with imagination would lie awake at night thinking about stuff like that."

Joel swallowed hard. Mr. Twigg held his gaze for a couple of seconds longer. "Like I said, a pound a week, first month payable in advance, and then everyone can go about their business with no unpleasantness, see?"

Joel saw very well. "I don't have that on me."

"Then I'll come back for it tomorrow," Mr. Twigg said. "At ten. Make sure you're here."

"I've a client at ten."

"So have my envelope ready. See you tomorrow, Mr. Wildsmith. Pleasure doing business with you."

He ambled out, leaving the door ajar. Joel went to shut it, and stood for a moment, breathing hard.

He was being shaken down. So what was he going to do about it?

Police? Mr. Twigg hadn't told him not to go to the police, but Joel suspected he was expected to know that for himself. Would the police act on the implied threat, or fob him off as they had his pawnbroker friend? Would they look at his record? Could they do anything useful at all?

If he spoke to Aaron—

No. It would be nice to have a CID man he could whistle up, but for that, he would need not to have told him to fuck off.

And suppose the police did their job and arrested Mr. Twigg, what then? The Sabinis had plenty of men. Would Darby Sabini accept the loss, or would Joel get jumped in a dark street one night? He didn't think defiance would feel like a moral victory after someone had pulped his right hand with a boot heel or a brick. Joel could feel it, feel the dry, grainy texture and the dull edge smashing down...

"Fuck," he said aloud.

He sat down and put his head in his hand. What to do? Pay up? He could manage a pound a week, probably, but it would put his state-of-the-art prosthetic out of his reach for months more, maybe years. The thought of waiting longer so some bastard gang boss could drink gin at his expense filled him with a sick, helpless fury.

And just like the other times he'd been the helpless target of abuse, he'd have to get used to it, because there was damn all he could do about it.

Chapter Twelve

Aaron was bone-weary as he made his way back to Lisson Grove after yet another long and miserable day. The last week had been one of the most sapping of his life.

DI Davis had piled work on his desk, not just the canal-workers' union, about which Aaron had carefully found nothing to object to, but two other cases. He had been scrambling to keep up with those and the entirely stalled Marks investigation; he'd done damn all to confirm his suspicions about DDI Colthorne.

He felt useless, and Aaron hated feeling useless. He'd joined the police because service was purpose, and if he couldn't achieve anything there, if he wasn't any good to anyone—or perhaps he was even worse than useless, propping up an organisation that was rotting from the head—and all for a job that had cost him so much...

Aaron didn't want to think how much it had cost him. He'd been trying not to think of that for months now, since his father's death. Not to think of Challice sobbing because other women's pain was being used to beat her down, or of people who asked for help and went unanswered while their so-called protectors lined their pockets, or of good men—they *were* good men, he insisted to himself—like Sergeant Hollis, bullying Joel for Aaron's benefit, or Inspector Cassell, dismissing an act of sexual violence if the victim was the wrong sort.

He'd wanted to make things better in a world that

screamed for help, and he'd sacrificed so much for that and been so lonely, and he wished he could say, *It was worth it*.

He *had* achieved things. He'd caught Wilfred Molesworth, put away a lot of men who deserved it, done things that needed doing to keep people safe. He knew that intellectually. But his belief in the job was slipping through his fingers like sand, and all the faster because of his constant drumbeat of regret over Joel.

He had made such a damned mess of that. He shouldn't have taken Joel out for dinner at all: it had been too much temptation. He'd wanted to blurt it all out, tell him everything, unburden his soul of his fears and worries because Joel felt absurdly like someone he could trust. He'd wanted to go back to that wretched bedsit more than he wanted air. And when he'd learned he couldn't, he should have left him at Shafi's, rather than trailing after him like a dog and then abruptly blurting out a refusal without explanation. No wonder Joel had been offended.

He wished he could have gone back with Joel. He wished more that he still had him as a friend. He had a feeling that he wasn't going to have any friends at all left by the end of this.

He had started composing a letter of apology, one to send if everything either got resolved or went badly wrong, and had managed two paragraphs over three days. He was so tired.

He plodded up the stairs to his flat, head low, contemplating dinner without enthusiasm. Another omelette, he supposed: the thought didn't appeal. Then he saw the envelope.

It was jammed at the base of his front door, which was

exceedingly tight-fitting: he kept meaning to get it looked at. A white rectangle on the mat, no inscription. He opened it, and pulled out a sheet of paper adorned with an ill-controlled scrawl.

Angelos now

JW

Aaron ran down the stairs and back out into the cold, having taken a full seventy seconds to change his shirt and tidy his hair. He hadn't shaved, although he tended to sport a five o'clock shadow and it was well past that hour; he didn't want to waste the time. The thump of breathless excitement at Joel's unceremonious eruption back into his life was irresistible.

Angelo's Italian restaurant was on the corner of the Grove: it was where he'd thought about taking Joel for the ravioli. He strode in and was greeted by the proprietor. "Mr. Fowler, good to see you! Your friend has been waiting—" Angelo made a face to indicate an excessive time. "I give him bread."

"Thank you," Aaron said, and followed him to the table where Joel sat with a half-demolished plate of bread, a half-drunk glass of red wine, and the expression of a deeply unhappy man. "Joel. Good evening?"

Joel just glared. Angelo pulled Aaron's chair out for him. "A drink, Mr. Fowler?"

"Red wine, please," Aaron said. "And a few moments before we decide, thank you."

Angelo whisked away. Aaron examined Joel's face and said, "Did we have an appointment that I forgot?"

"No," Joel said. "Obviously. I realise you probably don't want to see me."

"Of course I do."

"Really? Because at our last meeting you told me to fuck off, and then I told you to fuck off, only I actually used the words, so—"

"I didn't say or mean any such thing," Aaron said. "Though I dare say it seemed that way, so I can't complain that you were annoyed. Are you less annoyed now? Because you don't look it."

Joel breathed out very hard. "I am extremely annoyed, and also upset and terrified. I need to tell you some bad things, if you're willing to listen."

"Of course. Do you want to talk here?"

"In the restaurant? You probably know best about that. I expect even if we're being watched, a public place is preferable to your flat."

Cold snaked down Aaron's spine. "Do you think you're being watched?"

"I don't know. I took an absurd route to shake anyone off, two tubes and a bus, but that won't help if they're already here."

"I don't think that's the case," Aaron said. He lifted a hand as Angelo brought over his wine. "Angelo, is there anyone new in tonight? Unfamiliar faces?"

Angelo glanced round. "No? All regulars. You want I tell you if someone else comes in?"

"If you would. Joel, do you know what you want to eat?"

"We're going to eat?"

"Well, I'm hungry, and I've never known you be anything but." He shot a glance at Joel's left arm, saw he wasn't wearing the prosthetic. "The ravioli is excellent. It's a first course but if you'd like a larger portion—?"

"Fine."

"The ravioli as a main course for my friend, please, Angelo, and the veal for me. If we could have privacy?"

Angelo shook his head in sorrow at Aaron's inability to order Italian food properly, and moved off. Aaron said, "Right. What's going on?"

Joel eyed him. "I notice you're not surprised that I'm talking about being watched and followed. And the owner chap wasn't surprised at the question either. If you knew this was going to happen, you could have bloody told me!"

"I don't know what's happened. Talk to me."

Joel swallowed a mouthful of wine in a Dutch-courage manner. "Four days ago, the Sabini gang sent round a man to shake me down. Protection racket. A pound a week, with a month payable in advance, to be protected from, in effect, him taking a brick to my remaining fingers."

His voice crackled with anger and fear, unless that was the buzz of fury in Aaron's ears. He forced down the wave of rage and self-reproach. "Did he touch you?"

"No. I paid up. Four quid in advance."

"And have you gone to the police?"

"Of course not."

People so rarely did. Aaron knew all the reasons. "Go on."

"This morning I had another visit, same man. He said Sabini had changed his mind, and if I could pay four quid a month I could pay ten."

"Good God."

"I said, is it going to keep going up, because that's some inflation you've got there. He said yes, it was. I—got a bit upset. And he waited for me to, uh, finish being upset, and then he said Darby Sabini might let me work something out, if I had sufficiently useful information for him."

"What information?"

"That's what I said. He said I needed to talk to Mr. Sabini about it. I said I didn't know anything useful. He said, what about your pal the copper?"

Aaron's fingers tensed convulsively on the stem of his wine glass. He made them relax before he snapped it.

"I said, what pal is that," Joel went on. "He said, the one who keeps coming round here, who took you out for curry just the other day."

"Ravioli for you, signore!" Angelo announced from over Aaron's shoulder. He deposited the plates, waved the pepper grinder around, and departed.

"This smells marvellous," Joel said, prodding his plateful. "Shall I go on or would you rather eat first? It seems terribly ungracious to spoil both our appetites with unpleasant things. Although, once I've told you, you might wish I'd just got on with it."

"If we don't eat, Angelo will be offended. I come here at least once a week and I can't lose my favoured-customer status."

Joel forked up a single parcel, and chewed cautiously. "Mph," he said with his mouth full. "God, that's good. No, you're right, mustn't upset him."

They ate in silence for a few moments. Aaron was ravenous, perhaps more so because Joel had sought him out.

"I'm glad you came to me," he said. "I made a pig's ear of our last meeting and I'm sorry."

Joel's eyes snapped up to his. He had a mouthful of pasta, so Aaron took his opportunity to keep talking. "You have probably gathered that I haven't been having an easy time, but I handled things poorly, and I apologise. It wasn't anything to do with you."

Joel swallowed. "Thanks. And I'm sorry too. Partially."

"Partially?"

"You had every right not to come back to mine if you didn't want to, or to change your mind about it. Throwing myself at you doesn't oblige you to catch me. But it felt easier to be cross about that than to say what I was actually upset about, which was prickish of me, and I am sorry. Not partially."

"If you would like to tell me what you were actually upset about," Aaron said with caution, "perhaps I could apologise specifically?"

Joel gave him a level look for a couple of seconds longer than felt comfortable, then let out an abrupt breath. "Look, I'd let myself hope for—well, more that you just coming up for a couple of hours. And I realised I shouldn't have, and it hurt a bit. That's all. Well, it's not all, because then I was an arsehole about it."

The words were a fist to Aaron's chest. How he'd failed, what he'd missed. "I'm sorry," he said again, uselessly, because he wasn't sure what else to say in the face of that bare truth. He didn't think Joel wanted to hear *I'd have hoped too, but I didn't have the nerve.* "I'm sure my behaviour was confusing. I don't really know how to, uh, conduct this kind of thing at the best of times, which these are not. But if it helps, I wanted to come up that night more than I can say. It wouldn't have been a good idea."

Joel gave a tight imitation of a smile. "Indeed it wouldn't, because there was a man watching my house that night, who I have to suppose was a Sabini. Did you know that was going to happen?"

"Not when I invited you to dinner, no. Rahim warned me just before we left Shafi's. He said he'd just had a visitor—a Sabini—who had told him to report back on who I was eating with."

"Shit. Really? Shit."

"I assumed, as long as I didn't go back to your flat, there would be nothing to report and no problem. It would have been more sensible to part at the restaurant door, but the truth is, I didn't want to. That evening was the only good thing that's happened to me in some time and I didn't want it snatched from me before it had to end."

"That's nice," Joel said. "Glad to be of help. It's made my life considerably worse, but the food was wonderful, so I dare say it's swings and roundabouts." He stabbed a bit of pasta with his fork, and added, "Ignore me, I'm being a bitch. This isn't your fault."

Aaron was uncomfortably sure he was wrong about that. "I didn't intend to bring you harm. In retrospect I was a fool, but I didn't expect what's happening now, or anything like it."

"No, I dare say not. And as you say, lucky you were warned. How come restaurant proprietors are so helpful to you?"

"I've evicted a couple of tiresome customers, both here and at Shafi's. I like to stay on the right side of good food."

“Wise.” Joel had cleared his plate. He ran a piece of bread over the remaining sauce, with a look of regret that might have been because he’d finished, or because they had to talk about this again.

Aaron set himself to it. “So. You were watched that night, and shaken down. Who was this man?”

“He called himself Mr. Twigg. About my height, twice as wide, looked like a right bruiser. Broken nose, and something horrible had happened to his right ear.”

“A prostitute tried to chew it off when he assaulted her,” Aaron said. “Eddie Twigg, a close colleague of Darby Sabini. Blast: I was hoping someone was taking their name in vain. And are you going to see Darby?”

“I’m supposed to do that tomorrow. He’s expecting to hear all about you. I said to Twigg there was nothing to tell, that you were a miserable sod with no friends who had to pay people to eat with you , and I went for the free meal. He just laughed and said good story, tell it to Darby.”

Aaron made himself eat the last mouthful of veal, though it was more fuel than pleasure now. “Tomorrow. What will you say?”

Joel’s eyes narrowed. He shot a glance round then said, very low, “Well, I thought I’d mention that you gave me details of an ongoing case and then sucked my cock. That should sort everything out nicely for us both. What the hell do you think I’m going to tell him?”

Aaron wasn’t sure how this level of aggressive sarcasm could make him feel so warm inside. “All right, but you’ll have to give him something. Darby Sabini is an alarming man. You didn’t ask for any of this and you’re entitled to protect yourself.”

"I was rather hoping you'd protect me, actually. And I haven't finished, by the way, because after Twigg left, as if today wasn't shitty enough, I got this."

He pulled out a letter. Aaron took it, murmuring thanks as Angelo came to take the plates away. It was in his cousin Paul's hand.

Mr. Wildsmith

You are a liar, a scoundrel, and a slanderer. Your lies have damaged my reputation and caused me material harm and I intend to seek financial redress in the courts unless you make a full public apology and acknowledgment of your dishonesty in mutually agreed terms.

You are reliant on Aaron Fowler lying in court to protect you. Be assured that he will not be able to. His dealings with you are entirely unbefitting a police officer, he has no right to meddle with my private affairs in an official capacity. And your relationship with him is not one that he will wish to admit in court. If he is foolish enough to try I will not concern myself with his reputation when I destroy yours.

Yours sincerely

Paul Napier-Fox

"Christ," Aaron said.

"Indeed. I've a few questions."

"I'm sure you do." Aaron wasn't sure what to say. The sheer barrage on so many fronts was overwhelming. "I'm sorry. I had no idea they would go at you like this."

Joel sat back. "I'd like to know what's going on, please, since it's very much my business now. You can start with who 'they' are, because don't ask me to believe it's pure chance I've had your cousin and the Sabinis come down on me at the same time."

"I'll tell you if you like, but not here."

"Where?"

"My flat? I doubt it makes a difference now."

"That somehow makes me feel extremely unhappy," Joel said through his teeth. "Could you possibly do or say something reassuring?"

Aaron wished he could think of what that might be. "Pudding?"

"What?"

"They do delicious puddings here. Would something sweet help?"

"My life is falling apart and you're recommending pudding."

"Feeding you has always helped so far," Aaron pointed out, and there was a tiny relaxation in Joel's face that emboldened him to add, "They do a thing called dolce Torino—sponge biscuits, chocolate and hazelnuts. It's delicious. And sweet tea is good for shock, so—"

"—therefore pudding must be?" Joel finished. "I'd call you an idiot except that I didn't have any lunch because of all the fuckery and actually I am in no hurry to find out how my life is going to be upended for the, what, fourth time, so yes, why not, let's have pudding. You're paying."

Angelo arrived in response to Aaron's raised hand. Aaron asked for a dolce Torino for his friend and another glass of wine for them both, and got a raised eyebrow from Joel. "Are we making a night of it?"

Yes, Aaron could have said, in a different life. *I'm going to watch you eat chocolate and make those noises of pleasure that go straight to my groin, and we're both going to have that second glass and go back to my flat, and then—*

"Dutch courage," he said. He nodded thanks as Angelo brought wine and sweet. "Try that."

Joel took a spoonful. His face convulsed. "Oh God. Oh my *God*. This is— Can I eat all of this?"

"I don't think I'm up to fighting you for it."

"Well, you're bigger, and trained, and you have more hands. But I'm motivated, because this is in the top three of things I have ever put in my mouth. Mph."

Aaron wanted, urgently, to ask about the other two. He resisted, despite his companion's uninhibited moan, and just sipped his wine and enjoyed Joel's near-sexual relationship with his pudding until the plate was scraped clean.

"That was amazing," Joel said, accepting that it was over with clear reluctance. "You know how to treat a man."

"This and Shafi's are my favourite places in London."

"I can see why. Thank you for sharing them with me."

"I'm glad you enjoyed them both. I may never be able to eat here again without hearing the noises you were just making, but it's a small price to pay."

Joel stuck out his tongue, as if that had been banter rather than a devastating truth. Aaron's toes curled in his shoes. "I suppose we should talk now."

He let them both in to his flat, and poured whisky. It might be unwise on top of two glasses of wine, but he wasn't sure if things could possibly go any more wrong.

Joel took the seat he had last time, and clutched the glass Aaron handed him. "I'll be honest," he said. "I'm frightened.

And you're not going to tell me I've nothing to worry about, are you?"

"I don't think I can do that."

Joel nodded slowly, and knocked back half the whisky in a swallow. "Gah. Why do people say that helps? It doesn't help. All right, then, tell me what I *do* have to worry about."

"I will, but I'm not sure where to start."

"The beginning?"

"I don't know where that is, unfortunately. I feel as though I was dropped into this half way through."

"Then start with your cousin Paul. Who I'm sure you said was going to leave me alone, so what's this letter about?"

Aaron grimaced. "Paul doesn't like me, and I'm sure he's angry with you, but he's far lazier than he is vindictive. This letter is out of character."

"Well, it would be: he didn't write it," Joel said. "It was dictated to him."

Aaron had a bad feeling he was right about that, but he said anyway, "Based on—?"

"Oh, look at it, it goes in waves. Scribble, pause, scribble, pause. It just *looks* dictated, all right? And anyway, is that how your man-about-town cousin usually expresses himself? It sounds like a lawyer talking."

"Not a lawyer," Aaron said reluctantly. "A policeman."

"... Shit."

"Yes."

"Oh God. Just tell me."

Aaron took a deep breath. "Paper number seven. The man you said was a monster, with no moral compass and blood on his hands. He's my superior officer. Divisional Detective Inspector Colthorne, the head of G Division."

"Jesus fuck," Joel said. "*Fuck*. Have you told anyone?"

"Told them what? And who? The Commissioner of the Met is highly resistant to accusations against his officers. There was that case just recently, Sergeant Josling in Soho. He reported another sergeant for taking bribes, and was dismissed in disgrace for slandering a brother officer."

"I read about that."

"The man he accused is notorious for having his hand out. Everyone in Soho knows he was bang to rights, but Horwood wouldn't hear it, so the Home Office deliberated behind closed doors, threw the charge out, and got rid of Josling instead. And that was just for a sergeant; any sort of accusation against a divisional inspector will need full chapter and verse to stand a chance."

"So what do you have?"

"Absolutely nothing," Aaron said. "Sweet Fanny Adams, if you'll excuse the phrase. Plenty of suspicions, nothing concrete."

"Hang on. You're not basing all this on my reading?" Joel asked.

"I've seen your work. I believe it."

Joel's lips parted silently. "Oh."

"I don't understand it but I believe it. Which is alarming, but here we are. But the truth is, when you spoke about number seven, I knew it would be Colthorne, even before I checked. I don't like him and I don't trust him, and there's any amount of little things that have been adding up."

"Like what?"

"You recall that business with Dapper Melkin, when I was in the papers?"

"You Valentino, you." Joel was trying for a normal voice, but he looked very pale. "Yes?"

"The defence brief accused me of being in cahoots with the Sabinis. You said yourself, there's talk they have an in with King's Cross nick. I think that's DDI Colthorne. I think he's been quietly giving them a helping hand for a while, which may explain why they're returning the favour now."

"Running his errands. Bothering me."

"Exactly. I suspect he was setting me up to take the fall there, or at least to look suspicious or unreliable. There's been a lot of odd things, like him accusing me of being a publicity seeker—I wonder if he arranged that flurry of pieces in the press—or bringing up all sides of my family in the worst manner. Italian blood, Society connections and a union firebrand father: he and his lapdog DI Davis remind my colleagues of it all the time. At this stage—God, I've been at King's Cross for two years, and I truly don't know if any of them would stand up for me. And I can't prove any of that is his fault, as I can't prove anything at all, but Rahim said the man who asked about me was a Sabini man, and I sent that telegram to you from work."

"From the police station?"

"I can't think of any way Darby Sabini could have known what I was doing that evening, unless someone in King's Cross nick was watching me. And I can't think why Darby would care, unless someone important had asked him to find out."

"Find out about DS Fowler's boy friend," Joel said hollowly.

"I'm afraid so. I think, if Colthorne suspects he's got that on me—"

“Oh God. Could he? Is that my fault, my record?”

“Not if he’s talked to Paul,” Aaron said. “As he must have done if he dictated that letter. I, er, had something of an affair at school.”

“Ooh, did you now,” Joel said, a pale shadow of his usual teasing. “Well, shit. So what’s the plan? Darby Sabini puts the frighteners on me, extorts more than I can pay, then lets me know I can get out from under if I grass you up?”

“You spill your guts to Darby, he takes it to Colthorne, Colthorne dismisses me for gross misconduct. I won’t stand a chance,” Aaron said flatly. “I involved you in an ongoing investigation and you’ve got an indecency conviction. I could try to fight it but the insinuations and the press reports would destroy me, even if I was cleared.”

“Yes, but hang on,” Joel said. “How would that make you look like the Sabini nark in King’s Cross?”

“I don’t think that’s his aim any more. I think that was the original plan, but I have since stumbled on something that made it urgent for him to discredit me immediately and comprehensively, even if he has to put himself in debt to Darby Sabini.”

Joel’s eyes were huge. “What thing?”

“You said yourself. The murder he committed. Possibly murders.”

Joel grasped for words for a couple of seconds, then downed the rest of his whisky in an emphatic manner. Aaron shoved the bottle over; Joel shoved it a half-inch back. “If I drink until I feel happy, you’ll be sending me home in a wheelbarrow. Are you sure about this?”

“No,” Aaron said. “I can’t be because it’s all shadows and suspicions. What I know for certain is, in the last couple of weeks my DI—you read his hand too, he's the obedient bully—has been piling work on me. I've been strongly discouraged from pursuing the murder case in which I suspect Colthorne's involved. You've been harassed both by the Sabinis and by my cousin Paul, and Paul is an idiot and a snob. He wouldn't write a letter at Darby Sabini's dictation, but he would gladly take help from a gentleman and not question why it was offered. I think Colthorne is the puppet-master behind it all, and I think it's because he knows or fears I'm on to him."

"How? And how would he know about me?" Joel demanded. "We've only met a handful of times, it's not as though we've been kissing in public!"

"I was wondering that too. But Sergeant Hollis knows about your conviction, and the business with Paul. If Colthorne asked him questions, he'd have no reason not to answer. And my DC on the murder case spoke to him in a way which I suspect made him realise he could be in trouble. That was unfortunate."

"Unfortunate?" Joel yelped. "*Unfortunate?*"

"You know what I mean."

"I bloody don't! Or, yes, I do but that is not the fucking word! How are you so calm about this? You're talking about a sodding murderer trying to use me to ruin you! And that's shitty for you, but if your cousin sues me for slander, or the papers make a field day of Corrupt Policeman Pays Fraud Graphologist, or we get done for gross indecency, or Darby Sabini decides I'm annoying, I am *fucked*! This isn't fair!"

"I know."

"No, you don't!" Joel shouted. "No, you don't know that because this is happening to *me*! You aren't the one who's had thugs turn up and take your money, and if you get attacked you've got two hands to fight with, so you do *not* know! All I did was a fucking reading! It was your idea to pick on me because of your shitty cousin, it was your idea to shove a lot of shitty people's handwriting into my face, and now I've got gangs and the Met using me as a football, and I've already been to prison once! Stop ruining my life!"

Joel's voice was rising and choked with tears and his distress was unbearable because it was, indeed, all Aaron's fault. He reached out without meaning it, driven by nothing but the urgent need to offer comfort, and Joel flung himself into his arms.

Chapter Thirteen

Well, this was embarrassing.

Joel had a tendency to be overwhelmed by his feelings. He knew it, hated it, and resented that he never seemed to get better at noticing he was doing it in the moment. He overreacted, and said stupid things, or humiliated himself with tears, and then had to pick up the pieces. He'd spoiled more than one promising love affair in the past with an explosion of feelings he could have kept to himself.

And he'd just exploded on Aaron, who was probably in at least as much trouble as himself, and instead of telling him to shut up or calm down, Aaron had opened his arms and somehow Joel was now wrapped in a strong embrace, his wet face pressed against a damp but sturdy shoulder, with Aaron whispering meaningless reassurances into his hair.

He tried to pull away, albeit not very hard. Aaron just tightened his arms. "It's all right, Joel. It's all right."

Joel appeared to be clinging on to him. Could he make more of a fool of himself here? "Sorry," he mumbled into the cloth of Aaron's jacket.

"You've every right to be angry. It is my fault."

"It's Colthorne's fault. I'm only shouting at you because you're here and I'm scared."

Aaron's hand slid up to the back of his head, into his hair. Joel wondered if he was even aware he was doing it. "If it's not my fault, it's my responsibility. I'm so sorry. I didn't want, I never wanted to hurt you."

Joel squirmed so he could look up into Aaron's face. Those dark eyes were devastating at close range, with the warm depths of a cup of coffee, and just as liable to keep him up at night. "You didn't. It's not your fault. I wish it wasn't like this."

"So do I," Aaron said, a whisper of a voice.

"If it wasn't." God, he oughtn't say this. "If it wasn't like it is—"

"If it wasn't, I'd ask you to stay," Aaron said, in a voice that sounded to be dragged out of him. "I haven't stopped thinking about you since that night. I couldn't stop thinking about you before it."

"Christ. Aaron—"

Joel had no idea which of them moved first. Maybe it was both of them, because Aaron's mouth was crushed to his, and they were kissing frantically, desperately, teeth colliding and lips pressed so hard they'd bruise. Joel locked his left arm round Aaron's waist, grabbed his head, pulled them both backwards so they sprawled on the settee. Joel under, wrapping his thighs round Aaron's hips, Aaron's weight on him and his hands clutching Joel's face. Kissing like starving men, or like frightened, despairing, slightly drunk ones.

After a few frantic moments Aaron pulled a little away, and rested his forehead on Joel's. "God. You."

"We could have half an hour," Joel said. "Can't we? I've been here long enough to fuck anyway, if anyone's watching, and if they're not, then—"

"To the devil with it," Aaron rasped. "I want to taste you again."

"Yes please. Please do."

Aaron's hand scrabbled at his buttons. Joel squirmed under him, giving him access, inhaling sharply as his prick sprang free. Aaron took it in hand, very lightly, almost hesitantly, and glanced up.

He had liked direction before. Joel said, "Use your tongue. Just your tongue, for now."

Aaron's fingers loosened. He leaned in, and ran his tongue over Joel's prick, tentative at first, then firmer. Slow, careful licks, following veins and ridges, circling the head, pressing at the slit, until Joel was panting. "Fuck. Yes. You can use your lips."

Aaron's mouth curved. He leaned in, and kissed Joel's cock, a sweet, soft kiss. It was ridiculous. Joel wanted to cry.

He didn't have time for that. Aaron was using his mouth now—just the lips, circling, tasting, not sucking, and Joel was about to levitate off the settee with need. "Oh God. Suck me, right now."

Aaron made a pointed questioning noise. Joel said, "*Please.* Please, pretty please with bells on—fuck!"

That was Aaron plunging down on him, taking him urgently, still not using his hand, just a mouth that was wild and wet, perfectly tight and perfectly right.

"Oh, you miracle," Joel whispered. "I love it. More."

He meant harder but Aaron went deeper, taking Joel almost alarmingly far down. He made a tiny choking noise, pulled back, did it again, and now Joel was hanging on by his fingernails, mind going white, nothing in the world left but the sensation of DS Fowler learning how to get a man down his throat. "Oh fuck Jesus Aaron, Aaron—!"

He shot, shuddered, collapsed. Aaron held on like grim death throughout, and this time, he swallowed.

"Hand it to you," Joel mumbled, when he could remember English again. "Quick learner."

Aaron sluiced his mouth with a sip of whisky, then leaned over for a kiss. "I have been rehearsing that in my head for some time."

"It worked."

Aaron grinned, and relaxed on top of him, except for a very insistent erection. Joel squirmed a bit, to show he'd noticed. "Aaron?"

"Mmm?"

"Tell me something. In all that thinking you've been doing about me. What are you doing when you come?"

Aaron made a choking noise. Joel slid his hand over his arse. "I want to know. I mean, you've been thinking about me with your prick in your hand, right? So what are we doing?"

"It doesn't matter," Aaron whispered.

"It does. If you want something, I want to give it to you."

Aaron made a sound that was almost like a laugh. "What I want is to be naked in bed with you all night. To learn every inch of your skin. But that isn't going to happen, is it?"

"I'll stay if you want me."

"I want you, but you can't stay." Aaron's neck muscles corded briefly, a man swallowing tension. "Can I touch you?"

"Yes. However you want."

Aaron pushed himself up on his knees, and tugged Joel's open trousers and drawers down his thighs. The cloth was constricting, and he looked very big as he knelt over Joel, and Joel's heart was thundering now. He wondered if Aaron was going to turn him over, to fuck him here on the settee, without anything but spit. He was hardening again.

"Jesus," Aaron whispered. He ran his hands over Joel's bared skin, belly to thighs. "Do you think you might manage a second time?"

"If you care to make me."

Aaron's hands closed on his prick. Joel watched his face, his intent dark eyes, his slightly parted lips. His hands were firm, one nudging between Joel's thighs in exploration as the other worked him.

"This is very dedicated of you," Joel managed. "In the circumstances."

"You asked me what I thought about. I thought about the sounds you make, and how your hips move, all of it. I want to memorise how it feels to make you come because that is what I'm going to be thinking about for a very long time."

Joel stared up at his face. Aaron gave a twisted sort of smile down. "So if you can tell me how best to get you there..."

"I need to feel you too. Wait." Joel squirmed and turned under Aaron, muttering directions, until he was face down, Aaron's hand under him, round his prick, Aaron's weight on him, and his bare erection hot against Joel's arse.

"Oh God," Aaron whispered. "I'm not sure what I'm doing."

"I want you all over me. Between my legs, or inside me, or rubbing like that, whichever you please, but I want to be humping your hand, and under you, and listening to you pleasing yourself. Can you do that?"

Aaron was moving gently, rubbing against Joel's skin. "Like this?"

"Heavier. Don't hold yourself up."

"I don't want to asphyxiate you."

"I want your full weight," Joel growled. "I want a big strong policeman on my back and between my legs. Have you got that?"

There was a tiny silence. Then a heavy hand came down on Joel's back between his shoulderblades, pushing him into the settee.

"Fuck. That's it. Oh Jesus, yes."

He could feel the tension in Aaron's muscles. He was pushing hard now, strong thighs over Joel's, frotting against the crease of his arse, fingers gripping Joel's prick and bony against his belly, and Joel did very much wish that they had a jar of petroleum jelly and a couple of hours, but this was perfect too.

"Joel," Aaron whispered. "Is this what you like?"

"More."

Aaron came down on his forearm, across Joel's back, his full weight now. Joel attempted a wriggle just to see, and God, he really was trapped under the larger man. Aaron was pushing, driving, and they almost might be fucking, both of them rocking and grunting, hot breath and flesh and friction. Aaron kissed Joel's neck with force and teeth, burying his face in the crook, panting anguished breaths, and Joel needed to come again, he desperately wanted to give Aaron that. "Oh Christ. Talk to me. Touch me. Tell me what you want and sodding do it."

"You," Aaron gasped in his ear. "I want you, and I want—"

Joel yelped. That was because Aaron had straddled him, hoisted his hips, and thrust between his thighs. Oxford style, but with his legs caught like this it felt so tight and hot and hard. “Christ, yes, fuck me like this,” he gasped, and Aaron growled, “I’ll give it to you as long as you want it,” and that was it for Joel. Coming a second time, bucking in Aaron’s unbreakable, painful, glorious grip, begging, “Yes, Jesus, please,” as Aaron drove him into the settee and sobbed into his ear.

They lay together. Joel couldn’t have moved at gunpoint. His bones were liquid, his thighs sticky, Aaron a dead weight on his back, and he quite wanted to cry again.

“That was bloody lovely,” he managed.

Aaron didn’t respond. He might be actually dead, and Joel couldn’t blame him. He lay with his face in upholstery, wondering if they could just lock the door and stay in here forever.

At last Aaron shifted. “Joel.”

“Mmm.”

“Joel.” He didn’t seem to have anything more to offer. “Are you all right?”

“Yes. Don’t move.”

“I meant—”

“It was exactly what I wanted. You were perfect. I’ve spunked all over your settee and you should clean it up or the stain will be a bugger to get out.”

“Housekeeping tips too.”

“I’m a man of many talents.” He took as deep a breath as he could manage in the circumstances. “And I would like to stay here as long as you’d have me, but...”

“But,” Aaron said. “I know.”

“What do we do?”

“The best thing for us both would be to get you well out

of the way. If you can't be used against me, that would be extremely helpful. Go somewhere, use an assumed name, keep your head down. Somewhere outside London, preferably a longish way. Do you have any friends you could visit?"

Joel's entire acquaintance lived in London these days. "No, but I'll go somewhere. For how long?"

"I don't know. It could be some time."

Some time, when he was already four quid in the hole and wouldn't be able to earn without advertising. *Out of the way*, when Aaron was right here with his lonely eyes, and desperate, passionate handwriting, and a mouth that looked luscious with Joel's cock in it. It wasn't fair.

"If you say so," he managed, like a sensible grown-up. "If that's best. Can I contact you? How will I know when I can come back?"

Aaron hesitated. "That's a good question. It depends on how vindictive Colthorne might be, and on—well, what happens here."

Something clicked in Joel's head. "Happens here? To you?"

"About all this."

"And what will that be?" Joel enquired. "Does DDI Colthorne give up being mean to you if he can't put the thumbscrews on me?"

"I doubt that."

"Then what will my going achieve? Just that he'll need to find a different way to sack or frame or murder you? Is that what you have in mind? Aaron Fowler, are you being a martyr?"

"I'm not—"

"Yes you *are*. Get off me." Aaron half lifted; Joel squirmed furiously round. "You're sending me off so you can sacrifice yourself, aren't you?"

"For God's sake, Joel, why should you be caught up in this?"

"Why should *you* be? We haven't done anything wrong! Except, you know—" He waved vaguely. "Why aren't you fighting this? Firebrand Fowler might have been a martyr at home, but I never heard he turned down a scrap!"

"Because I don't have anything to fight with! Do you not think I've tried?"

"No, I don't! You haven't talked to me till now, and you haven't talked to anyone who might listen. Have you?"

"Who's going to listen, still less help? The Commissioner won't want to know, and Colthorne's been setting me up as untrustworthy or unreliable for God knows how long. I can't think of anyone I could safely talk to, in case they go back to him. There's nobody I can trust. Christ, I'm a fool." The words sounded like they hurt. "I've spent six years of my life in the Met. Six years, my father, so much lost time, and all for what?"

"For justice," Joel said. "To stop bad people. That was what you joined for, that was what you wanted to do and good for you, so why don't we do it now?"

"We?"

"You asked who'd help you. There's me."

"That is—something," Aaron said carefully. "It means a very great deal, as an offer. But I don't know what you can do."

"Let's sodding find out, shall we?" Joel was fizzing with something—rage, hope, a good fuck, who knew. "What do we have to lose? You're fucked, and what am I supposed to do if I run away? Sit around wondering if your murderous boss has murdered you yet, and if he'll come after me next? Change my name and find something completely new to do with my life, for the however-manyth time it is? I've started again so many times—after prison, after my hand, after being kicked out—and I'm bloody tired of it!"

Aaron winced. "I'm sorry."

"I don't need you to be sorry, I need you to be fighting! I want— Oh, bloody hell, I'm just going to say it. All I've been doing for so long is living with things. Keeping on with them, putting up with them. And then I met you and now this, you and me, it doesn't feel like 'living with' at all. It's *living*. Actually having things that matter instead of the days just passing. I want more of that. I want all I can get, even if we can't get much."

Aaron's lips had parted. Joel set his shoulders and pushed on. "I don't know if you feel that too. Maybe you don't, and we barely know each other really, and probably if we had longer, I'd annoy the hell out of you. But even so, I want more time with you, and if we have to fight for that, then let's fight, all right? You're a good copper, I'm a graphological genius, we can try."

"And if we fail?"

"Then let's fuck DDI Colthorne *right* up on the way down. Because—" He took Aaron's hand. "Because you and I deserved a chance."

"Joel." Aaron's eyes were wide.

"If that's too much—"

"It's not too much," Aaron said, and grabbed his face. His lips hit Joel's hard, and they were kissing again, as hungrily as before, awkwardly tangled on the settee in a chaos of bare flesh, inconvenient cloth, stickiness, and just for now, it was perfect. Just for now, Joel could cling to his hard biceps and feel Aaron's desperate clutch, and neither of them was alone.

Aaron pulled away after a moment. He looked slightly stunned. "Joel. Are you serious?"

"Yes," Joel said stubbornly, because he was aware of his nerves jangling behind the bravado. "I want you for as long as I can have you, and I want to fight this because it's not right and I'm *sick* of these bastards getting away with murder and bullying and the rest. Not to mention that was four quid I won't see again."

"You've no idea what you're getting into."

"Bloody right I don't. You're the policeman, you solve the crime. I'm here for moral support, handwriting analysis, and the occasional Frenching to keep your pecker up." He grinned at Aaron's choke. "Look, I read that arsehole's hand. I really do understand that we're in a lot of trouble. But running away won't achieve anything for me that I care to have any more. I'd rather play than fold."

Aaron touched his face with a gentle finger, a wondering expression. "The odds are bad. And the stakes are very high."

"I know," Joel said. "But if the war taught me anything, it was that if you keep going, you might get through. And not to raise your hand for attention, that's a terrible idea. And *also* that tea fixes most things, so get the kettle on, because we're going to talk about this."

Aaron made a pot. They sat together on the settee, Joel curled against Aaron's broad chest, Aaron's arm round his shoulders.

"Gerald Marks. A private detective by trade. In particular he was hired a few years ago by the Beech family after their son hanged for murder." He recounted the case: a wealthy art dealer found beaten to death; a bloodstained poker and a pile of cash under the bed where a drunken man slept.

"Was he covered in blood?" Joel asked.

"He was not. It was argued that he had had the presence of mind to wash himself and dispose of his bloodstained shirt—one was missing—but had forgotten about the poker."

"And where did Colthorne come into it?"

"He was investigating the case, but he had played cards with Thaddeus Knight, the victim. He stated that at the outset, making it clear they had played legally in a private house and he didn't owe the man money. It was less than ideal but he was kept on the case due to the pressure of wartime on manpower. Beech swung. His family hired Marks to look into it, but he didn't get anywhere. The family emigrated two years back."

"And the case was seven years ago, so why would Colthorne care now?"

"Good question." Aaron made a face. "Marks didn't forget the Beech case; we know he discussed it with his landlady. He came into money in the last weeks of his life, and we can't trace its source. And then he received a fatal wound to the back of his head, his office was searched on the night of his death by someone who had his keys, and his notebooks and all his files relating to the last few months are missing."

"That sounds dodgy as hell."

"Doesn't it just. But the coroner's report was inconclusive, there were no witnesses, and he was very drunk. It's hard to pursue a murder case with no evidence of an actual crime and no suspect. Certainly, DDI Colthorne didn't want me to. And when he was telling me so, he asked me if we'd found Marks's 'papers'. But I had only said his notebooks were missing."

Joel curled his mug against himself. "So what are you thinking? Marks kept working on the Beech case, found something in the last few months that would look bad for Colthorne...blackmailed him? Is that where the money came from?"

"It's a theory."

"Not one that's very flattering to Mr. Marks."

"He was a drunk, he needed money, and his clients had left the country," Aaron said. "Or, more charitably, perhaps he suspected that Colthorne would be able to quash any investigation, so this seemed the only retribution available."

"And then Colthorne kills him instead. Having got him drunk first?"

"I retraced Marks' steps to a pub. The barman recalled him buying several doubles and thinks he was sitting with someone, but he couldn't come up with a description beyond a middle-aged man."

Joel scowled in thought. "So would Colthorne kill Marks himself or have one of his gang friends do it?"

"I should do it myself, in his shoes."

"Then he searches Marks' office for any papers

pertaining to himself, or Sammy Beech, or both, and… doesn't find them? Or finds them and takes them?"

"They're gone, so someone's taken them."

"But if Colthorne had them, why would he need to go to these lengths against you? Or any lengths at all, really? Surely he'd just need to burn the evidence."

"I can only conclude he thinks I know a lot more than I do. Which is absurd, because if I had Marks's evidence, I'd have taken it to Scotland Yard or the Home Office already."

"But he thinks you could get it," Joel pressed. "He must do, because he's trying to force you out one way or another. Destroying your reputation via me, or making your life miserable. So can't we try to find whatever Marks had? Because if you got hold of the evidence he's murdered at least one person and framed another, I don't think him spluttering accusations about your friend the queer graphologist would hold much water."

Aaron reached over and kissed the top of his head. It was the kind of casually affectionate gesture anyone might make, except this was Aaron, and Joel's whole heart hurt at it. He made himself glower anyway. "Was that an 'aren't-you-sweet' kiss?"

"Perhaps a little," Aaron said. "I entirely agree that finding Marks's papers is vital. It's the finding that's the hard bit, in part because Davis, the DI, has been running me off my feet."

"What happens if you take tomorrow off sick?" Joel asked. "Go search his office again, and his rooms."

"I…could do that. And I might talk to Challice, the detective constable who was with me. I think I can trust her. She was the other hand you read, the Head Girl character."

"Oh, yes, I liked her. And I'll talk to Darby Sabini."

"Joel—"

"I can't avoid him: he knows where I live. Suppose I tell him you're a complete fool for graphology?"

"Rather than for a graphologist?" Aaron asked, and there went Joel's heart again, squeezing painfully, because Aaron flirting ineptly was so much better than the most practised seducer. "No, but what do you have in mind?"

"What if I claim you're convinced I have mystical powers? You think you'll be solving crimes like billy-oh with me as your secret weapon, and I'm taking your money, and that's why we've been seen together. That wouldn't be illegal for you, would it?"

"It could probably be presented as a form of misconduct," Aaron said thoughtfully. "In fact...with the right spin, it might be enough for Sabini to believe you've given him something useful to pass on."

"I'll say that, then. You talk to your constable, if you think you can. And your cousin?"

"Oh, I *will* be talking to my cousin," Aaron said, with intent. "Although not yet, if you don't mind looking as though you're capitulating."

"That's fine. Should I reply to him?"

"Hold off. Darby Sabini is enough for now. Are you sure you're willing to do this?"

'Willing' might be overstating it. Joel didn't have any great desire to cross a senior policeman or a gang boss, to risk pain or prison. Actually, he'd have preferred all of it to go away, but life didn't work like that.

"One of the men in my ambulance division was an older chap," he said. "Boer War injury, not fit to fight, volunteered for us instead. I said, you surely didn't need to come out, do you enjoy wars or what? He whacked me round the head. And then he said, 'It won't be over till someone's lost, so here I am, helping 'em lose.'"

"You could so easily not," Aaron said hoarsely. "You could so easily walk away."

"Problem is, it wouldn't be easy." He put his hand over Aaron's. "Which is your fault, by the way."

"Dear God, Joel," Aaron said, and pulled him over again.

Chapter Fourteen

Joel had to return home eventually, much against his will. He wanted to be with Aaron, together, touching, giving each other strength; he also really didn't fancy the walk. That was his hard luck, because the Tube and buses had long finished running, so he trudged along two and a half miles of dark, cold, empty streets, jumping at every shadow. He got stopped twice on the Euston Road by uniformed policemen commenting meaningfully that he was out late, and although he knew that Colthorne was CID, and was fairly sure he was outside G Division, it brought his heart into his mouth both times.

He replied pleasantly anyway and had a bit of a chat with both constables. He might want witnesses that he was going home to spend the night in his own bed.

The cigarette-smoking watcher was outside his house again when he got back. Joel considered a smart remark, and decided against it. He just let himself inside, went to bed, and lay awake in the cold, trying to smell Aaron on himself and sweating ice about the next morning.

He'd been told to present himself at the Griffin public house in Clerkenwell at noon. He got there at ten to, and was conducted in by a couple of men who looked like boxers, to the saloon bar and a table where a broad-shouldered man sat.

You couldn't call him pretentious. Darby Sabini, king of the racecourse gangs, wore a flat cap, a collarless shirt, a high-buttoned waistcoat, and a dark suit that had seem better days. He had a broken nose, and looked like a bricklayer in his Sunday best.

"Well, now, Mr. Wildsmith," he said. "Sit down. You're very prompt, I like that. Will you take a drink?"

He had a pint of stout in front of him. Joel wondered if this was some sort of trap. "If you think I'll be staying that long, Mr. Sabini. I honestly don't know why I'm here or what I can do for you."

"We'll find out. Pint, is it?"

"Just the half, please. I had a couple last night," Joel tried, and saw no recognition in the shrewd eyes. Maybe Aaron's place hadn't been watched. That would be good.

Darby waved. A pint of bitter arrived. "Thank you," Joel said, and took a polite sip, which unfortunately revealed that his hand was shaking. A dribble of beer ran down the tankard, and pooled on the sticky table.

"Right," Darby said. "So, Mr. Wildsmith, what is it you do?"

"I'm a graphologist. I analyse handwriting. Tell you people's characters."

"You any good at it?"

"It's a living. You know how it is, Mr. Sabini." He lifted his truncated left arm. He'd decided against the prosthetic in case the hook was taken as an offensive weapon.

Darby nodded slowly. "I do know. And you didn't answer me. You any good at it?"

Joel took a split second to weigh up the alternatives. "Pretty good, yes."

"Let's see, then." He waved again, and a lean youth brought over a letter. "Why don't you tell me about this?"

Joel took the paper with trepidation. He couldn't get anything off the barely literate since the hand had to be second nature for the personality to express itself, and he feared that wouldn't be the case given his surroundings. He also had panic lapping at his ankles, fogging his brain. He took a couple of deep breaths before he dared look.

It wasn't wonderful. The hand wasn't fluent, but maybe practised enough to let character come through. Hopefully. If Joel could just relax and let it happen. He was very aware of his thundering heartbeat, and the numerous eyes on him.

If you fuck this up, he won't believe anything you say. Get it right. Get it right.

He wasn't helping himself. He tried to think of Aaron saying something calm and soothing in his deep voice. Aaron probably faced down characters like Darby Sabini all the time. Imagine going back to him and saying, *Sorry, but after all that big talk I broke down and couldn't get a word out.*

He'd been in a fucking war; he was not going to collapse in a Clerkenwell pub. He inhaled so hard his nostrils stung a little, and looked at the paper, taking his time, turning it over and back, thinking.

"Determination," he said after a moment. "That's the strongest thing I get: this is a very determined person. I think it would be pretty hard to make him do anything he didn't want to do, there's a *lot* of willpower here. That's impressive, but maybe, sometimes, a bit too much of a good thing? I wonder if he might stand in his own way now and again, by digging his heels in when he could afford to give a little." There was a rustle from the silent watchers; Darby gestured and they shut up. Joel tensed his toes in his shoes, steeling himself. "That's the main thing, but there's also...there's a real expansiveness here, you can see it in the broadening of the vowels. I think he's likely to be a very generous man, there's nothing small about him. A man you could turn to. Or at least, if he decides to help, he'll do it properly. That's part and parcel of the determination, of course: he decides what he thinks is best, or right, and he does it. He'll make a judgement and then carry it out, whether that's to help people or, you know, the opposite. That's really what I'd say here: this is a good friend and a bad enemy. I wouldn't want to get off on the wrong foot with him, myself."

He held the paper out. Darby didn't take it. "You got that off the handwriting."

"Yes. It's what I do."

"Off a letter to my mother."

"Yes, it—" Joel stopped short. "Uh. That was *your* hand?"

"That's right."

Joel opened his mouth, moved it soundlessly, then said, "Excuse me," grabbed the glass of beer, and took a hefty gulp. The laugh exploded around him, and he was relieved to see Darby looked as amused as anyone.

He hoped to God he'd judged that right. It had been a reasonable punt that Darby had produced his own writing: for one, he probably wasn't surrounded by literates, and for another, it was an aggressively pigheaded thing to do, and aggressive pigheadedness had been clear on the page. Joel had carefully skipped the other observations that came to mind, such as *vicious* and *self-centred as a spinning top*, in favour of what he knew about Darby Sabini from Clerkenwell gossip.

Broadening of the vowels indeed. Aaron would laugh, assuming Joel lived through this to tell him about it.

"A good friend and a bad enemy," Darby mused. "Well, I'd like to think it. What do we reckon to this, boys?"

There was a chorus of mostly approbation from the watchers, but one man said, "So what's the trick? How'd you know all that?"

"I don't *know* anything," Joel said. "Certainly not about Mr. Sabini. But the way a man writes tells you a lot, or it does me. I bet you can judge a man pretty well?" he appealed to Darby. "You look at his eyes, the way he holds himself, the way he talks back, and you know what you think, yes?" He waited for the nod he knew would be forthcoming; people rarely said, *No, I'm a terrible judge of character*. "Well, I do it off handwriting, not faces. That's all."

"Useful," Darby said. "Sounds like something the coppers would like."

"Oh, it wouldn't stand up in court. I've been assured of that."

"Have you, now. Let's talk about that. All right, you lot, clear off."

The hangers-on vanished, leaving them alone, although Joel didn't feel any less threatened for it. "So," Darby said. "Eddie Twigg told you what I want."

"He said you wanted to talk to me about Detective Sergeant Fowler. May I ask why?"

"No. So I hear you and Mr. Fowler are pretty close, he takes you out to dinner, that sort of thing. Tell me about that. And I know what you did time for, Mr. Joel Wildsmith, so don't mess me about."

"Sorry, what?" Joel said blankly. "Are you implying— Oh, come on. He's a *policeman*."

Darby Sabini's jaw hardened. "I know that. Now you tell me all about you and him."

There was sweat sliding down Joel's backbone; he had no idea how an empty saloon bar without a fire could be at once so cold and so stuffy. "Mr. Sabini, I'm sorry, but if you're after dirt on Fowler, you'll need to ask whoever he's doing the dirty with, because it's not me. I'm not tupping a copper! I'm not stupid and I'm not going back inside if I can help it, so—"

Darby slammed a hand on the table. Joel's terrified yelp as he recoiled was entirely unfeigned. "Are you lying to me, you little pansy?"

"No!" Joel said, his pitch rising. "Who's been saying this? Why's anyone talking to you about me?"

"Nobody cares about you," Darby said, with chilling unconcern. "I'm asking about Fowler."

"I've no idea who he's screwing! It's not me, that's all I know!"

"And when he took you out for a nice Indian meal—what about that?"

"That? Oh my God, is *that* what this is about?" Joel pantomimed relief with a hand on his chest. "For goodness sake. That wasn't a candlelight meal for two, Mr. Sabini, it was work. He reckons he can get me to solve his cases."

Darby's eyes were cold pools you could drown in. "Are you taking the piss?"

"That's what I said to him! I said, I'm not magic! The only way I can tell you if someone's committed a crime from looking at their handwriting is if they wrote a full confession!" Darby grunted at that, which was a relief. Joel did not want him worrying about his powers later on. "But he wouldn't listen. He wants to get ahead, and he reckons I'm a secret weapon. You know how people want to believe things and you can't tell them anything else? Well, he's decided I'm about four times as good as I am. He offered me a retainer if I agree not to consult for any other police clients."

Darby leaned back. "You got many of those?"

"None at all," Joel said. "So I told him I had several and he'd need to double the offer."

"Hah!" Darby gave a proper laugh this time. "And?"

"He's thinking about it. Which— I'm not a nark, Mr. Sabini. I don't *want* to consult for the Met. Well, it isn't for the Met, it was 'in a private capacity', but it's still working for the busies, isn't it? But like you say, I've a record, and if a detective sergeant is telling me what I need to do for my own good, I don't have much choice. The dinner was him being nice about it, and I don't want him to be nasty, but..." He gestured helplessly. "I suppose you've called me here because you don't want me to do it, and I understand that, I truly do, but I'm between a rock and a hard place. I can't just tell CID to piss off." He looked plaintively at the gang lord. "What should I do?"

"Maybe I can tell him to piss off for you," Darby said. "If you give me the information I need."

Joel perked up. "Could you? What do you need?"

"Enough to get rid of Mr. Fowler for good."

"But I don't *have* anything like that," Joel said, and heard the very real crack of fear and frustration in his voice. "Honestly, if I could get rid of him, I would."

"And what's to stop you saying he made a pass? Who's to know?"

Joel had been afraid of that. He grimaced. "Well, him? He's bigger than me. Got more hands. And the last time a policeman made a pass at me, I ended up doing two months, so I don't want anything to do with all that."

"Then what have you got to offer me?"

"Nothing," Joel said wretchedly. "I did say, Mr. Sabini, and I'm very sorry. Well, except that Mr. Fowler did say not to tell anyone? But—"

"Tell anyone what?"

"About me working for him. He said he's shown me confidential documents so I need to keep my mouth shut about all of it, and that I couldn't put it in my advertising—'Consultant to the Metropolitan Police', you know, which, if I *have* to do it you'd think I might at least get the benefit, but he said no. He said that my readings wouldn't stand up in court, and a decent defence brief might even get a case chucked out just because he'd involved me, and then he, Mr. Fowler, would get in trouble. So I wasn't to tell anyone he was consulting me, and especially not that I'd seen any documents."

"What documents?"

"A couple of written statements and some letters," Joel said earnestly. "He said they were evidence in an investigation, but he didn't say what. He wanted me to tell him if someone had committed a crime. Which, as I said, I can't do."

"Well," Darby said slowly. "Well, now."

Joel gave him hopeful eyes. "Is that useful? Because I honestly don't know anything else."

"We'll see. I expect you'd be willing to swear your affydavy to all that, would you?"

"Where?" Joel said, with panic he didn't have to feign. "I'm not going back to court. Or crossing a copper, either. He's a sergeant, Mr. Sabini!"

"I wouldn't worry about that," Darby said. "I don't reckon it'll get as far as court. I reckon I bring this to certain people and your problem goes away like that." He clicked his fight-thickened fingers.

"You can do that? Really?"

"Fowler's only a sergeant. Some of us have friends in high places, sonny."

"Yes, but *I* don't, and you're talking about me swearing to things and getting on the wrong side of CID, and now I don't know what's going on! Mr. Sabini, please." Joel let his voice wobble. It didn't take much acting. "Could you just tell me? Because I don't want any of this, and if I do have to do something I'd rather not get it wrong, and I don't *understand*. Please?"

Darby clicked his tongue, with almost fatherly patience. "Here's how it works, son. You want rid of Fowler, right? Well, say there's a certain other person of the same mind, in a position to do something about it. I pass on what you just said to him. If it's enough for him to see Fowler off, well, that fixes my pal's problem, and it fixes your problem too. Simple as that. See?"

"So this other person says 'You've been a bad boy, consulting graphologists when you're not allowed,' and that makes Mr. Fowler back off me?"

"That's right. So I've done you both a favour. And...?" He gave Joel a meaningful look.

"And now me and your important pal both owe you a favour?"

"You're a bright boy," Darby Sabini said. "All right, you can pop off now. Make sure you're ready for a chat when I tell you, and don't you worry, I'll sort it out. We'll talk more about that favour you owe me in a while. I could use a man of your talents."

"Of course, Mr. Sabini," Joel said faintly. "Whenever you like."

Joel would have liked nothing more than to fling himself into Aaron's arms, blurt out the whole horrible conversation, and be reassured that he'd done the right thing and wasn't going to find himself in permanent hock to a gang lord. Or worse. He and Aaron had agreed the lie he'd tell Sabini, but now his mind was filled with the awful prospect of being asked to testify, of his words being used against Aaron.

He'd had to give Sabini something, though, and he'd got at least circumstantial confirmation of their suspicions. A high-up in the Met gunning for Aaron, getting Darby Sabini to lean on Joel, owing a gang lord favours.

Joel wasn't the stuff of which righteous avengers were made. He'd never felt he had the time and resources to look after anyone much beyond himself. But he was properly outraged now, not just for Aaron—honest, dedicated Aaron who cared about doing the right thing—but as a matter of principle. This was *wrong*, and he was angry in the sick deep-down way he'd been angry about his trial and conviction, with the impotent rage that came from watching powerful people wreck lives for advantage or profit or fun.

He fretted the rest of the day away, and was grateful for a

couple of clients to distract him. He used the rest of his time putting his things in order and packing a bag so that, if need be, he could run.

He wasn't to contact Aaron unless it was an emergency. He didn't expect to hear from him that day, and duly didn't; he did hope for something the following afternoon, say. Or evening, or night, but the clock ticked remorselessly on and no word came.

By the third morning Joel had chewed off all the fingernails he had available and was cursing the Germans for depriving him of the other five. Ought he try to get in touch with Aaron? Why wasn't he saying what was going on? Had he found anything? Was he keeping Joel out of it to protect him, and how hard would Joel need to kick him?

It wasn't that he didn't want to be protected; he absolutely did. But he wanted even more to be useful. He wanted to be Aaron's partner in this, and he wanted to know what was going on, because Aaron ought not to be facing this alone.

When the knock came, he ran for the door. Whether it was a telegram from Aaron, or Eddie Twigg, or Darby Sabini himself, he needed to see *something* was moving.

It was none of those. It was a young woman in a long sensible serge skirt.

"Mr. Wildsmith? I'm Detective Constable Helen Challice. May I come in?"

Joel stepped back. Miss, or Constable, Challice entered, shut the door, looked around with every evidence of disapproval, and said, "I need to talk to you, Mr. Wildsmith. DS Fowler sent me."

"Is that right," Joel said. This was the woman copper

Aaron had said he'd talk to, that he felt he could trust, but Joel wasn't inclined to extend the benefit of the doubt to anyone right now.

She was eyeing him up shrewdly. "I expect you want to know if I'm telling the truth."

"Er—?"

"About DS Fowler," she clarified, as though Joel were slightly slow. "He said you probably wouldn't take my word that I was here on his behalf. He told me to say—let me get this right—'dolce Torino'. I suppose that's Italian for something? Anyway, he said that would prove I was from him, a sort of password. It's all terribly cloak and dagger."

That was the chocolate sweet Aaron had watched Joel eat with an expression of such naked longing that Joel had all but thrown himself on the table there and then. "Yes, I see," he said carefully. "Why did he give you a password? I mean, why are you here, and not him?"

"Because he's in rather a lot of trouble," Constable Challice said. "May I sit down?"

"Of course, sorry. Tea?" he added automatically.

"He said you'd thrust tea on me," Challice remarked. "He said you wouldn't be able to help yourself. If the house was burning around your ears, he says you'd put a kettle on the flames."

"Yes, all right, you're definitely from him," Joel muttered. "What trouble? Is he all right? How do you take it?"

"No tea. Sit down." The instruction came in the sort of voice that took a man right back to school, and Joel dropped into the nearest chair as though she'd cut his hamstrings. Challice took the other seat and folded her hands neatly in her lap.

"Well," she said briskly. "First of all, DS Fowler has given me a series of quite remarkable allegations about DDI Colthorne. I understand you know that."

"Yes."

"DS Fowler believes that the DDI was behind the murder of Gerald Marks, because he feared Marks had something on him. Was perhaps even blackmailing him."

"Yes."

"Do you believe that?"

"DS Fowler believes it, which is what matters," Joel said. "He's the copper, he knows about the case, and he thinks it's what's going on."

"And what do you think?" she said implacably.

"I think he's an honest man. I know that someone is leaning on me to get at him. And I understand this started after the Marks murder, which Colthorne told DS Fowler to stop investigating. So yes, I believe it."

She nodded slowly. "Interesting. Because the thing is, DDI Colthorne has accused DS Fowler of gross misconduct, on both personal and professional levels. He's offered to let Mr. Fowler resign quietly for the good of the Met, if he signs a full statement admitting to disgracing his office. If he doesn't resign, the DDI will take it to a formal disciplinary."

"He's trying to shut him up. Isn't that obvious?"

"Unless DS Fowler knew he was going to be accused, and trumped up this story against the DDI first in an effort at self-protection."

"But he didn't," Joel said. "And it would be quite a rubbish effort, wouldn't it, if he couldn't provide any proof. Who do you believe?"

Challice regarded him levelly. "Well, that's the thing. You

see, DS Fowler tells me that the charges against him are all based on your testimony."

"Mine?"

"DDI Colthorne says that you have accused DS Fowler of sharing confidential evidence relating to active investigations—"

"Did he, by God," Joel said. "*Did* he. We've got the swine."

She raised a questioning brow. Joel said, "The people leaning on me? One of them was Darby Sabini. He called me in to demand dirt on DS Fowler, so Fowler told me to say that he'd given me confidential evidence relating to active investigations. Only, he never did that, and I haven't claimed he did to anyone *except* Darby Sabini. So how come your DDI Colthorne is accusing him of exactly that?"

Challice took that in. Then she said, "The DDI also said you accused the DS of indecent behaviour."

"I did not! Sabini wanted me to—told me to, even—but I didn't, so that's a sodding lie. Excuse my French."

Challice considered him. For a fresh-faced young woman, she had the eye of an inquisitor. "So you think the Divisional Detective Inspector is corrupt, and he's making Mr. Fowler a scapegoat to avoid exposure."

"Yes!"

She let out a breath that sounded long-held. "So do I. That man gives me the screaming ab-dabs."

The knuckles and joints of her interlaced fingers were white, Joel saw belatedly. God knew what guts it must have taken for a young woman to join CID, how precarious that particular experiment was, how much she might feel riding on her success or failure. How unpleasant a lot of people probably made her life.

"Do you want to be involved in this?" he found himself asking.

"I don't imagine any of us do," she said. "If you haven't made personal accusations against Mr. Fowler—"

"I have not! Can you please tell him, I have *not*."

"He asked me to tell you he doesn't believe it for a second."

That was a punch to the heart. "Really?" Joel asked like a fool. "That is—did he mean it?"

"I assume so, since he said it. But the DDI presumably expects you to back up his story if it comes to the crunch."

"I won't."

"DS Fowler says, either you'll be forced into it or you won't be in a position to speak at all."

"What does that mean?"

"He thinks you should get out while you still can. He said to tell you, 'We tried'."

"We have *not* tried," Joel said, suddenly furious. "We certainly haven't tried everything, and now I've got proof your precious Divisional Detective Inspector is getting information from Sabini, so I am not running away and letting him win!"

"Good. What do we do about it?"

"We, you and Mr. Fowler?"

"We, you and me, Mr. Wildsmith," Challice said crisply. "Mr. Fowler is in deep trouble and it would be a very bad idea for him to embroil himself further in the Marks case, speak to Darby Sabini, or contact you. That leaves us. Given you seem to be in this to your eyebrows, I was rather hoping you'd be able to give me some ideas."

"Me? You're the police!"

"Yes, and look how well we've done," Challice said. "Mr. Fowler's the most honest and decent man I've met in—well, in the Met—and the DDI intends to ruin him. I don't want that to happen but I'm dratted if I know how to avoid it. I asked DS Fowler and he told me not to get involved for my own sake."

"He would," Joel said. "Stupid pri—uh, prig."

"Quite. Talk to me, Mr. Wildsmith. I didn't have long with the DS, so you'll need to fill me in."

Joel did his best. Challice was a sharply intelligent listener, and swiftly grasped the situation as he presented it. He didn't know if she'd also grasped the parts he wasn't admitting.

"So Sabini wanted to you make indecency allegations, and you refused," she mused. "But the DDI nevertheless said you'd made them. That's quite a bluff."

"Is the DDI saying it because he thinks he can scare Aaron—Mr. Fowler—with the mere accusation, or because he thinks he can make me say it?" Joel asked. "Because if it was the latter, I'd have thought Darby Sabini might have had another word with me already, to let me know what I was obliged to do."

"And he hasn't?"

"No," Joel said thoughtfully. "This Colthorne chap: nice as pie until he doesn't get what he wants, and then the temper comes out?"

"Very much so. Where are you going with this?"

Joel thought back on the conversation with Sabini, the various hands he'd read. "Sabini likes to be a man who does favours. Once I started appealing to him for help, he was generosity itself. But he doesn't like taking orders. I'm just wondering, if Colthorne told him to get an accusation of indecency out of me, and all Sabini brought him was an accusation of inappropriate graphology, would that have gone down badly? Would Colthorne maybe say *Go back and do it properly*, sort of thing? They both need to be the big man in the room, can't be challenged—"

"Have you met DDI Colthorne?" she demanded.

"I read his hand."

"Hmm. DS Fowler told me about that. It sounds plausible knowing the DDI, but does it get us anywhere?"

"Only that if Sabini took the hump, Colthorne might have done himself out of an ally," Joel suggested. "Temporarily, at least. So perhaps he decided to bluff his way through, and hope Mr. Fowler wouldn't care to fight a whole barrage of accusations." Especially if Paul Napier-Fox had blabbed about Aaron's school indiscretion. Joel didn't propose to bring that up. "You wouldn't do that if you felt certain you could frame someone up properly. But you might do it if you were on shaky ground and didn't want to give them leisure to counter-attack."

She nodded slowly. "So we should do that, then. DS Fowler still thinks the answer is in Marks's notebooks."

"Or papers. Colthorne mentioned papers. And I told Sabini that DS Fowler had showed me letters from an ongoing investigation—"

"Whereupon Colthorne launched the attack. Hmm." She drummed her fingers on her knee. "We searched Marks's office and rooms very thoroughly. I can't think he had another place; he was barely able to afford the life we saw. If he stashed them somewhere, we haven't found it."

"If he was afraid enough to move his files, he surely

would have wanted to put them somewhere they'd be found if anything happened to him," Joel said. "Or, perhaps, with someone who'd act if he turned up dead?"

"Nobody has contacted us to my knowledge. He wasn't married, no family." She frowned. "I might visit his landlady again. She clearly cared about him; I wonder if he'd have confided in her. She didn't want to talk to me, though, and was very distrustful of the police. I wonder—"

"If Marks told her not to trust the fuzz," Joel said breathlessly. "With Colthorne involved, wouldn't that be something Marks would say?"

"Yes, it might. Which creates a problem for me, of course."

Their eyes met. Joel swallowed. "Suppose—not that I want to tread on your toes or insert myself into official business or any such—but suppose I talk to her?"

Challice considered that for what felt like a very long time, then said, "Yes. Suppose you do."

Chapter Fifteen

Aaron stared at the walls of his flat. He couldn't seem to make himself do anything else, because his life had fallen apart around him and all he could do was brace himself for the coming blows.

The meeting with DDI Colthorne had been dreadful. It was truly terrifying to have a man lie to your face when you both knew he was lying, but he didn't care that you knew because you had no power to object. Colthorne had listed Aaron's supposed acts of misconduct with a little, cruel smile, enjoying every second of his discomfort. *I can crush you*, was the message, *and I will.*

As indeed he could, if Joel had caved.

Aaron knew that was possible: sometimes there was simply no choice. He didn't really expect Joel to stand up to Darby Sabini if the man made it a matter of physical threat, or to DDI Colthorne if the prospect of another prosecution for a longer sentence was on the table. He wouldn't expect that of anyone.

He hoped Joel was all right, for the sake of what they'd had and what might have been. He very much hoped the man took his message of trust as he intended it: a statement in principle, not a rebuke if he'd faltered.

Or maybe Joel hadn't caved, and Colthorne was lying, but even then, Aaron didn't see there was any way out for himself. He hadn't found any sort of proof against Colthorne to back up his suspicions—except the accusation that Joel had made to Sabini, but he didn't want to find himself in a situation where he and Colthorne exchanged accusations. He knew who'd lose.

And, in truth, he wasn't sure he could face the fight. He knew all too well how it would go. He had involved himself in private affairs in his official capacity; he had brought an obvious charlatan into a police investigation; he had spent a lot of his free time with Joel, with all that implied. It could be so easily twisted into a web of corruption and villainy, and the mud Colthorne threw would stick. Sergeant Hollis was noticeably avoiding Aaron, which indicated where he thought his bread was buttered.

The sensible thing to do would be to sign the resignation, take the private shame to avoid the public humiliation and then find something to do with the rest of his life.

He didn't want that, or at least, not like this. A reckoning with his profession was probably long overdue, but he wanted it to be on his terms. He didn't want to leave as a tainted man; his reputation mattered to him. And mostly, he did not want to see Colthorne carry on his merry way, unchecked and unpunished. That could not stand. He just had no idea how to prevent it.

So he stared at the walls, feeling them close in around him, feeling his neck muscles cramp, feeling his options narrowing and his life with it, until there was a knock at the door.

He answered for lack of better ideas, and was faced with a boy who shoved an envelope into his hand. It was a telegram, and it read SHAFIS NOW DONT BE FOLLOWED.

It was only mid afternoon. Aaron knocked at the restaurant door, and was quickly admitted by Rahim Mohammed. It felt extremely cloak and dagger.

"Your friends are here, Mr. Fowler," Rahim said. "Let me bring you a drink."

Joel and Challice were seated at a table laden with nibbles and snacks for a small army. Aaron stared blankly at them. "Challice? What are you both doing here? I told you—"

"Shut up, sit down, look at this," Joel said, his voice quivering with excitement. "*Look.*"

Aaron took the paper he held out. He recognised the handwriting very well indeed.

I, John Colthorne, promise to pay Thaddeus Knight the sum of four thousand four hundred pounds...

"What the," he managed. "What."

"It's his note of hand," Challice said. She was vibrating almost as visibly as Joel. "The DDI owed Knight a fortune as of the third of March 1917. Knight was murdered on the fifth. And Mr. Colthorne claimed that they only knew each other casually and played for small sums. Four thousand four hundred pounds isn't *casual.*"

It was something like ten years of a DI's salary. Aaron passed his hand over his face and felt the tremor. "If Colthorne didn't declare that as an interest—he can't have, he'd have been treated as a suspect—"

"So he killed Knight, framed up Sammy Beech, and lied through his teeth so your lot let him lead the investigation," Joel said. "Sees Beech hang and sits back feeling safe—"

"Until Marks comes up with this. Where did he find it? Wait: where did *you* find it?"

"Marks's landlady, Mrs. Trotter," Joel said smugly. "I did her a couple of readings and said rude things about the police, after which she ate out of my hand. Marks gave her the file and notebooks for safe keeping about a fortnight before his death, with strict instructions not to trust the police. She was supposed to post them to Beech's family in Canada if anything happened to him, but he hadn't passed on the address. She was just holding on to them, so we had a nice talk, and she agreed to give them to me."

"Joel," Aaron said helplessly.

Joel grinned at him, ochre eyes crinkling with glee. "Thank Helen. It was her idea to go back to the landlady."

"Joint effort," Challice said. She and Joel both had tin cups of lassi: they clinked them together. "Although we mostly owe this to Gerald Marks. Knight had left a briefcase in the lost property at Paddington, would you believe? Apparently Marks found out earlier this year that he sometimes did that as an alternative to a safety deposit box, and spent God knows how long going through every lost property in London. And, if you need any more, his latest notebook says he tapped Colthorne for two hundred pounds. That was eight days before he died."

"We've got him." Aaron couldn't quite believe it. "We've *got* him."

"Damn right," Joel said. "You have to have some of these things before I eat them all, by the way, they're incredible."

Aaron took a pakora from the plate Joel offered him and dipped it in fragrant sauce, thinking hard. "This is astonishing from you both. What I'm wondering is how we work it. It can't disappear into a Home Office confidential enquiry."

"They wouldn't, surely, sir," Challice said. "It's *murder*."

"Strictly speaking, this only proves that Colthorne owed Knight money and lied about it. It's obviously bad and the inference is clear but the higher-ups might well conclude that a prosecution would struggle to prove murder at this distance. And there's still no concrete evidence that Marks was murdered, and the defence could make hay with that. Colthorne lied about his gambling debt from the best of motives, the conviction of Sammy Beech was made on strong evidence and has not been quashed, he paid Marks's blackmail and intended to continue doing so as penance, and this entire prosecution stems from a drunkard slipping and falling on a rainy night."

"Oh," Challice said, deflating. "Do you think so?"

"It's what the defence will argue. Whereas the prosecution will need to cast Colthorne as an out and out villain, a murderer given high authority in the Met for years under the noses of his colleagues and superiors. The Commissioner won't like that at all." He grimaced. "I'm also aware that if this comes from me, Colthorne might argue a disaffected officer trying to get revenge for his own disgrace. That could muddy the waters to the point where a prosecution might seem very hard to achieve."

"Helen said he threatened you," Joel said.

"Unpleasantly. He said I could look to have my various wrongdoings all over the papers."

"Not via me. I told Sabini what we'd agreed and nothing else. If Colthorne said more, he's a damned liar."

Joel sounded ferocious. And he hadn't caved. He'd stood

up to Darby Sabini and lied to his face, for Aaron, and quite suddenly Aaron felt something crack inside.

"Aaron? You all right?"

"Yes. Yes. I just— I don't know what I did to deserve you. Either of you. I have never felt so alone in my life as I did this morning, and all the time you two were doing this when you should have been watching your own backs."

"I *am* watching my back; that's why we're meeting here," Challice pointed out. "You're not wrong, Mr. Fowler. We don't want this to be bogged down by the DDI accusing you; the Commissioner would never tolerate all that dirty linen in public."

"Could you do it?" Joel asked her.

Challice picked up a bit of battered onion and turned it in her fingers. "Would anyone listen to me? A detective constable, a woman, with a story like this? And...to be quite frank, bringing down a fellow officer is the kind of thing that ends careers, sooner or later. Everyone might agree he's a bad apple, but nobody likes a nark."

"That's true," Aaron said. "Not to mention, if you do it, I expect all women officers will be treated as potential snouts for a while. No. My career is over, whatever happens; I'll do it, and take whatever shrapnel comes my way."

"No," Joel said. "That's not fair."

"It's all right." It wasn't all right as such: it would be hellish and humiliating and he'd be all over the newspapers. But it had to be done, and Aaron felt a certain lightness at the decision, as though he'd let something slide off his shoulders. "I told you at the beginning of all this I'd do something about number seven, and I intend to. The question is how we make this work. Who I can go to who won't be swayed by the Commissioner's obduracy or Colthorne's claims about me, and who's prepared to face the trouble this will cause."

"One of the Big Five?" Challice asked.

"The Detective Superintendents of the Met, based at Scotland Yard," Aaron explained to Joel. "As far as I know they're all decent men, but the DDI is on good terms with them. He's been widely tipped to make a sixth. And any investigation would still have to be cleared by the Commissioner."

Joel frowned. "Maybe if the information was already out there, it would be harder to brush it under the carpet?"

"Out where?"

"In the papers."

"That's a good idea," Challice said, sitting up. "Do we know any journalists? What about those ones who called you Valentino, Mr. Fowler?"

"Oh, bugger journalists," Joel said. "What about the editor of the Tribune?"

"You know him?"

"No, but I broke up his daughter's engagement to an absolute arse a few weeks ago, so I'd say he owes me a hearing."

"You mean Paul?" Aaron demanded.

"His fiancée was Barbara Wilson, daughter of Tony Wilson, who edits the Tribune. Did you not know that?"

"I try to avoid learning anything about Paul. Can you get me an introduction?"

Joel tapped his fingers on the table. "I could do that. But... All right, hear me out. Suppose I tell him I found the information myself?"

"You?"

"Let's say Marks consulted me. Wanted to check if Colthorne's handwriting on the IOU was real, something like that."

"But he didn't."

"I'd like to see anyone prove that," Joel pointed out. "Then he died, and I asked your advice, as the only copper I know. You persuaded me to let you look into it, but Colthorne found out about your investigation, and that's why he's been going at you and me. And now Sabini is involved and it's got too much for me, so I'm giving up on the police and handing it to the Tribune."

"That's genius," Challice said through a mouthful.

"No, it's putting yourself in the firing line," Aaron said. "You can't do that. If you get in the papers—the things Colthorne might throw at you—"

"Are the same things he'll chuck at me if he goes after you. I'm already in this, Aaron, like it or not. It's just sensible."

Aaron's stomach was a hard knot. "Don't. I don't want you to do this."

"Why not? This could work very nicely for me. I'm going to give the editor of the Tribune a whopping great scoop, and get any amount of publicity that money can't buy."

"Along with the full and probably hostile attention of the Metropolitan Police! Do you have any idea—"

Joel thumped his left arm on the table, which made it obvious he wasn't wearing the prosthetic. Challice gave a slight exclamation that she suppressed almost at once.

"Yes," Joel said, a little loudly. "Yes, I do in fact know that attracting attention isn't always a good idea. Do you know why I was waving for attention when they shot my hand off?" He looked between Aaron and Challice. "Because we went out after a bombardment, and I had found a man who might have a chance, and I needed someone to help me get him back. Well, we needed two men as it turned out, because my stretcher-carrying days ended quite dramatically at that point, but I *did* get two men, and they *did* take him back, and he lived. I wish it hadn't happened like it did—Christ, I do—but he's alive, his kids grew up with a father, and we still send each other Christmas cards, so I can't wish it hadn't happened at all. Sometimes you just have to do the thing."

"We all have to make sacrifices," Aaron said. His mouth was dry. "But you've done enough."

Joel opened his mouth, then shot a look at Challice. "Helen, could you possibly give us a moment?"

"I need to powder my nose," she said promptly. "And also to find out what this yellow sauce is, and see if they'll let me have the recipe. Do excuse me."

"*Joel*," Aaron said through his teeth as she departed.

"No," Joel said flatly.

"No what?"

"No to all of it. No, I am not making a great sacrifice because I'm playing martyr. I couldn't be any less of a martyr; I'm just not a shirker. No, I am not going to hold this over your head forever, and fuck you for suggesting I would."

"I didn't—"

"You thought it somewhere deep down, so shut up. No, I am not going to ask for anything in return, and also no, I am not going to *refuse* anything in terms of appreciation, such as you buying me another very large meal here, because this isn't a transaction. This is—this is us, Aaron. You and I working together as seems best. *I* take this to the Tribune, *you* endeavour to shield me from the consequences, *we* do our best to bring Colthorne down. Grammar."

"But you're trying to protect me," Aaron said. "I know you are."

"So what if I am?" Joel demanded indignantly. "We'd literally just met when you chased down that bastard Sefton and saw off your cousin for me. Why can you do it and me not? Or, to put it another way: Are you the only one who gets to do things for other people, and nobody can do anything for you? Because I'll give you one guess who that sounds like."

"You are the most aggravating man who has ever walked the earth," Aaron said with feeling.

"Thank you; I try."

"And you are probably right," he made himself go on. "If this becomes public knowledge Colthorne is finished as a copper, no matter what the courts may say, and you probably can make that work better than I could. It's still taking on a great deal. May I say I'm grateful?"

"No. I don't want your gratitude, your thanks, or your obligation," Joel said. "I simply want wholehearted admiration of my courage, integrity, and intelligence, which can be demonstrated by a good shagging at any time."

Aaron started to laugh. There was so much to worry about, and so much to be done, but the bubble of bewildered joy had to come out and he couldn't help it. He put his elbow on the table and his hand over his face, and he shook with laughter even as Challice returned and demanded what the joke was.

A lot happened after that in quite a short time. Mostly, Joel went to see Mr. Tony Wilson, editor of the Tribune. The conversation touched on a number of potentially sensitive issues, including how little either Aaron or Joel wanted to be part of the story. DDI Colthorne's response was agreed to be unpredictable.

The Tribune took two days to consult its lawyers, and then, late on a Tuesday evening, Aaron went to the unofficial chief of the Big Five, Superintendent FP Wensley, at Scotland Yard and let him know the front page the Tribune would be running the next day.

Joel woke up very early on Wednesday with a sick feeling in the pit of his stomach. The Tribune's editor had assured him that the presses could not be stopped, but he had still lain awake worrying that the Home Secretary might have been nobbled, an injunction issued. He wished Aaron was there to roll his eyes and explain that wasn't how it worked, but Aaron would not be coming anywhere near him for some time.

The only thing more frightening than the idea that the story might have been spiked was the prospect that it was running. Joel lay in his single bed and listened out for the cries of newspaper sellers. When he heard what sounded like 'Sammy Beech', he let out a long breath, got up, and went to fish out his smartest clothes and his medals. He had a feeling he'd need them, and indeed, the barrage of journalists started very soon afterwards.

Joel gave every interview he could, having commandeered his thrilled landlady's downstairs parlour. He did not mention Darby Sabini, or Aaron. He repeated again and again that Mr. Marks had come to consult him, that he had felt unhappy about the man's death. They all asked him why he'd passed on the information to the press rather than the police. He asked them all, "What would you do in my place?"

It was long and exhausting. Towards the end of the day, some of the questions became more hostile, with a journalist from the Daily Express touching on whether he had a grudge against the Met, and asking pointedly if he'd ever been convicted of a crime.

They'd known that would come, and agreed that blaming his aberration on distress and illness after a traumatic war injury would be the path of least resistance. Joel hated that with every fibre of his being. He wanted to name Constable Sefton as an exploitative bully, to point out he had harmed nobody, to ask why it was a good use of police time to poke into his private life rather than rooting out the murderers in their own ranks.

He needed to focus on protecting Aaron, and on making sure Colthorne couldn't muddy the waters. He needed to say, *I was ill, unwell, I didn't know what I was doing. It was an inexplicable lapse, a momentary madness.* Common sense dictated he should.

Common sense collided with Joel, and lost.

"I've a conviction, yes," he said. "Served my time, paid my debt to society. Who fed you that line?"

"Sorry?"

"I was just wondering, did you go looking into me of your own accord, or has a little bird in the Metropolitan Police been singing in someone's ears?"

The journalist reddened slightly. "I'm establishing the facts, Mr. Wildsmith."

"The facts are that DDI Colthorne owed Thaddeus Knight a fortune and lied about it when he investigated the man's murder. That when Gerald Marks found evidence to that effect and told DDI Colthorne about it, *he* mysteriously died, and that DDI Colthorne didn't mention any of that to the investigating officer," Joel said. "Those are the facts. Not my facts, just facts, because I'm only the messenger here. Frankly, you can leave me out of all this and I'll be happy."

"You don't want press?"

"Well, if the story says Handsome, Talented Graphologist Offers Reasonable Rates..." Joel said, and got a reluctant grin. "No, I don't want press, because this isn't about me, it's about three dead men. And DDI Colthorne, of course. I hope some of your mates are asking him questions too?"

"We're pursuing the story," the journalist said, a little defensively.

"Someone else gets to talk to Colthorne while you're stuck trying to make two paragraphs out of me? Did you piss off your editor?"

The journalist glowered. "About your conviction—"

"You're swimming against the tide, mate." Joel could feel sweat springing round his neck, but he was digging his heels in now. "You don't want to be the one repeating Colthorne's lines of defence when everyone else is exposing his wrongdoing. Some people are going to look pretty stupid for believing him." He paused, inspiration striking. "Actually, I could name you one."

"Who's that?"

"Someone a lot more interesting than me," Joel said, making very direct eye contact. "It depends if you'd rather write scandal about a graphologist nobody's heard of, or a Bright Young Person who's made a complete tit of himself."

The journalist weighed that up, and grinned. "Go on."

The next day all the papers ran the story on the front pages. The Daily Mail had managed to reach Sammy Beech's family by telegraph; The Times had dug up some old friends of Thaddeus Knight; the Mirror had an immensely frank interview with Marks's landlady.

The Express had the Paul Napier-Fox story as an exclusive. The journalist had gone straight to him and extracted a full admission that Colthorne had dictated the threatening letter. Paul tried to claim he'd gone along with it because Joel had unfairly maligned his integrity, but the journalist had also contacted Barbara Wilson, who did a gleeful job of eviscerating his character and morals. That would teach the swine to bully Aaron as a child.

The news had also had the effect of putting Joel's profession in the public eye, and the letters begging for appointments started coming by the second post. Joel refrained from replying quite yet. The last thing he wanted was to be accused of profiteering from murder. He did, however, open them all just in case Aaron had written.

He desperately wanted to know what was going on at the

Met. Commissioner Sir William Horwood had come up with a lot of pap about investigations taking time and the proper channels, but he'd be lucky. The brewing scandal had already been dubbed the IOU Affair by the press, and two of the papers were running observations about the rumours of a Sabini connection to King's Cross CID. Joel just hoped Darby Sabini didn't blame him for that.

Aaron had managed not to be interviewed by anyone, but there were a couple of blurry photographs of him entering Scotland Yard, grim-faced. He was of course featured in the story as the investigating officer on the Marks murder; he'd be answering a lot more questions behind the scenes, Joel knew. But they had wrenched the story from Colthorne's hands, and prevented it from being quietly covered up, and on the whole, he was proud.

Thursday came and went with more interview requests, a twentyfold increase in the number of letters, and still nothing from Aaron. Joel, who hadn't left the building since Tuesday, was increasingly bored and frustrated. He wanted to see Aaron and to hear what was going on. He wished his landlady had a telephone.

He'd paid her son to get him all the papers. The lad duly delivered the Evening Standard, which had a sidebar about the story on the front page pointing to a spread on pages 2 and 3. Joel turned to it and almost dropped the paper.

Sergeant In IOU Affair, Marks Murder Case Leaves Force

Detective Sergeant Aaron Fowler, who led the investigation into Gerald Marks' death, abruptly left the Metropolitan Police this morning, according to reports. It is unclear if he resigned or was dismissed. The Standard's requests for more information were not answered...

"Shit," Joel muttered. Had Aaron been pushed too far? Or was this Colthorne getting the upper hand? He hadn't made a statement beyond the obligatory one about not commenting on active investigations and expecting all allegations to be cleared up shortly.

Aaron would surely get in touch now. Joel would just have to sit tight and wait for the next post; there was usually one around five-thirty.

It came and went without a letter. Joel paced up and down his room feeling like a kennelled dog. Had he fucked this up? He might have fucked this up. He'd insisted on taking the lead, but maybe that had made Aaron seem incompetent or incapable. Perhaps Colthorne had been able to use Joel's record and his words to Sabini against Aaron. Maybe he oughtn't have thrown Aaron's cousin to the wolves?

Maybe Aaron was just being highly cautious and not contacting him like they'd agreed, and Joel should stop working himself into a tizzy for no reason.

He made himself a resentful bacon sandwich for supper. The last post arrived at eight; if he didn't hear from Aaron by then, he'd stop worrying. Or he'd throw caution to the winds, run out to a telephone box, and call him. One of the two.

He heard the rattle of the letterbox and the soft thump of a cascade of paper falling to the mat, and went downstairs to collect what would be overwhelmingly his letters. He put them on the stand to sort through them, and almost knocked over the whole pile as Aaron's hand leapt out at him. He ripped open the letter, fingers fumbling in haste, and shook it out of the envelope.

Joel—

Please come to my flat as soon as you get this. Things have gone badly wrong. Don't speak to anyone. Come at once.

Aaron

He stared at the familiar hand, a cold feeling of dread coalescing in his stomach. Then he sprinted upstairs for his coat.

Chapter Sixteen

The knock at the door came in the middle of the afternoon. Aaron didn't open it. Perhaps that was an excess of caution, but he hadn't been making friends recently. He called, "Who is it?"

A high-pitched adolescent squawk from the other side. "Telegram."

That was surely from Joel. Perhaps it was urgent. Perhaps Joel needed him. They'd agreed to keep apart until this was over, however long that might be, but if Joel had reason to get in touch, Aaron had to respond. Not to mention that Aaron had had an appalling day and he wanted Joel, even at the remove of a telegram, with a longing that hurt.

"Can you leave it on the mat?" he called

"Telegram!" the uncomprehending voice squeaked again.

Damn it. He wasn't going to risk the boy taking it away. "One moment."

He opened the door. DDI Colthorne smirked at him.

Aaron went to slam it, but the DDI's foot was in the way, and as Aaron tried to kick it, Colthorne raised his hand. He held a revolver.

The DDI gestured. Aaron moved numbly backwards; Colthorne kicked the door shut behind him. "Hands on your head. This is loaded; don't imagine otherwise, and don't think I won't shoot. You are going to do as I say."

"Sir—"

"Shut up. You'll write a letter, to my dictation. Play the

fool and I'll blow out your brains. Sit down and keep your hands where I can see them."

Aaron sat at the bureau, hands on his head. Colthorne rested the muzzle of the revolver against his skull, cold and heavy, while he had a look for the gun Aaron didn't own, then pulled out pen and paper. "Write as I say. 'Joel. Please come to my flat—"

"No."

The metal ground viciously into his scalp. "If you refuse, I will pull the trigger. If you speak one word more, I will pull the trigger. And then I will leave you lying in your own blood and brains while I send a telegram to your boy friend, and he'll come running just the same. Do you understand me, Fowler? Now *write*."

Three hours later, Aaron was lying on the carpet full length, face down.

It wasn't comfortable, but he wasn't doing it by choice. Colthorne had ordered him to the floor once he'd written the Judas letter to Joel, and they'd both been here in silence ever since.

Aaron hadn't asked about what he was doing here, or his plans, or anything else. Colthorne had made it clear he didn't want to talk, and Aaron wasn't inclined to push him. The DDI presumably needed him alive, at least for the moment, but you could hurt people a lot before they died and Aaron didn't want to offer the provocation.

He was, he knew, probably going to die tonight. It was the only available conclusion. Perhaps Colthorne was seeking vengeance, or perhaps he was having another go at pinning his crimes on others, and wanted Joel and Aaron to —what? Write out confessions of something or other, assert they'd lied or forged the documents, set up a joint suicide afterwards to avoid awkward questions?

It didn't stand a chance of working to Aaron's mind, but he didn't suppose Colthorne thought in the same way he did. And after all, why not take the chance, even if it meant racking up two more bodies? They could only hang you once.

Because Colthorne was surely going to hang. A witness to Marks's death had popped up, and another to Colthorne's visit to Marks's office, thanks to the barrage of publicity. There would be enough evidence to mount a prosecution for the detective's death, if not Thaddeus Knight's killing or Sammy Beech's judicial murder. Public feeling would demand it.

Did Colthorne really believe he could get away with his crimes even at this late stage? Perhaps he simply wanted vengeance on Joel and Aaron first. It was hard to say.

Either way, Aaron had helped him. He'd written what Colthorne had told him, the words that would summon his lover, his absurd, brilliant Joel who had lit up the last few weeks in a way that Aaron had never experienced, for the convenience of the man who intended to murder them both. And now Aaron was lying on the floor, waiting for it to happen.

He was uncomfortably aware of his bladder, but didn't want to risk asking to get up. He rather hoped Colthorne was getting sleepy, though even if he was, it wouldn't do much good. Aaron had been lying still for the best part of three hours; he'd be stiff as a board when he tried to rise, and there was very little to be done against a man with a gun.

At last, the electric bell went. It was the doorbell, not the one for the front door of the building. Apparently Joel had got someone to let him in. Aaron felt a wave of fear so intense it left him nauseous.

"Is that the downstairs?" Colthorne demanded, rising.

"No. He's at the door."

"Get up. Open it. And keep your mouth shut or I'll kill you both," Colthorne said, very low, stepping to one side.

Aaron hauled himself off the floor. His knees hurt from the enforced stillness. The buzzer went again; Colthorne gestured angrily.

Aaron limped to the door, trying to loosen his muscles. Colthorne could see his face, he'd be able to see his mouth move if he tried to mime a warning.

So he'd shoot Aaron first, that was all. Joel would not set foot in here if Aaron could stop him.

He took a deep breath, pulled the door open, and saw DC Helen Challice.

"Good evening, sir," she said merrily, stepping in without invitation, so that Aaron automatically recoiled. "I thought I'd come to say hello. And the DDI! Marvellous! We're all here for a lovely chat. Oh goodness." She cocked her head like a bird, looking at the revolver in Colthorne's hand. "Why have you got a gun in your hand, sir?"

"Why are you here?" Colthorne gritted.

"I wanted to see the DS," Challice said calmly. "So I came. With my friends."

She walked all the way into the sitting room, followed by Sergeant Hollis and a uniformed constable whose name

Aaron couldn't recall. They both stared at Colthorne, at the revolver he held.

"Get out," Colthorne said, but it didn't have nearly enough force.

"You should put that away, sir," Hollis told him, voice very level. "Not safe in a domestic environment."

Colthorne's face was trying for rigid, but his throat worked spasmodically; Aaron could see the muscles twitch and jump. He was running calculations in his head, trying to find a way forward, but there was none at all, not any more, except self-destruction. His eyes flicked to Aaron, and Aaron could see the thought, the *At least I'll take him with me*, filling his mind—

"Please give me the gun, sir," Challice said and stepped forward, directly in front of the revolver.

There was an endless, horrible moment in which nobody breathed, then Colthorne lowered his weapon. "I am your Divisional Detective Inspector," he said thickly. "Mind your damned business, girl. There will be a reprimand."

He turned on his heel and strode out. Nobody moved for twenty seconds or more, and then Challice said, "Are you all right, Mr. Fowler?"

"He's been holding me hostage for three hours," Aaron said through a cracking throat. "I don't think he's a danger to the public, but if anyone forces a confrontation—"

"We'll get after him," Hollis said. "Challice, call it in to the Yard and the nick. Come on, Farrell. And—I'm sorry, mate," he told Aaron. "Colthorne said things about you that I oughtn't have listened to."

"That's all right. Thank you."

The two uniformed men left at a jog. Aaron told

Challice, "Use my telephone. Warn people. Put a man outside Joel's lodging house, he might go there. Where is Joel?"

"At the Italian restaurant on the corner; we thought Colthorne oughtn't see him. He wasn't awfully happy about it. Shall I get him?"

"Call the Yard first," Aaron said, and sat down hard.

Challice made the calls, speaking urgently, while Aaron drank a lot of water and had a few private moments to recover his composure. She went out after that, and Aaron waited for what seemed like hours, although it was barely long enough for the kettle to boil before she returned with Joel in tow.

Aaron wanted nothing more than to grab him, to grapple him close and kiss everything he could reach and never let go. He said, "Hello."

"Evening," Joel said. "Is that tea? Oh thank God. So I was right?"

"Joel got your letter and telephoned me, saying he thought you were in grave danger," Challice told Aaron. "It seemed obvious what *that* was likely to be, so I found some help. It was a bit touch and go, because all I had to show was a perfectly ordinary letter, but luckily Sergeant Hollis remembered Joel, and Malcolm was happy to help. Constable Farrell, you know. He's very sweet. Really, they both were."

"And you didn't twist their arms *at all*," Joel added helpfully.

Aaron would have liked to know more, but not at this moment. "Thank you. Thank you so much for coming, and thank you for seeing that, Joel." He couldn't help a shudder. "He had a gun to my head when I wrote it."

"Yes," Joel said, with an air of polite interest. "It did rather feel that way."

"I must say, I'd quite like to see this gift of yours in action, rather than just take everyone's word for it," Challice remarked.

"Helen, angel, you get free readings for life."

She gave Joel a beaming smile. "So I should hope. What now?"

"I'll make a complaint of wrongful imprisonment if it's required. Tomorrow." Aaron was absolutely exhausted, he realised. "Today has been rather wearing. You may know, I resigned earlier."

"Yes. I'm very sorry."

"It was unavoidable. You've been a joy to work with, Challice—Helen—and I'm grateful. I look forward to watching your rise; I expect we'll see you in Scotland Yard soon enough."

She glowed at him. "That's very kind. Do you want me to stay or send for anyone, in case he comes back?"

"No. No, I think I'll just lock the door," Aaron said, with a weak smile. "Thank you again."

"I'll just finish my tea," Joel said. "See you, Helen."

Aaron waited for her to leave with what felt like glaringly obvious awkwardness. He went to lock and bolt the door. Then he turned, found Joel right behind him with open arms, and walked into them.

"Jesus," he said into the mop of copper hair. "Jesus Christ. Thank you, thank you."

"I have never been more frightened in my fucking life," Joel said into his shirt. "Your *writing*."

"I didn't know whether to write it and risk you coming here, or refuse and have him put a bullet in my head there and then. I thought you'd realise, but I was so afraid you wouldn't."

"Course I saw it. Not a sodding idiot," Joel mumbled. "Did he hurt you?"

"He was waiting for you to arrive before he did that."

"Shit. Shit. And what now?"

"He's finished," Aaron said. "He wouldn't have come here like this otherwise. It's only a question of how much damage he does on the way down, but that's not my problem any more."

"No. What happened?"

Aaron sighed. "A bloody awful couple of hours with a variety of increasingly senior people wanting to know why I hadn't handled it all better and how I let you give the evidence to the press. Apparently I should have reported all my suspicions from the beginning. I asked, 'Like Sergeant Josling did in Soho?', which went down poorly."

Joel cackled. "Nice."

"Your pernicious influence. This whole thing is going to be a frantic flurry of finding someone to blame. The high-ups will say I should have spoken out earlier, while the rank and file will call me a snout even if Colthorne is found guilty in court. I didn't feel inclined to stick around for punishment."

"I don't blame you." Joel's arms were warm and tight around Aaron's waist. "But I'm sorry."

"No, it was time. My work was feeling increasingly like

an exercise in compromise and hypocrisy. Too many things I wasn't letting myself see in order to keep the faith. I believe in what I was doing, trying to do, but that's not enough."

"No," Joel said. "I wondered if you'd want to stay and change things."

"I wish I could, but that ship has sailed. I've brought down a copper, and no matter how he deserved it, that won't be forgotten by the men on the ground, still less the ones in charge. Six years of my life, my father—well. It's over, and that's all there is to it."

"I'm sorry. Or, I'm not sorry you've left, but I wish it had been on your terms."

Aaron held on for a moment longer, then loosened his grip and stepped back a little so he could see Joel's face. "We got Colthorne, though, and, as a philosopher once told me, you should take your wins where you can. So here we are, and now I need to reconsider a lot of things about my life."

"Such as what?"

"Such as how you can stay in it," Aaron said. "I've been thinking about what you said, how you were tired of living with things. I've been doing that too, and only barely at that. I haven't felt like a person for so long, and then you came along with your ridiculous talent and your appalling attitude and your hair. And —Christ, Joel. I spent three hours lying on the floor thinking I was going to die tonight, and I realised that you were what I'd miss. I was terrified at the evenings I wouldn't have with you, the meals we wouldn't eat together, the things we wouldn't see. It was unbearable. I want those things. Can we have them?"

"Excuse *me*," Joel said. "I had to whistle up a lot of coppers and get from King's Cross to Lisson Grove with your bloody letter screaming at me, not knowing if we'd be in time, and you think *you* were terrified? *And* I had a breakdown in Angelo's while I waited, but he was very nice about it. So yes, let's have meals and evenings, and also nights and breakfasts and everything else. Because I'm sodding sick of losing things, and I'm not losing you if I can help it."

"No, you're not," Aaron said hoarsely, and kissed him.

A short but intense period later, they ended up on the sofa, Aaron finger-combing Joel's hair, barely believing that they were together, touching. It felt like relief from a pain that had lasted so long, he didn't know what it was like not to feel it.

"You did all this," he said softly. "You changed everything. I'm so damned lucky I met you."

"You should thank your cousin Paul," Joel said. "Or maybe not. I don't know if you saw the papers?"

"You throwing him to the wolves? I did. Good work."

"I'd say it was an unfortunate necessity, but actually I enjoyed every minute of it."

"God bless you. Will you stay tonight?"

Joel looked up, ochre eyes wide. "Can I?"

"Yes. Nobody could expect you to return home alone, and to hell with it anyway. Stay with me, Joel. I want to go to sleep with you next to me, and find out what it's like to wake up with you. I'm quite sure you're foul-tempered."

"Find out," Joel said and leaned into him.

They were still on the sofa some time later, although definitely planning to get up at any moment, when the telephone rang. Aaron shoved Joel off and hauled himself up. "Hello? … Ah. Yes. Yes, I see. Well, that will cause comment. Thank you, Helen. Good night."

Joel looked up. "News?"

"Colthorne just shot himself on the doorstep of Scotland Yard."

"God, I can't stand bad losers," Joel said, which felt like all the epitaph Aaron cared to hear. "Shall we go to bed?"

It was such a simple sentence, with its domesticity, its casual plural, and it brought up every hair on Aaron's neck with pleasure. "Yes," he said. "Or, in a moment. I wanted to say, I have a proposal for you."

"Aren't we still reeling from the last one?" Joel remarked. "Go on."

"I told you my grandmother left me a legacy. I bought this flat, and the rest has been sitting in the bank doing nothing because I've had nothing to do with it." He took a breath. "How would you feel about a trip to Germany?"

Joel stilled. "Are you serious?"

"I need a break, time to think. You're going to have a lot of people bothering you that you don't want to be bothered by—"

"Happening already. You should see my postbag."

"And we deserve some time. I speak reasonable German. We could take a holiday, and see about that prosthetic you want. Visit the man so you can see for yourself what he can do."

Joel's mouth moved soundlessly. Aaron took a moment to appreciate that rare occurrence. "But— Really? But—"

"No?"

"No, yes, but— I mean, I've thought about it as a dream

for a long time, but what if the real thing isn't what I want? If we go all that way and it doesn't seem worth it—"

"Then we'll have learned something. We'll have tried."

"Right," Joel said. "Taking me to Germany is quite a lot of trying."

Aaron took his hand, curling their fingers together. "It's not gratitude, in case you're wondering. Still less obligation."

"What is it, then?"

Aaron considered his answer. He'd have liked to come up with a witty remark, or a playful jab of the kind Joel was so good at, but the only thing coming to mind was the truth.

"That I love you," he said. "I love you, I want us to live, and from now on, if you find yourself living 'with' anything, I want it to be me."

The smile that broke across Joel's face was bright dawn. "That sounds pretty good," he said. "Same. All right. Let's."

Author's Notes

Joel's graphology is of course fantastical. However, my grandmother used to read handwriting and I have to tell you, she wasn't all that far off.

A few factual bits and bobs...

A small wave of Indian restaurants opened in the UK in the 1920s, including Veeraswamy, which is still going strong. Shafi's Restaurant was a well-known home from home for Indians, particularly students, until the 1940s, but there is an amazing variety of claims out there as to the identities, names, and occupations of the original owners. In the absence of finding anything definitive, I've based my fictional version on the very brief mention in *Curry: a Tale of Cooks and Conquerors* by Lizzie Collingham. I would love to know more.

Charles 'Darby' Sabini's birth name was Ottavio Handley. He was the son of either Ottavio Sabini or Charles Handley; his mother wasn't sure, so he got named for both men, and then switched them up for his nom de guerre. It's possible to conclude he had issues.

Darby dominated much of London and the South-East's organised crime between the wars, running a 300-strong gang based in Little Italy (the Clerkenwell area of London). He made a fortune extorting bookmakers and nightclubs when he wasn't in savage fights with rival gangs or ordering people to be carved up with razors, but was apparently a very pleasant chap otherwise. The Italian and Jewish gangs of the area formed an alliance against other London and Birmingham gangs that lasted till the Second World War. Darby was interned as an enemy alien in 1940, despite being born in Holborn, being only questionably possessed of Italian heritage, not speaking the language, and never having set foot outside England.

Commissioner Sir William Horwood, who really did escape an assassination attempt involving arsenic-laced Walnut Whips because truth is always less plausible than fiction, was known for his dogged refusal to accept there could be wrongdoing in the force he supervised. He was instrumental in the disgrace of Sergeant Horace Josling, who had come to him to accuse a colleague of taking bribes. Horwood made Josling face an enquiry where he was aggressively grilled for two days, called self-righteous, and finally forced to resign for impugning another officer's good name. This rather backfired a few years later when the man Josling had accused got eighteen months' hard labour for, er, taking bribes. Josling was vindicated in Parliament and the press, and paid a large sum in compensation. He didn't get his job back.

The first woman in CID was Lilian Wyles, who joined the Met in 1919 and made Chief Inspector before her retirement. Her memoir *A Woman at Scotland Yard* is hard to get hold of (and upholds the less proud traditions of the Met in its occasional casual racism and misogyny), but is fascinating as a piece of social history.

The hideously mean-spirited quotation from the Ministry of Pensions in chapter four is, I'm sorry to say, real. So was Joel's hoped-for functional prosthetic hand; you can see the film online.

The graphological quotation in Chapter Two comes from *Analysis of Handwriting* by HJ Jacoby; regrettably, the whole book is like that.

Thanks time!

I'm deeply grateful to the Metropolitan Police Museum for use of their extensive reference library and all the assistance given by their very helpful staff.

Huge thanks to KJ Charles Chat (now on Discord!) for title brainstorming, and particularly to Metylda who came up with the winner.

As ever Lis Paice and May Peterson gave me early reads, confidence boosts, and invaluable help.

Many thanks to James Egan at Bookfly Design for the lovely cover and to Garrett Leigh at Black Jazz Design for the print layout.

About The Author

KJ Charles is a recovering editor turned full time writer. She lives in London with her husband, two kids, an out-of-control garden, and a cat with murder management issues.

KJ writes mostly historical romance, mostly queer, sometimes with fantasy or horror in there. She is represented by Courtney Miller-Callihan at Handspun Literary.

For all the KJC news and occasional freebies, get my (infrequent) newsletter at kjcharleswriter.com/newsletter.

Find me on Bluesky @kjcharleswriter.com

Pick up free reads on my website at kjcharleswriter.com

Join my Discord group, KJ Charles Chat, for book nerding, good conversation, sneak peeks, and exclusive treats.

www.ingramcontent.com/pod-product-compliance
Lightning Source LLC
Chambersburg PA
CBHW071744190726
48292CB00003B/863
9781912688272